Who, Me?

Fog Bows, Fraud, & Aphrodite

A Macavity & Me Mystery #2

by

Charlotte Stuart

ISBN 978-1-950613-70-0

Published by Taylor and Seale Publishing, LLC
3408 South Atlantic Avenue
Unit 139
Daytona Beach Shores, FL 32118

Cover design and layout by Chris Holmes

Publisher's Note: This is a work of fiction. Names, characters, places, and incidents are a product of the author's imagination or used fictitiously. Locales and public names are sometimes used fictitiously for atmospheric purposes. With the exception of public figures or specific historical references, any resemblance to actual people, living or dead, or to businesses, companies, events, institutions, or locales is completely coincidental. Any historical personages or actual events depicted are completely fictionalized and used only for inspiration. Any opinions expressed are completely those of fictionalized characters and not a reflection of the views of public figures, author, or publisher.

To sail boaters and cat lovers—

may the sun break through the fog bows in your lives.

And in memory of Barbara Whitson, member of the Every Six Weeks Ready or Not Book Club. She is missed.

Acknowledgments

I would like to thank Taylor and Seale Publishing for their continued support, with special thanks to editor and author Veronica H. Hart and to my agent, Donna Eastman. Most of all, I want to thank my readers. I enjoy writing humorous mysteries and sincerely hope that you find some positive energy and a few laughs in my books.

As a pro bono management consultant for small non-profits, I've repeatedly witnessed commitment to mission and persistence in trying to perform miracles on a shoestring budget. Unfortunately, there are those who would take advantage of any organizational weakness for personal gain. I apologize to nonprofits everywhere for using such a weakness as a catalyst for my mystery. We all owe a debt of gratitude to the nonprofits striving to make our world a better place.

Please check out my website: www.charlottestuart.com

WHO, ME?
Fog Bows, Fraud & Aphrodite

by

Charlotte Stuart

A yawn is a silent scream for coffee.

Chapter 1

A Midnight Swim

I got involved because I drank too much coffee the night before. I'd stayed up late Friday night working on a project and woke up after just a few hours because I had to go to the bathroom. The brass porthole next to the toilet on my 40-foot sailboat was open, and as I stepped inside the cramped space, I heard angry voices. Two people screaming at each other from the aft deck of the *Knotty Lady*, less than thirty feet away.

"Why do you have to be so . . .," a male voice blasted, like an angry tuba. It was Arthur, the owner of the boat. He must have turned away as he spoke because I lost the actual words at the end of his accusation. But his tone was menacing, a dormant volcano about to erupt.

I craned my neck to look out the small opening, banging my head against the stick I use to prop open the porthole. In the dark all I could make out was the outline of the awning on the boat in the next slip and some shadows on the glassy night water.

"You are a twisted SOB," a woman's voice retorted with enough venom to make me cringe. I tried to remember if I'd seen anyone with Arthur lately, and a vision of a well-dressed woman in inappropriate shoes for walking a wood plank dock came to mind. I couldn't picture her face. All I remembered were the spikey red high heels, the kind of shoes that squeeze the joy of walking out of your feet and beg for attention from horny males and shoe-obsessed females.

"Be *reasonable*—" I heard his attempt to calm things down as clearly as if I'd been standing next to him. Somehow, after such an angry exchange, I didn't think asking her to be reasonable was going to work. Especially not with that condescending tone.

"*Reasonable*?" she screamed, her voice hitting the bat range. "Reasonable?" she repeated in case anyone within a two-mile radius hadn't already heard her.

Sounds of movement and a few muffled grunts followed. Then silence settled like a summer fog over the marina, interrupted only by the slap of rigging on sailboat masts.

Was the argument over? Were they making up, like some couples do after a heated exchange? Or had the woman left Arthur standing there alone on the aft deck, his plea for reason swallowed up by the night? It was possible they'd taken their argument inside the boat, denying me the satisfaction of hearing what happened next, like turning off the TV before the finale of an emotionally charged drama.

I don't like nosy neighbors, and I certainly don't want to be one, but given the heat of the exchange and the sudden end of the argument, it seemed like I had an obligation to find out if everything was all right. What if their fight had become physical? What if the grunting sound had been someone punching out the other? Maybe I should have yelled something out of the porthole to let them know there was a witness. It seemed a little late for that now. Another option was to call the police. But if I did, what would I say—that there had been a fight but it was over?

A little voice at the back of my head was warning me not to overreact. And although the voice sounded suspiciously like my mother's, it probably wasn't bad advice. I needed more information before calling the police.

Meanwhile, I still had to go to the bathroom.

After relieving myself, I put my ear next to the porthole again, held my breath, and listened for all I was worth. No one was shouting. No one was apologizing. No one was moaning in pain. The only thing I could hear was what sounded like hard-soled shoes pounding wood as someone paced back and forth on the deck that I couldn't see.

Then I heard a muffled voice yelling something from inside the boat. It's strange how you can sense an attitude without actually knowing what is said. Based solely on tone, I considered the pacing and the yelling to be hostile acts. Whatever was happening wasn't over. Maybe I *should* call the police. Or maybe I should keep my nose out of someone else's business. If it was simply a loud argument, did I really want to call in the cavalry?

It was too bad that I had a tarp cover securely tied over the back deck of my boat that would require considerable adjustment in order to get a look at the next couple of floats. Although if the argument continued inside the boat, I wouldn't be able to see anything anyway.

My boat is moored on the inside of a cement pier that butts up against the end of an old wood dock lined with rows of covered slips. The cement extension was once a fuel dock, but those days are long gone. There is one overhead light nearby, just sufficient to cast a hazy glow over everything. If I got dressed and strolled down the dock to check things out, there was a problem—Arthur and his sparring mate could see me. It would be hard to hang around hoping to hear something that would help me make up my mind about the level of threat their argument posed without calling attention to my presence. But I needed to get closer in order to find out what was going on.

In retrospect it was probably a crazy idea, but at the time it felt like a viable option. I love to swim. And since I couldn't approach the *Knotty Lady* on foot and remain out of sight, a midnight dip seemed like the perfect answer.

I carefully pushed back the hatch and climbed out into the cockpit. It had been warm the day before, and my swimsuit was still hanging from a cross-brace. As I slipped out of my nightgown and started to pull up my clammy swimsuit, I almost changed my mind but I knew the chilly discomfort would end as soon as I got into the water. I'd taken late-night dips before to cool off when the heat of the day lingered.

My plan was to slip under the canvas cover and ease myself into the water, then swim over to the *Knotty Lady* to reconnoiter. But plans have a way of sometimes missing details needed for flawless implementation. In this instance, I had done too good a job of securing the canvas cover to the cleats I'd added for the purpose, so I didn't actually "slip" between the boat and the canvas cover and lower myself silently over the edge. Instead, the tarp pressed against me, pinning me against the railing. My struggle ended with a plop into the cold nighttime water that was not much louder than a kid doing a cannon ball into a pool.

For a few seconds I clung to the side of the boat waiting for someone to yell, "What's going on out there?" When nothing happened, I swam over to the boat between mine and the *Knotty Lady*, pausing near its stern to listen. I could hear indistinct voices coming from inside the *Knotty Lady*. After only a moment's hesitation, I swam closer to the hull, staying out of sight under the dock.

What happened next made me wish I'd been less worried about being visible and more concerned with line of sight. I couldn't see what was happening on the back deck, but I heard a door open, sounds of a struggle, and, moments later, a loud *splash*.

Something heavy had gone into the water!

Tiny ripples spread out from the stern. Except for my own raspy breathing, the marina descended into an eerie silence. There were no more voices coming from the *Knotty Lady*. No pacing on the aft deck. Nothing.

Had someone fallen or been pushed into the water? If so, why didn't I hear sounds of them returning to the surface. Unless . . .

It was time to call the police.

I quickly swam back to my boat only to realize that I had removed the boarding ladder and left it on the dock after securing the cover the day before. There was no way I could pull myself up over the side on my own. And the dock was way too high. The nearest dock ladder wasn't far away, but it was at the corner of the "L," right under the light and visible to anyone on the *Knotty Lady* who happened to be looking. I needed another way up.

There are only four liveaboard boats at the marina. Two on each dock. I obviously couldn't ask Arthur on the *Knotty Lady* for assistance, so I would have to swim over to the other dock and see if I could find a ladder or, as a last resort, rouse two liveaboard friends to help me get out of the water.

It was too dark on that side of the marina to see much of anything from the water, and I was apparently too rattled to remember where the ladder was. There was no other choice. Judd and Logan were about to get a 2:00 a.m. visitor.

Logan is a good friend. He and his partner, Judd, live on the Carpe Diem, a 47-foot ferro-cement sailboat tied along the outside of the dock across from the covered moorage slips. Their bunks are located in the bow, so I swam there and pounded on the hull as hard as I could. Fists on cement from an unstable position in the water aren't too effective. But I kept on hammering away, trying for some syncopation so they would know it wasn't a piece of wood sloshing against their hull. If I had known Morse code, I could have tried that.

When I finally heard some mumbling from inside, I pounded more rapidly, trying to bounce the boat a little. I thought I heard someone say, "What the hell," but by then my own noisy breathing and attempts to avoid swallowing lake water was dominating my world.

Moments later I heard a hatch open and someone called, "Anyone there?"

I swam over to the side of the boat and softly said, "Down here." I didn't want my voice to carry across to the other dock.

"What? Did someone say something?" It was Logan. He sounded groggy. Well, I couldn't blame him.

"Down here," I said a little louder, slapping the side of the boat. When nothing happened, I splashed some water up on the deck.

"Huh?!"

"What's happening?" Judd called from inside.

"Not sure," I heard Logan say.

"Logan, I'm in the water." I didn't want to shout, but I was getting cold and irritable. "Down here," I repeated, this time with feeling and slightly more volume.

Logan's face suddenly appeared over the side of the boat, peering down at me. "Bryn? Is that you, Bryn?" His face disappeared and I heard him say, "It's Bryn, she's in the lake."

Then two faces were looking down at me. "Bryn," Judd said. "What are you doing down there?"

"Do you have a ladder?" I asked. "Or can you pull me up? I'm getting cold."

Logan leapt into action, leaning over the edge and extending his hand. But Judd was still puzzled. "Did you fall in?" he asked.

"Just help me up, okay?"

Judd leaned down next to Logan, and the two men grabbed my wrists and hauled me aboard like they were landing a large fish. "I guess that means you don't have a ladder, huh?" I was shivering and not feeling very coherent.

"But what . . .," both men began at once.

"I need to use a phone," I said. "Right now."

"Sure, of course. But why swim over?" Judd was clearly not at his best when awakened from a sound sleep.

"And I could use a towel." I was dripping all over their deck, feeling more and more chilled now that I was being attacked by the cool night air.

Logan ran to get me a towel and a telephone. As he disappeared below, I noticed a police car pulling into the parking area for the marina. "I just need the towel," I called down to him.

Judd turned in the direction I'd been looking. "You were going to call the police?"

"There was a fight," I explained. "On the *Knotty Lady*. I swam over to investigate and then couldn't get back on my boat."

"You swam over?" He sounded as puzzled as if I'd said I had hopped a hot-air balloon to survey the marina from above.

"I'll tell you the whole thing later. First I need to talk to that police officer."

Logan reappeared and handed me a large towel that I gratefully wrapped around myself. I wondered who had called the police. Maybe Carol, a part-time liveaboard, or some passerby. People sometimes walked the docks late at night for reasons known only to them. Well, I would find out soon enough.

I started to step off the boat, but Logan put his hand on my shoulder. "Wait, I'll come with you," he said. I glanced at him and shook my head. He looked down at himself as if suddenly aware that he wasn't wearing anything but a pair of black boxers with little red chili peppers on them. "Just give me a minute to grab some pants."

In less than a minute, we were headed down the dock, Logan buttoning his shirt, me barefoot and dripping wet, gripping my borrowed towel, and wondering how I was going to explain myself.

Chapter 2

Sabrina and The Naked Lady

The parking area consists of a single row of unmarked spaces at the top of a short flight of steps just off the narrow road above the marina. The steps run alongside a three-story wood building that has seen better days and provides cheap office space to me and several other tenants, including our landlord. The second floor is at street level. The officer was standing at the bottom of the steps next to the row of lockers tucked under the parking area. He was talking on his phone as we approached him. When he looked up and saw us coming, he seemed startled. "I'll get back to you," I heard him say as we drew near.

"Are you here about the, ah, disturbance?" I asked.

"What disturbance?" He was eyeing me like he'd never seen a sopping wet woman wrapped in a towel before.

"Didn't someone call you?"

"Call me?" He had an annoying way of turning my questions back on me.

"Yes," I said firmly. "About the disturbance."

"Why don't you tell me about this 'disturbance.'"

Logan took that moment to jump in. "We were going to call you, well, the police . . .," he began, then paused.

"About . . .?" the officer prompted.

Since Logan didn't know anything about what had happened, he turned to me and nodded as if to say, "Tell the man why he's here."

"Look, Officer." I leaned forward, trying to read his badge, but it wasn't a well-lit area.

"Dodd," he said, taking a step back, as if he thought I might be contagious.

"Well, Officer Dodd," I began again. "There was a loud argument on a boat just down the dock from my boat, and I was concerned when I heard a loud splash. As if something . . . or, ah, someone went into the water."

"A person? You think someone jumped off a boat into the water?"

"Well, jumped . . . or . . . was pushed or . . . maybe was thrown overboard." There, I'd managed to vocalize my worst fears out loud. Although I wasn't sure the "thrown overboard" phrase captured my vision of a body being tossed into the water.

Logan and Officer Dodd opened their mouths as if to say something, but nothing came out. They simply stood there staring at me.

Finally, Officer Dodd cleared his throat and asked, "Did you *see* what happened?"

"No-o-o-o."

"But you thought you heard something."

"I *did* hear something."

"And where were you when you heard whatever it was you thought you heard?"

"I was in the water near the bow of the boat where the incident took place. The *Knotty Lady*." I pointed in the direction of the boat.

"And," he looked me up and down, "perhaps you can tell me what you were you doing in the water?"

"I can explain," I said. "But don't you want to check out the boat first?"

"Yeah," Logan chimed in. "If a body was dumped in the lake, don't you want to check it out?"

Whoa, Logan, I thought. Although I appreciated his unquestioning support, that was much too graphic given the lack of evidence. "I don't know what happened," I said. "I just know there was a heated argument followed by a loud splash. Something heavy definitely went overboard off the stern."

"Well, I suppose I could take a look." Officer Dodd's obvious reluctance to walk down the dock to verify or disprove the incident made it clear that he thought it was a dubious claim made by a woman crazy enough to be swimming in the wee hours. "To be on the safe side," he added without enthusiasm. Perhaps Logan's reference to a body being dumped in the lake had forced his hand.

Logan and I guided him down the dock to the *Knotty Lady*. It was dark inside. I knocked on the side of the boat, and we stood there waiting. When nothing happened, the officer stepped aboard. Just as he was about to knock on the door of the cabin, Arthur opened the door and looked out. "Can I help you?" he asked. He had on a pair of Captain America pajamas. Not exactly what you would expect someone to be wearing if he had only a short time before tossed a body of a woman overboard.

"This lady . . .," Officer Dodd motioned toward me, "claims there was a loud argument here. Know anything about it?"

Arthur looked at me and shook his head as if mystified by the allegation. Then he turned back to the officer. "I have no idea what you're talking about." He was a good liar. An incredibly good liar for someone in superhero PJs.

"Wasn't your, ah, girlfriend here about an hour ago?" I asked. "Is she still here?" I added as an afterthought. And not in the lake—

It seemed obvious to me that he was having a hard time deciding what to say. He hesitated just a little too long before responding to my question. And, instead of opting for the truth, he went with what I knew to be another lie. "No, I've been here alone all evening."

Officer Dodd turned toward me. "Well?"

"I heard you arguing with someone," I persisted.

"And you called the police?" Arthur sounded incredulous.

"Well, no, actually I didn't." But I would have, so perhaps that didn't count.

Arthur seemed to realize for the first time that I was wearing a towel and looked wet. "Were you swimming?" he asked.

"Yes, I like to swim when I can't sleep." There, that sounded like a good reason . . . didn't it?

"Well," Arthur said, "Maybe you heard someone on another boat. Or someone's television. You know how sound travels over water." All three men nodded "yes." It appeared as though I had even lost Logan's support. Of course, I knew that water affects sound waves, especially on calm water, but I also knew what I'd heard and where it had come from. Arthur was definitely lying . . . and it appeared as though he was going to get away with it.

We all stood there, a silent tableau waiting for someone to speak. No, that isn't accurate: everyone was staring at *me*, waiting for *me* to say something. But I couldn't think of anything to add to what I'd already told them. Finally, Officer Dodd mumbled something about a waste of time, stepped past us, climbed off the boat, and headed back down the dock toward his patrol car.

My brain started functioning, and I remembered something I should have asked. I jumped off the boat and hurried after him with Logan close behind. "Wait a minute," I called. He slowed down but didn't stop. I came alongside him and asked, "Didn't you come here because someone called you about all the shouting?"

He paused long enough to say, "No one called; I was just stretching my legs."

I stopped and tried to absorb what he'd said. He'd been taking a break. There wasn't another witness. Just me and Arthur's emphatic denial. Without more information, I couldn't think of anything else I could do or say to convince anyone that they should believe me and not Captain America.

Logan took my arm and led me back toward my boat, the *Aspara*, named for a fictional bird from *Islandia*, a utopian novel that made the act of sailing seem magical. Tonight, however, there was little magic, just harsh reality. How I wished I could ask for a second take of the evening's events. In take 2, I could have shouted for the two combatants to "shut up." Or maybe I could have screamed that the police were on their way. Either action might have resulted in an end to their argument. Then I wouldn't have gone for a swim and ended up being humiliated by Arthur's denial.

"Want to get dressed and come over for a cuppa or a drink or something?" Logan asked when we reached my boat. I declined, assuring him that I would give him and Judd the full story tomorrow, or today, depending on what day it was at almost 3:00 a.m.

"I'll hold you to that," he said as he left me there feeling alone and miserable.

After stripping off my swimsuit and toweling my hair, I went back to bed. My thoughts were a jumble of random replays of scripts and images from the last couple of hours. The fight, the midnight swim, Officer Dodd questioning my credibility, Arthur standing there looking innocent in his Captain America PJs. My last thought as sleep welcomed me into oblivion was that the woman on Arthur's boat was right: he was an SOB.

I was awakened by birds shrieking at each other right next to my boat. A peek at my clock told me it was 6:28 a.m. The grating, hoarse *kraa* of a crow and the noisy choking complaint seagulls make when defending territory suggested there was a fight in progress. Crows and seagulls are sworn enemies when it comes to claiming any food left out or put in an unsecured container. And there is always some looky-loo who wanders down the dock and tosses bread, chips, candy—whatever they have handy that's edible—to any birds that happen to be around. Okay, I admit it, I occasionally feed my favorite duck. She's a regular visitor and usually hangs around for a while to keep me company when I'm out back reading. It beats having to walk a dog, and my cat, Macavity, gets along just fine with Mallard. Not a very original name for a pet duck, but it's satisfyingly descriptive.

After tossing and turning and trying to go back to sleep, I gave up and dragged myself out to my Keurig. Why I don't make a whole pot of coffee in the morning since I usually end up drinking two or three cups, I can't explain. All I can say is that I have a one-cup limit that doesn't seem too effective.

As reality seeped into my brain, I started thinking about Arthur standing there in his Captain America PJs, lying his head off. I couldn't let him get away with that. Especially if he'd dumped his girlfriend in the lake, in *my* marina, in *my* swimming hole. But not even coffee could jumpstart my brain. I sat there, thoughts swimming around, going nowhere, like Bubbles IV circling his fishbowl.

It was Saturday. I didn't need to be anywhere, and I didn't have any special plans. Maybe I should just let myself drift for the morning, let my thoughts settle, have a bowl of cereal, perhaps take a nap. Cereal sounded good. Of course, to have cereal required milk, and, when I checked my fridge, I didn't have any. Which turned out to be moot because I didn't have any cereal either. I really did need to make a grocery run.

Okay, a nap on an empty stomach. But first, I had obligations to attend to.

I poured some cat food into a bowl for Macavity. He had apparently given up on breakfast and gone off somewhere. Perhaps, unlike his owner, he had weekend plans. He would return when he got hungry, demanding food and attention before resuming his wandering.

Next, I dropped a pinch of food into the fishbowl for Bubbles IV, my current goldfish resident, watching to see if he was going to eat. He'd been acting a little off lately. That's why I had him in the boat rather than in my office—to keep an eye on him. Although I wasn't at all sure what I was going to do if he took a turn for the worse. I'd never heard of anyone taking their goldfish to a vet.

As I watched, Bubbles IV nibbled at a few flakes before they sank to the bottom of his bowl. Then he continued the circuit of his watery home.

My duties done, I took a book and headed for my bunk. The story started with an intriguing action scene, but apparently that wasn't enough to stave off sleep. I awoke to a chorus of frog talk, my cell ringtone letting me know that someone was trying to get in touch. After fumbling a few tries, I managed to tap the right button. It was Logan.

"Hey, we were thinking of going out to breakfast. Want to come? You could tell us about last night." Hint, hint.

"Who's buying?"

"You are. After all, we hauled you out of the lake."

"In that case—"

"Okay, we'll spring for the 'special' at Beth's. *If* the explanation for your early morning swim meets the 'reasonable man' standard, currently referred to by most as the 'reasonable person' standard so as not to leave out fifty percent of the population."

"Are you dividing the world into men and women or into the reasonable and unreasonable? Puts a different slant on it, doesn't it?"

"Hmmm. I have to think about this one."

"Give me a couple of minutes, and I'll meet you at the head of the dock, okay?"

I hung up and quickly got dressed. On my way out, I checked to make sure the screen over Bubbles IV's home was secure just in case Macavity came back and wanted a fish-oil supplement for breakfast. Then I paused, trying to decide if he was still looking sluggish. Even if I couldn't administer any life-saving measures if he took a turn for the worse, I felt guilty about leaving him to die alone. And, deep down, I was convinced he was about to die. In my experience, that's what pet goldfish do.

As I stepped into the cockpit, I found my wet swimsuit and borrowed towel crumpled in a heap next to the hatch. After hanging them up to dry, I pushed back the canvas flap and found myself blinded by early morning sun. Mornings really can be obnoxious.

Arthur leapt off his boat just as I turned the corner and started toward the head of the dock. It crossed my mind that he'd been waiting for me to walk by. He didn't look particularly upset, but he was fidgeting. You *should* be nervous, I thought. I don't like liars, especially ones that make me look foolish. I can do that for myself.

"Hello, Bryn," he said as if we were two friends who just happened to run into each other.

"Arthur," I acknowledged, stopping to look him in the eyes. We were about the same height. I stood up straight, shoulders back, and flicked my red hair away from my face in what I considered an intimidating gesture. Like a horse pawing the ground. Or a goose hissing before an attack.

He looked down, a flush slowly creeping up his neck. I always like it when people have a physical tell.

"Bryn," he said again, his mouth moving as if words were struggling to get out.

"Arthur," I mocked. My tone was hopefully just the right blend of sarcasm and irritation.

After a few seconds of uncomfortable silence, very long seconds, he finally looked up. "I'm sorry," he said. "Really, I am."

"Why don't you tell me what you are sorry about . . .," I prompted, wishing I had turned on the recorder on my phone. Legal or not, it would have been satisfying to get him on record as a liar.

"Well, you understand," he stammered. "I didn't want to admit that I'd been fighting with Sabrina." He paused. Somehow, he didn't look like a guy who would have a girlfriend named Sabrina. On the other hand, maybe he didn't anymore.

"So, you admit that she was here last night and that the two of you were arguing."

He hung his head like a boy confessing to his mother that he had done something naughty. Did tossing your girlfriend's body in the lake qualify as *naughty*? "Yes," he said softly.

I had never given Arthur much thought before. He was an average looking guy with the perpetual hangdog aura of someone who had been teased and bullied as a kid. I might have gotten past that, but he was also a power boater. In my experience, sail boaters and power boaters are seldom simpatico. Even so, lying to the police didn't fit my image of him. Unless—

"Where was she when Officer Dodd came by?" Was this the point where he made a full confession?

"She had already left."

Via water, I wondered? My liar antenna was quivering, but he sounded so sincere. Just like he had last night. "What's Sabrina's full name?" I asked.

Arthur looked apprehensive. "Why do you want to know?"

"Well, I thought I might look her up," I replied. "To verify your story."

"No, you can't do that," he said quickly.

"Why not?"

"Because, well, because she wouldn't like it." His eyes were pleading with me to understand.

"Do you want me to go back to the police?" I pulled my phone out of my pocket and held it up. "With this?" I said. He didn't need to know I hadn't recorded anything. You gotta love technology.

He blinked at the phone in disbelief, then slowly seemed to accept the inevitable. "You won't bother her, will you? She's already mad enough."

"That's certainly the impression I got last night," I agreed. "And you were a bit hot under the collar yourself."

"I don't know what came over me. It was just so . . . so upsetting."

"Okay, she was mad and you were upset. Loudly mad and furiously upset. I got that. So, tell me her last name."

"I'd rather not."

"I'll find out one way or another."

Arthur paused, weighing my threat. Finally, his shoulders hunched and he said, "Valdez. It's Sabrina Valdez."

"And why was Sabrina Valdez," the woman with the high heels and sexy name, "upset?" I asked.

Arthur shoulders hunched even more. A few more inches and he would collapse in on himself. It was clear he knew he'd lost the battle. Very softly, he said, "She didn't like my naked lady."

"Naked lady?" For an instant I thought I'd misunderstood what he had said.

"Yes. A modern sculpture of Aphrodite I bought at an art show." He suddenly perked up a little. "Gorgeous. Very detailed. Aphrodite is said to have had the power to inspire desire, you know." From the glint in his eyes as he spoke about his statue, his knockoff Aphrodite had obviously channeled the power of desire to him. Then he deflated again. "Sabrina claimed it was a corruption of the original. No longer a work of art, but, well, you know."

"You bought it at an art show?"

"Well, it was an arts and crafts show. Some of it geared to adults. You know—"

Actually, I didn't know, but I could guess. "So, you showed this modern version of Aphrodite to her and she got, ah, angry?"

He nodded. "She said it made her uncomfortable." He paused. "But it was so beautiful, and the marble so cool and smooth." I could picture the little creep running his hands over the nude body, suggestively. No wonder Sabrina said it made her uncomfortable. Although what she saw in Arthur in the first place was a mystery. And why was he referring to Sabrina and the statue in the past tense?

"So, where's this 'naked lady'?" I asked, not sure I really wanted to know. It was Sabrina's whereabouts that I was concerned with.

"She dropped it overboard." He looked and sounded totally devastated by the revelation.

"She dropped it overboard?" Could the statue going into the water have been the splash I heard? "Maybe you'd better tell me what happened from the beginning."

"It's just like I've told you. We argued about the statue and she grabbed it and took it out back and held it out over the stern. I thought she was just trying to make a point. I couldn't believe she would actually let go of it. I mean, she may not have considered it art, but it was expensive."

Could he possibly be making this stuff up? "What did *you* do?"

"Nothing. Like I said, I couldn't believe she'd actually drop it in the lake. My Aphrodite. Gone. Just like that. Then Sabrina left without saying another word."

No final comment, just a splash, and she left. Arthur frozen in disbelief. It *was* possible. She could have changed from her heels into some soft-soled shoes or even left barefoot. That might have been why I hadn't heard her leave. But the entire exchange seemed bizarre. First a nasty argument. Then a malicious act. Followed by a silent withdrawal. If it had been a scene shot for a movie, it would have ended up on the cutting room floor.

I glanced down the dock and saw Logan and Judd headed toward us, so I decided it was best to end the exchange. I could look up Sabrina Valdez and check out Arthur's story later. After I'd had a free breakfast.

"Okay, Arthur." I signaled to Logan and Judd to wait, that I was coming. "Have to run."

Beth's is a small cafe nestled in an industrial area among a handful of marine related businesses and other small start-ups with unrecognizable names that gravitate to the dead-end street along the water for its low-rent options. Just the other side of the dead-end is a new industrial complex that includes a number of restaurants with views and menus that cater to people in business attire. But Logan, Judd and I are regulars at Beth's. Even though Judd is a successful lawyer and Logan is a university professor, we prefer our blue-collar café with its stained menus and hearty fare to the yuppie atmosphere just a few blocks away.

Logan and Judd wanted instant information, but I was hungry and put them off until we had our orders in. Then I gave them an overview of what had happened, from the argument to the disquieting splash to the silent aftermath. I also told them about Arthur waylaying me this morning and his explanation for why he'd lied to us the night before.

"Do you believe him?" Judd asked.

"Well, he did give Officer Dodd the runaround. But if what he told me this morning is true, I can understand why he wouldn't want to confess to it. Still, I intend to find out which is fact and which is a blatant lie."

"How?"

"By locating Sabrina."

"If she isn't in the lake, you mean." Logan started biting his lower lip, a habit of his when he's trying to think of something witty to say.

"Yes. I'm going to look for an email or telephone number for her."

"Think it will be a waterfront location?" Judd looked disappointed when neither Logan nor I acknowledged his attempt at humor.

"If I can't find her easily, I'll go back to Arthur and threaten him some more."

"You threatened him?" Judd raised his eyebrows.

"Just with going to the police."

"Your intent is simply to verify that she's alive?" Judd sounded more like a lawyer than a friend at the moment. But I didn't mind; I needed to think things through.

"That's it."

"Even if you locate someone named Sabrina Valdez, how will you know if you have the right person? There could be more than one, you know," Logan said.

"I may have to ask her if she knows Arthur." That would be awkward, but probably necessary.

Logan was chewing his lower lip again. "Give it up," I said, looking directly at him. "There's no connection between Sabrina and the enchantress known as the lady of the lake from medieval times."

Logan held up both hands. "I don't know what you mean."

"Of course you don't."

We finished our breakfasts, and Logan reluctantly paid for mine. I knew he would. Not everyone would understand why I swam over to the *Knotty Lady* in the wee morning hours, but Logan did. He can be as impulsive as I sometimes am. And as curious. If he'd heard what I'd heard, I had no doubt that he would have jumped in the lake to get a closer look.

On the way back to the *Aspara,* I thought of one more thing I could do to either disprove or verify Arthur's story. But that would have to wait until dark.

Chapter 3

Diving for Treasure

I found two Sabrina Valdezes in the online white pages, and although I hate to pay for information that I believe should be free, I reluctantly used my credit card to get the two telephone numbers and addresses. My first effort to reach Sabrina #1 failed to yield more than superficial results because the person who answered hung up on me before I could finish telling her my reason for calling. Still, she had sounded older than Arthur's Sabrina should have, so I put a question mark by her telephone number and tried the second number. There was no answer, but the message voice sounded like a possibility. I didn't leave a message. But my suspicious nature was piqued.

Next, I turned to social media. Neither Sabrina nor Arthur had a Facebook page. LinkedIn only had one Sabrina Valdez listed for the area. I didn't recognize her face, but I did recognize the name of the large professional services firm she worked for. It specialized in audits, taxes, risk assessment, and who knew what else. They occupied a large part of one of the downtown high-rise buildings. If I didn't get through to her by telephone, I could always go by and check her out at the firm. One way or the other, I was going to verify whether Arthur's Sabrina Valdez was among the living.

I spent the rest of the day running errands, reading, talking to Macavity, and restlessly pacing back and forth in my tiny galley/sitting area. At one point while I was trying to read, Macavity climbed up into my lap and stared at me with his two different colored eyes, something he does from time to time for reasons known only to him. I tried to stare him down with *my* two different colored eyes, but he always wins. His eyes were the reason I'd rescued him when he was only a kitten. I don't believe in fate, but my serendipitous visit to an animal shelter with a friend had resulted in me getting a kitten that I didn't want and her leaving empty-handed. If not fate, then what?

Every so often I want to scream at time to slow down, to stop the clock on a special moment, or to go back in time for an hour or even for five minutes to re-enjoy a live concert or the first bite of an exquisite meal. On the other hand, there are also times when I want to race into the future, to slip past an unpleasant situation or to simply get on with the task at hand. That was what I was experiencing Saturday evening as I anxiously waited for darkness to fall, trying not to look at my phone to see what time it was, again. I kept thinking about what it must be like for someone living in the Arctic Circle during the summer when the sun never sets.

Macavity must have sensed that something wasn't normal and decided to take advantage of the situation to wheedle a few extra treats out of me. He likes his food, but like most cats, he will only eat what he wants to, and I have to guess at his preferences by trying out different things. Since he has me wrapped around his fuzzy orange paw, I play the game. But he keeps changing the rules. His current passion was for Temptations Seafood Medley Cat Treats. After I finally stopped doling them out, he leapt up next to me on the settee and exposed his white belly for me to rub.

The seconds and the minutes passed slowly, imperceptible movement, like a snail crossing a path. But because I wasn't in the Arctic Circle, the sun eventually did disappear behind the horizon, and darkness descended like a curtain coming down on a stage. Only the show wasn't ending; it was about to begin.

At one time I'd been into scuba diving, and I still had most of the gear for it, including a wetsuit, fins, weights, mask, and an LED light you can attach to your hand. The light provides a relatively wide-angle beam in dark water, and since I didn't have a large area to explore, I thought it would be sufficient for what I had in mind. Jacques Cousteau I'm not, but I was confident that I could find the statue of Aphrodite if she was where Arthur said she was. In fact, I was surprised he hadn't mentioned trying to retrieve it himself—*if* it was really there. The lake is only about twenty feet deep in most of the marina with a fairly solid bottom interspersed with areas of sticky mud. Maybe he would eventually try to salvage it, or maybe he wouldn't bother because he knew it wasn't there.

A second nighttime swim, this time with a pair of goggles and a good light, and I would know whether Aphrodite was at the bottom of the lake. I refused to let myself consider the other possibility, that I would find the body of a real woman.

I waited until midnight. Arthur's boat was dark. I didn't know if he was home or not, but I didn't intend to make much noise. And it was highly unlikely that he would come out on his back deck, peer into the water, and notice my light. Besides, nighttime swims might be unusual but not illegal. And as far as I knew, a marina tenant didn't have special rights to the water under their boat.

This time I made sure my boarding ladder was in place, and I loosened the cover over my back deck so I could slip into the water out without making any noise. There was a light breeze, and the sound of rigging slapping aluminum masts echoed throughout the marina, punctuated occasionally by the rattle of tin roofs on the covered moorage spaces. Cover for my clandestine operation, I thought, as I lowered myself into the cold nighttime water. This time I was wearing a wetsuit for both camouflage and warmth, a weight belt to maintain neutral buoyancy, and swim fins for speed and efficiency of movement. Once in the lake, I adjusted the weight belt and my mask before diving underwater toward the end of the finger float where Arthur claimed Sabrina had dropped the marble statue.

My first attempt wasn't very graceful or productive. I bounced off a piling as I was trying to get my light to turn on, then ran out of breath. The second dive was a miracle. As I swam downward, my light instantly illuminated something sticking up out of some muck below the stern of the *Knotty Lady*. When I got closer, I could make out the head and the top half of Aphrodite's torso, the detailed body exposed to any sea creatures that happened by. An underwater erotic art display. Or pornographic sideshow, depending on whether you perceived her as alluring or lewd.

I was pleased not to see a real body, but, at the same time, I felt somewhat deflated. As if the presence of the statue supported the idea that I had overreacted and cried wolf without justification. Still, as long as I was there, I decided that I might as well rescue the lady in the lake. Not that she looked like a lady. More like a seductress with a wardrobe malfunction.

I reached down and tried to pull her out of the mud. It took several more dives and a lot of pushing back and forth before she was free. Then I took the 3/8 line I'd wrapped around my waist and secured it under her armpits. I had to make one more trip to the surface for air before I managed to get her prepared for the ascent. Then I tied the other end back around my waist so I wouldn't lose her.

Dragging a heavy marble statue along the bottom of the lake turned out to be more difficult than I'd anticipated. It must have weighed at least twenty pounds, maybe more. If I kept doing what I was doing, it seemed to me that it would take forever to retrieve the statue. It was time to rethink my approach.

Treading water, I considered the possibilities, including leaving Aphrodite where she was for someone else to find. But it was proof. Proof of what exactly I wasn't sure. But I had invested time and energy into the retrieval effort and didn't relish giving up. Foolish or not, I wanted to recover Arthur's statue.

Finally, I decided to continue pulling the marble vixen as far as the next finger float. From there I would hoist it up to the float and carry it back to my boat. That was all there was to my plan. I hadn't thought about what I was going to do with it after that.

With each dive I managed to move the statue another foot or two. I was running out of steam and motivation by the time I reached the finger float. After taking a few minutes to catch my breath, I secured the line from around my waist to one of the cleats near the end of the float. Then I swam back to the *Aspara*, climbed aboard, and removed my diving gear. It was time to salvage my sunken treasure.

The moment I pushed back the flap on the tarp cover, a barking dog charged me. I quickly pulled the flap into place and waited while the dog continued to bark.

"What do you have there, Riley?" I heard a male voice say. Riley's barks became softer and slowly transformed into obsequious snarfles. "Hey, it's okay," the voice said. "Nothing's there. Come on, now."

Great, that was all I needed. Someone taking a late-night stroll on the docks. It happened from time to time, especially on the weekend, but I had hoped it wouldn't happen tonight.

I sat there in the hazy glow of light that managed to seep through the cover over my aft deck, waiting for the footsteps to fade. Then I gave it another few minutes before coming out of hiding. There were still no lights on at the *Knotty Lady*. But it was possible the barking had awakened Arthur—if he was there. I would have to be stealthy, and quick.

It felt oddly satisfying to creep over to the other finger float in my black wetsuit. Like a character out of some Bond movie. Not one of the Bond girls to come dripping out of the lake all curves and seductive pursed lips, but a professional colleague of Bond's who had performed a successful clandestine operation. Of course, the statue wasn't some mysterious artifact to be returned to a museum or a stolen piece of art from a billionaire owner willing to cough up big bucks for its return. It was just a tacky piece of erotic kitsch that had been the catalyst for a bitter argument about artistic taste or, should I say, lack of taste?

The rest of the maneuver went smoothly. There were no barking dogs, no Arthur leaping out of the darkness at me, no flashlight suddenly spotlighting my late-night activity. I simply untied the line from the cleat and pulled up the statue, pausing a few times to rest. In spite of its buoyant force, the damned thing was heavy. Then I lugged it back to my boat.

Staring at the marble figure in the privacy of my tarp covered cockpit, I couldn't decide whether this was conclusive proof that Sabrina was alive or not. Maybe he had hit her over the head with the statue and both had gone into the water. The statue's shape and weight could have caused it to sink into the lakebed, whereas an unweighted body might have drifted off. At any rate, one part of Arthur's story checked out.

After mulling over what to do with Aphrodite, I decided I would hold onto the statue until I verified Sabrina's continued existence. Then I could either admit I had hauled it up and give it back to Arthur, or I could simply leave it on the float next to his boat and look surprised when he asked me if I knew anything about its reappearance. Either way I couldn't keep it on my boat. There wasn't any place to hide it.

After changing clothes and emptying out my laundry bag, I put the statue in the bag and headed down the dock with the bag over my shoulder, like Santa with a "for adults only" gift delivery.

The padlock on my locker opened with a squeak that seemed as loud as a gunshot in the silent marina. But moments later I had the statue concealed in the jumble of stuff inside my locker and was headed back to the *Aspara*. Another late night. I was exhausted. Tomorrow I would have to get back to normal. Whatever normal was.

Chapter 4

Whose Biological Clock Do I Hear Ticking?

Sunday morning I awoke to the sound of frogs clearing their throats. Or farting. Or partying. It's hard to tell with frogs. Reality finally pierced my almost awake haziness as I felt Macavity kneading my arm with his claws as he was either chasing or running away from the frogs. Then I remembered that we didn't have frogs in the marina. It was the ringtone on my cell phone. What had seemed cute after a couple of glasses of wine now just seemed weird. And I had taken so long to realize that it was my phone that the person on the other end had given up. Or they had been switched over to voicemail.

I looked at my alarm clock. It was 7:00 am. Who would be calling me at seven on a Sunday? Oh, that's right, I had a mother.

Sure enough. When I finally located my phone and checked for messages, there it was—my parents' landline number. Although I also have a father, I was fairly certain the call wasn't from him. He was probably still trying to hide under the covers while my mother hustled about doing whatever she did before the rest of us were totally awake.

I skipped the message and hit redial. "Where were you?" my mother asked. "I just phoned you."

"I know. That's why I'm calling you at seven in the morning on a Sunday." I knew she was immune to sarcasm, but I still had to make the effort.

"So, you agree?"

"Agree to what?" This was dangerous ground. I should have had my first cup of coffee before calling her back.

"You *are* coming to dinner today?" Why was that even a question? The whole family always came to dinner the first Sunday of each month. I don't remember how the dinners first started, but it was a tradition that we honored, because if we didn't, my mother hounded us and generally made life miserable. So, Dylan, my brother, his second wife, Angelina, and their twins, Noah and Emma, dutifully showed up at 3:00 for an early dinner. Sometimes Dylan's older daughter by his first wife also joined us. But Catrin somehow managed to make her attendance voluntary instead of mandatory without making my mother crazy. I wish I knew how she did it.

"Yes, of course I'll be there today."

"And you agree to dress up a little?"

"Why would I do that?" I always wore jeans and a T-shirt to dinner at my parents', or sometimes a sweater if it was cold.

"Didn't you listen to my message?"

"No, I thought it was better to call you back right away."

"That was thoughtful," she reluctantly acknowledged. "Well, it's because we will have a guest joining us."

"Did you call Dylan and Angelina to tell them to dress up?" I had a feeling I knew what this was about.

"No, Angelina always looks so nice."

"Dylan is a bit sloppy at times," I pointed out.

My mother sighed, one of her long-suffering sighs that used to make me feel guilty. Well, okay, it still makes me feel guilty, even after all these years, but I'm working on it.

"All right," I conceded. "I'll clean up my act a bit. How about a T-shirt with an inspirational quotation instead of something humorous?" *Humorous* in my world was usually labeled as *distasteful* by my mother's standards. One dinner she had complained to the entire family about my Bette Midler T-shirt that said, "I wouldn't say I invented tacky, but I definitely brought it to its present high popularity." At least I never wore anything to the family dinners that had to be censored for the kids.

I admit to not being a fashion plate. I don't wear make-up or high heels, but I do comb my hair and wear what used to be called "business casual" when meeting with clients. Unless I'm consulting with a high-tech company. Which I frequently do due to their prevalence in the area. Then I only dress up for the initial meeting. After that I wear whatever fits in with what I observed their employees to be wearing. For the most part, the high-tech world values comfort over fashion. I seldom have to search around much in my closet to find something that seems appropriate.

"Bryn," she began in a tone I recognized. Before she could give me the "why are you such a difficult child" speech that hasn't changed substantially since I was seven years old, I quickly capitulated.

"Mother, don't worry. I'll wear something that you will be okay with." I paused, then asked what I knew I shouldn't: "So, who are we having over?"

"Oh, it's just the son of a friend. No one you've met before."

I considered putting up a fight, but quickly thought better of it. My biological clock wasn't ticking, but my mother's ticked on my behalf. I was almost 40, never been married, never even been close to a trip to the altar, and that was just fine by me. Why my mother cared when she already had three grandchildren was beyond me. Although I suspect it has more to do with the vision of *her* perfect life than of mine.

I arrived a few minutes before 3:00 pm. Everyone else was already there. The twins greeted me at the door with sticky hands, yelling a fair facsimile of "Bryn, Bryn," competing with each other for my attention. Noah in his little sailor suit and Emma in her pink dress. No gender stereotyping in our family.

As soon as I made it inside, mother pulled me over to introduce me to John, a tall, serious looking man in his early forties with thick glasses and a very conservative suit with a vest. I couldn't remember the last time I'd seen a three-piece suit up close. The only good news was that he wasn't wearing a pocket watch.

To fulfill my obligation to dress up, I had pulled my straight, long red hair back into a French braid and was wearing the only red sweater I had. It was a gift from Dylan and Angelina, and I had no doubt who had picked it out. A very nice sweater, but I look terrible in red. Even in flats I was almost as tall as John, but from the way he was looking at me—like a starving man staring in a bakery window—it probably didn't matter.

"You two have a lot in common," my mother said. "John works for an auditing firm as a consultant." Got it, Mother—all consultants are alike. A separate breed of professionals, no matter what their specialty.

I was saved from having to explore our common interests by Dylan and Angelina. They came into the dining room from the kitchen, arm in arm, Angelina all frilly and floral, laughing at something her clever husband just said. They were followed by my father, a retired engineer whose only sin in my eyes was agreeing to name me Bryn Geneva Baczek. My mother liked Welsh names, and Geneva was my grandmother's name. That, combined with an unpronounceable last name, had been a life-long burden. I often varied the pronunciation when correcting people. Not to confuse anyone; it was my way of getting back at the gods of naming protocols.

The dinner wasn't terribly painful. The food was good. John was too shy to be obnoxious, and the kids were their usual attention-seeking distraction. When my mother asked if I was working on anything interesting, I knew it wasn't because she cared; it was an invitation to show off for John. I didn't take the bait, so she tried to fill in for me, but she doesn't really know what I do, so that didn't last too long.

For a moment I fantasized about telling everyone at the table about my two nighttime swims. I could picture the flutter of disapproval—my mother because she would be afraid it was a turn-off for John, my brother because he always disapproved of everything I did, Angelina because it wasn't dignified, and my father because of safety concerns. Only the twins would approve, maybe even think it was cool and ask to go with me next time. Well, I wasn't about to prolong the conversation even to provoke everyone a little. My goal was a quick departure before John and I were directed to go out back and sit in the patio swing together. Like a scene from a 1950s romantic comedy. But since I wasn't wearing a retro skirt with a poodle dog on it and John would have to wipe down the swing before sitting on it with his immaculate clothes, maybe we would simply be directed to the loveseat in the living room where everyone could keep an eye on us as the rom-com developed.

No way that was going to happen.

As soon as the last bite was swallowed, I jumped up and started clearing the table, announcing that I had to leave right away because I had plans for the evening. My mother gave me the stink eye, but she held her tongue, grabbed some dishes and followed me into the kitchen.

"He's a nice man," she said defensively.

"Yes," Angelina agreed as she came in carrying an empty platter. She obviously hadn't taken time to stack any dishes. "No need to run," she added.

"She's afraid of commitment," my mother said. Before the two could become engaged in an in-depth discussion of my failed relationships, I kissed my mother on the cheek, waved at Angelina, and whipped out the back door. It was true that my love life was currently non-existent, but I didn't want to hang around for the dissection.

There wasn't much traffic, so I was home in time to try Sabrina #2 a couple more times. When she didn't answer, I turned to Macavity and Bubbles IV and said, "So, what are our plans for this evening?" When they didn't answer, I put the cookies I had snagged when leaving my parents' house on a plate and settled in to watch a movie on my computer. The movie wasn't great, but the cookies were delicious. I shared a few crumbs with Macavity, breaking my rule of not giving him people food. I considered dropping a few tiny tidbits into the bowl for Bubbles IV to see if that would cheer him up but decided it would probably just hasten his demise. He wasn't looking good, but then it's hard to tell if a goldfish is ill or just bored. When Macavity decided there were no more treats for him, he hurried off to make his nightly rounds of the marina, leaving me alone but not lonely. Well, maybe a bit lonely.

My office is in a smallish room on the second floor of the building at the foot of the dock. The windows look out over the marina with a peek-a-boo view of the lake. Monday morning, I managed to respond to my alarm and get dressed in time to get to my office by 9:00 am. To me that is a civilized hour to begin the day's work. Especially on a Monday. I barely had time to pour myself a cup of coffee from the Keurig I keep on a wobbly end table in the corner of my office when there was a discreet knock on the door. Since I usually go to my clients and seldom have anyone drop by, I assumed it was Hudson Hiller, our landlord, or someone looking for another tenant in the building. To my surprise when I answered the door it was Arthur.

"Hello," I managed.

"Hello," Arthur said back. "Ah, could we talk?"

I hesitated a moment before motioning him inside. It didn't seem to me there was anything to talk about. Unless he had come by to offer proof of Sabrina's continued presence on this earth. Or to ask me to erase the conversation I had allegedly recorded.

Curiosity won out over my inclination to say I was too busy to talk.

He looked around as he headed for the chair across from my cluttered desk. I admit the space is tiny, made to feel smaller by all of the bookshelves filled to over capacity with books and stacks of files. Since it was my workspace and not intended for client meetings, I didn't feel like I needed to apologize. Still, I couldn't help but feel a bit self-conscious about its disorderly appearance. My mother's housekeeping regimen was a forever curse. I've never been able to shake her example in my mind, even though I'm not even slightly tempted to emulate her in practice.

It took Arthur almost a minute of clearing his throat before he stated the reason for his visit. "I, er, I just wanted to explain about Sabrina. You see, we aren't actually friends. She's a business acquaintance." I knew that he worked for a large nonprofit associated with coordinating housing programs for the homeless, a group called the Affordable Housing Alliance. But that was all I knew about him. However, I was pleased to note that today he was referring to Sabrina in the present tense.

"Does she work for your group?" I asked.

"No, she's an auditor." My second auditor in as many days. "I'm the secretary/treasurer, so it's my job to manage the audit. In the past we've used a solo independent guy, but we've grown so much and our finances are a lot more complicated than they used to be, so I went to Zelen and Hobbs and chose Sabrina for her, ah, skill set."

I didn't ask what that skill set might be, but I did ask the obvious question: "So why was she on your boat?"

"She stopped by to pick up some papers."

"In the evening?"

"She said she was going to be with another client all day and wanted to have the papers to review early the next morning."

"So, you invited her to stop by your boat to pick them up?"

"She said it was on her way home."

"Let me see if I understand—she came on board and saw your statue of Aphrodite . . .?" I found the scenario hard to believe, although it *was* possible.

"You see, I was hoping . . ." His voice trailed off. It didn't take much imagination to know what he'd been hoping for.

"I got it. You wanted her visit to be personal and she wanted to keep it professional."

"She overreacted." He sounded whiney and self-justifying. If something had happened to Sabrina, it wasn't me he would have to convince.

"Why are you telling me this?"

"Because, well, because I want you to know that our argument wasn't a big deal. Just an unfortunate misunderstanding."

"Okay."

"Okay?"

"Sure."

He looked relieved, got up, thanking me profusely for being understanding, and left. If his story panned out, maybe I would put the statue in a stocking for him at Christmas. On the other hand, maybe I'd be putting it in a very large and heavy cake and handing it to him through prison bars.

Chapter 5

Sabrina, Where Art Thou?

The first thing I did after Arthur left was to look up the AHA, Affordable Housing Alliance, website. They had been in the news enough that I was somewhat familiar with their mission. In addition, I had done some consulting with a couple of their member groups. But I was curious about the larger picture, as well as who was on their board. You can tell a lot about a nonprofit by looking at the qualifications and connections of their board members.

Arthur was right about one thing, AHA was thriving, its large membership including some big movers and shakers. At the same time, however, the homeless population was also growing. With so many committed to solving the problem of homelessness, it seemed like AHA should have been making better progress toward reducing the number of homeless people on our streets. But, based on what I'd observed in the city and read in the news, they weren't even able to push the boulder halfway up the hill before it rolled back down on them. Still, you had to give them credit for continuing to try.

As I studied their website, I started to get a clearer picture of the scope and challenges faced by AHA. Homelessness is clearly a complicated situation, and finding solutions was undoubtedly made even more complicated by the fact that AHA's members included nonprofit and for-profit organizations, each coming at homelessness from a slightly different perspective.

Some of the nonprofits listed served special needs populations—from veterans to single mothers with children to non-English speaking immigrants. There were also social service and religious groups that were probably less focused on specific issues than simply trying to eliminate one tiny corner of human suffering.

Then there were the members of AHA who had a financial stake in the primary goal of eliminating homelessness: construction companies, architectural firms, property management associations, banks, and land developers. A couple members even owned and/or managed low-income housing developments. None of these connections was a secret though. And I'm aware that just because a group has a financial interest in a particular venture doesn't mean they aren't also motivated by social consciousness. There's nothing that says you can't make a profit off of good deeds. Someone has to provide the infrastructure for housing. Still, even with an umbrella group to coordinate things, the act of getting the homeless off the streets by providing safe and affordable places to live was a monumental undertaking. They probably had to count each small success as progress and each failure as a learning experience. Otherwise, how did they keep pushing the boulder up that hill?

In addition to listing its diverse membership and some fairly impressive statistics about the number of living units developed or preserved during the previous year, the AHA website also had bios of their board members. The large board included representatives from organizations directly involved in providing services and housing to low-income and special needs groups as well as people from large companies whose participation was likely part of an on-going philanthropic commitment to the community. Only a few board members had bios that were short on activities dedicated to helping people. Maybe they had just recently found their passion, or maybe they were in it to make a buck. If they contributed to the common goal, who was I to judge?

Next, I pulled up the website for Zelen and Hobbs. It was a huge international firm with a fairly good-sized workforce in Seattle. I was familiar with some of their work, having come across reports done by them for mutual clients. But I'd never actually worked with or for them. Their website mentioned a wide range of advisory, tax and audit services, including mergers and acquisitions, and risk analysis. The website also mentioned their commitment to pro bono work for nonprofits. I wondered if AHA was a paying customer or if they were getting free consulting. That was something I could ask Arthur, although I wasn't sure what bearing it had on the situation.

At the top of their home page there was a tab titled "Meet Our People." When I clicked on it and went to the section on Audit and Assurance, I quickly found Sabrina's picture. She was looking directly at the camera with her head slightly tilted, like a model who knows how to sell her good looks. I couldn't imagine how Arthur, in his wildest dreams, imagined he could connect romantically with an attractive professional like Sabrina. On the other hand, the laws of attraction can be as capricious as any other laws. Maybe that's what he had been counting on.

One thing was clear: Arthur was concerned about me trying to get in touch with Sabrina, whether because of what she might tell me or because she was no longer among the living—a critical difference. For my own peace of mind, it was time to get serious about confirming or disproving my suspicions. And I sincerely hoped it would be the former and not the latter.

I called Zelen and Hobbs and asked to be put through to Sabrina Valdez. There was a moment's pause before her voice message clicked in. Somehow, I wasn't surprised. Of course, it was possible she was in a meeting or just too busy to take an unsolicited call. One option was to leave a message and wait for her to call me back. But I was getting impatient. I called the main number again and said that I needed to get in touch with Sabrina Valdez immediately and asked if they had some way of contacting her. I wasn't sure what I was going to say to her if I actually managed to get through, but I could always claim to have the wrong Sabrina Valdez. After all, I knew that there was at least one other in the area.

Unfortunately, there was no paging system and no one apparently willing to run around and look for her, but I was told they would put me through to her supervisor. After a brief time listening to what seemed to me inappropriate rap music for a conservative firm, I connected with a live voice who informed me that Sabrina's calendar indicated she was in a meeting and the fastest way to get through to her was to leave a voice message. Unless it was a life and death matter . . .?

Okay, I was back to option number one: leave a voice message and wait around for her to return my call. The message I left implied I had a question about the work she was doing for AHA. I was fairly certain that would get me a call back. Once she verified that she was working with Arthur on an AHA project, I could say something about also leaving a message for Arthur and that I would get back to her if I couldn't get the information directly from him. That might not explain why I'd left her a message in the first place, but a busy woman like Sabrina would probably be happy not to have more work piled on her, whatever the reason. And Arthur wouldn't have to worry about me stoking the fire he had started.

I put down the phone, tapped a pen on a blank piece of paper, stared at my computer, and admitted to myself that I am a person totally lacking in patience when I want to get something over with. I could sit there and wait for Sabrina to return my call. Or . . . I could make a trip to Zelen and Hobbs and check out for myself whether Sabrina was in meetings or otherwise not available. If I combined a trip to Zelen and Hobbs with a little grocery shopping, I would get both answers and food. I was running low on staples, including Macavity's favorites. By making a run on the market, I would make Macavity a happy cat. I would do it for Macavity . . . sure.

My skepticism and persistence often serve me well, but in this instance, I knew I was rationalizing doing something that some might label as obsessive. Or none of my business. Or just plain stupid. On the other hand, until I knew for sure that Sabrina Valdez was happily attending a meeting, I wouldn't be able to concentrate on anything else.

The downside was having to get dressed up. I opted for a classic dark green jacket that had come from a nearby Goodwill, a light green silk blouse that was only slightly wrinkled, and a pair of black slacks that I had bought on sale. I don't like spending a lot of money on clothes, and from time to time I raid consignment shops and thrift stores for wardrobe additions. I figure that unless the former owner of a piece can identify some distinguishing mark, no one will know where I bought it. Not that I would care if they did. Although it might feel uncomfortable meeting someone while wearing one of their castoffs.

Parking downtown is both difficult and expensive, so I parked near a light rail station on the hill above town and took the train. I got off at a station that was just a short walk to the building in which Zelen and Hobbs occupied several floors. The main lobby was huge. A stairway to the left led to a Starbucks on the second floor that was open to the high-ceilinged lobby. I could smell the coffee and hear the chatter of small talk dimmed by banal background music. The aroma of coffee is like catnip to me; I had to force myself to keep walking past the steps, miraculously resisting the strong desire for a fresh brew.

To the right was a waiting area with several couches, a cluster of comfortable looking chairs positioned around a large coffee table, and a few more isolated chairs scattered randomly in empty spaces, each with its own small table. A young woman was seated on the couch, mouthing the words to something, maybe practicing for an interview. She was wearing a dark blue suit and a white blouse, safe interview attire. Her dark navy heels were resting beside her bare feet. I hoped she could slip them on in a hurry if and when someone came to get her.

Straight ahead, a young man at a long desk below a sign listing the residents of the building was guarding the entry gates leading to the bank of elevators. He looked slightly bored, his eyes wandering around the lobby as if searching for a distraction, settling on the shapely legs of the young woman on the coach. When I stopped in front of his desk it seemed to me that he turned in my direction very reluctantly. Still, once we made eye contact, he gave me his full attention. Going for the direct approach, I asked if Sabrina Valdez was in.

"Do you have an appointment?"

I knew the right answer: "Yes." I glanced at my watch. It was 11:45. "We're going to lunch." I hadn't planned to say that, but given the time, it seemed like a reasonable response. Since it was doubtful there were *two* Sabrina Valdezes that worked for Zelen and Hobbs, I wasn't sure what I was going to say if she answered and the receptionist told her that her lunch appointment was in the lobby. Maybe, "Oh, my assistant must have made a mistake." Something vague like that. Whatever—I didn't think it was a crime to pretend you had a lunch scheduled with someone. Unless she thought I was stalking her.

The receptionist dialed a number and we waited while it rang. And rang. And rang. "Sorry," he said, hanging up. "She doesn't seem to be answering. What is your name? I'll leave a message telling her you're here."

"Tiffany Riddle," I said without hesitation. Why, I have no idea. That's what happens when you don't plan ahead. And there was probably a camera somewhere. There's no such thing as anonymity anymore. On the other hand, if Sabrina called down to the desk and said she didn't know anyone named Tiffany Riddle, I would have succeeded in verifying her existence without making it awkward if we met some time in the future. Although, if that happened, departing without making a total fool of myself would be unavoidable. In general, I agree with my mother, the master of the "white lie," that one lie inevitably leads to another and it is therefore better not to lie in the first place. Fortunately, I don't consider certain acts of deception as lies. Rather, it's a matter of bending truth to your needs for the sake of expediency. Hopefully, the truth I was currently bending wasn't going to cause me too many problems.

I settled in on one of the chairs in the waiting area and flipped through my email. Then browsed news headlines. Then I considered playing mahjong but caught myself just in time. I didn't intend to stay there indefinitely. It had already been fifteen minutes. How long was I willing to hang around on the off chance that she would get the message that there was someone waiting to go to lunch with her?

While I was trying to decide what to do an irresistible opportunity presented itself. A group of people arrived and gathered around the reception desk. I got up and joined them, pretending I was waiting with them. Eavesdropping on their conversation with the receptionist, I learned that they were expected at Zelen and Hobbs for a lunch meeting. I casually took off my jacket, moved alongside one of the women and asked her for the time. Moments later I had not only confirmed what time it was, but I was with part of the group on the elevator headed for the fifth-floor offices of Zelen and Hobbs. That's where the group's lunch meeting was. What the heck, the fifth floor was as good a place as any to start my search for the elusive Sabrina.

When we arrived on the fifth floor, I parted company from my make-believe lunch companions and started wandering around, peering over cubicle partitions, and trying to peek inside offices of those lucky enough to have their own space. When that got me nowhere, I decided it was time to break down and ask for directions. But it seemed like anyone who wasn't at a desk was either on their phone or avoided making eye contact, as if too busy to be bothered talking to someone they didn't know. When I came across a young woman who looked me in the eyes and smiled, I leapt on the opening. “Excuse me,” I said. “But can you tell me where Sabrina’s office is?” I thought that by using only her first name it would seem like I might be a little confused but that I had a right to be there.

“Oh, you have the wrong floor. She’s one down. On four,” she added, pointing down. In case I didn’t know which way “down” was.

“Sorry,” I said, rolling my eyes. “I must have pushed the wrong button on the elevator. Thanks.” Better to be thought incompetent than sneaky.

“You’re welcome.” Maybe it was my overactive imagination kicking in, but in spite of her friendly helpfulness, I felt like she checked me out in case she had to describe me later to someone official. On the other hand, maybe she was admiring my jacket. Maybe she had once owned one just like it.

I spotted a sign that said “stairs” and took them down to the fourth floor. Then I headed in the same direction I’d been going on five. In case she’d meant the reference to “down” literally.

There were fewer occupied spaces on the fourth floor. Unfortunately, the nameplates on the cubicles and on the glass panels next to office doors were too small to read from the main aisle. They made me feel like I was failing an eye exam. Could you go back to line three, please?

I had just paused to get my bearings when I overhead someone say, “Have you seen Sabrina this morning? She was supposed to be in a meeting with the group from Warner’s.” Talk about lucky. I slowly pivoted around to see who had asked the question.

My eyes landed on an older, frumpy looking woman frowning at a young, equally frumpy woman sitting in a cubicle right next to an office with a name plate that *could* have said

Sabrina Valdez. I headed in their direction, pausing to listen while pretending to answer my phone.

"No, and she didn't leave a message for me either." The young woman sounded aggrieved. "How am I supposed to keep track of her calendar if she doesn't stay in touch?"

"Well, if she shows up, tell her to hightail it to the conference room on three. The meeting is continuing over lunch."

"Will do. Although I'm going to lunch soon, so if she doesn't deign to show herself within the next five minutes or so, then it's not my problem."

The older woman paused a moment, then shrugged. Not her problem either apparently. It seemed that Sabrina, the classy woman with the model's demeanor and fancy high heels, didn't inspire much loyalty among her colleagues, at least not with these two.

There was a voice in my head telling me that the smart thing to do was to acknowledge defeat and make my exit. But I was so close to Sabrina's office, and it was possible there was something in there that would help me figure out where she might be. And her assistant was about to take a lunch break. A quick look around and I would leave. If anyone caught me, I could say I was leaving her a note. In for a penny, in for a pound. Whatever that means.

There was a vacant cubicle nearby with a view of Sabrina's office and the woman who would hopefully soon go to lunch. I sat down at the desk and pretended to be responding to a text message. What I was actually doing was playing mahjong. I'm addicted. But I try to limit my playing to times like this when I need to while away a few minutes. I got so absorbed in a run of fours that I almost missed seeing the woman leave. As she streaked by, apparently eager to get away, I reluctantly clicked off the game and got up, assiduously forcing myself not to glance around. In case anyone was watching, I needed to look like I knew what I was doing. I marched straight over to Sabrina's office and poked my head around the corner before entering. Unless someone knew Sabrina wasn't there, they might think I was asking for permission to enter and not guess that I was heading into an empty office.

Sabrina's space was larger than my office, but not by much. The main difference was how orderly it was. There was very little on her desk, and what there was looked like it had been carefully placed with an eye to both function and aesthetics. The only papers were in an ornate wood box lined up with the edge of the desk on the left-hand corner. Next to the box was a stained-glass holder for her cards. I reached over and took a card as I went around behind her desk. Very nice card. Balanced design, bold colors, her picture in a small box in the corner. It was too bad it wasn't a picture of her high heels; I would have recognized them.

I wasn't sure what I was looking for. I already knew she had failed to show up for a meeting and that no one had seen her. But you never knew what you would find until you looked. I pulled open the top drawer of her desk and found myself staring at an appointment book. I didn't know people still used those. Almost everyone I know puts everything online. Even my parents do. Wishing I was wearing gloves, I used the bottom corner of my jacket to open the book. It wasn't easy. The pages didn't want to cooperate. They were begging for the feel of flesh rather than cloth. But with some effort, I finally managed to work my way to the page for last Friday. There were several times and names noted for appointments during the day. "AS" was written at the bottom of the page. "AS" as in Arthur Stanton? Continuing my push and pinch technique, I slowly turned some more pages. Nothing for Saturday or Sunday. Then on to today. The meeting she was missing was noted on her calendar. Nothing was scheduled for the afternoon.

Flipping to the back of the appointment book I found a list of telephone numbers. Quaint. There was also a post-it with some writing on it covering part of the list. I pinched the corner of the post-it with the fingernails of my left hand as I studied the list.

"Ahem," someone said. At least that's how I translated the sound. I looked up to see a young man in a moss green shirt standing in the doorway. I liked his shirt. I'm fond of green. It complements one of my eyes.

"Can I help you?" I asked, trying to sound confident and natural.

"I'm looking for Sabrina," he said.

"And I'm looking for some paper so I can leave her a note." I started rummaging through the drawer, regretting the fingerprints I was leaving all over the contents of her desk.

"Here," he said tossing me a small notepad that I miraculously managed to catch without falling on my face on top of the desk. Had I looked like someone able to grab a notepad out of the air, or had the gesture been a power play?

"Thanks." I shut the drawer, tore off a page from the notepad and tossed it back to him, hoping he would fumble and have to pick it up off the floor. But he handily caught it and put it back in a pocket. Then I reached for a pen in the cloisonné container on Sabrina's desk, pausing to appreciate what a lovely piece it was. "You want to leave a note too?" I asked since he was still hanging around.

"No, but I don't think we've met, have we?"

If he had to ask, and we *had* met, I obviously hadn't made much of an impression on him. Or was that a version of an office pick-up line? I glanced up to verify that I didn't recognize him. "No, I don't think so." He wasn't bad looking, but a little young for me. But then, maybe he wasn't interested in me as a woman but as a suspicious character. I scribbled a brief message: "Call me when you get in. TR." Then I stuck the note under her card holder, feeling only slightly guilty about ruining the symmetry of the contents on her desk.

As I moved toward the door, I expected the young man to step aside or leave ahead of me. Instead, he stuck out his hand and said, "I'm Tom Thompson."

I was tempted to ask him if his name was really Thomas Thompson, but I didn't want to say anything that he might remember later. I shook his hand, mumbled something about being late for a meeting and squeezed past him, glancing back to make sure he wasn't following me. He wasn't. He had gone into Sabrina's office, perhaps to check out my note. I saw an "exit" sign not too far away and made a beeline for it, surreptitiously looking over my shoulder to see if I was being observed before darting into the stairway. Then I took off like I was being chased by a Minotaur.

I got off on the second floor and looked around for a restroom. I needed to get out of sight and take a few minutes to figure out how I was going to make my exit without being noticed.

Once I found the restroom I had to go. It's the power of suggestion. Then I washed my hands, looked at my image in the mirror, momentarily worrying that that I had added a few gray hairs, relaxed the muscles in my face to achieve a "composed" look, and headed back to the stairway. My hastily improvised plan for leaving Zelen and Hobbs was to do the same thing I had done to get in: I would hang out near the elevators until a few people were leaving together and join them. I took off my green jacket again, glad that I had chosen a nondescript blouse to go with it.

Cell phones are great for making you look like you belong someplace. I "answered" my cell as I exited the stairway near the elevators and pretended to be talking to someone. Fortunately, I didn't have to wait long. It was, after all, the lunch hour. I smiled as I walked alongside a trio of women all talking excitedly as though they'd been forced to keep an oath of silence until that moment and were bursting with a pent-up need to communicate. I nodded and grinned as if I was in on their conversation. But I needn't have bothered. There was a different young man at the reception desk. Like his predecessor, he too looked bored. Apparently not the most exciting job in the building.

On my way out, I was tempted to make a quick stop at the second floor Starbucks for a cup of coffee, but decided it was better to put some distance between Tiffany Riddle and Zelen and Hobbs. It wasn't as if I wouldn't have plenty of other coffee shops to choose from; Starbucks had locations sprinkled throughout the city, some directly across the street from each other. All alike. All serving the same coffee and the same pastries and assorted snacks. Not much variety, but consistently dependable.

After walking a couple of blocks, occasionally looking over my shoulder, I felt comfortable enough to take a place at the back of a short line in a smallish Starbucks. The line moved quickly. I ordered a single tall Americano because I dislike always asking for a tall drip, even though it costs less and I like the taste. There were several empty stools at a counter facing the sidewalk. I took one off to the side, popped the lid off my coffee for ease of sipping, and watched the people all hurrying to wherever they were supposed to be. It seemed to me like no one except the homeless and infirm walked slowly these days. Taking time to smell the roses was definitely not trending. Of course, on city streets, the smells weren't always pleasant.

Well, I asked myself, what next, *Tiffany*? How do you solve the *riddle* of the missing Sabrina? I reached into my pocket for her card and discovered that I had also managed to hang onto the post-it that had been in her appointment book. I didn't remember putting it in my pocket. I must have done so reflexively when Tom Thompson surprised me while I was searching Sabrina's appointment book. Oh well. It was too late now to return it. Hopefully, Sabrina had a back-up. Assuming, of course, that she was still around to need the information.

As I studied Sabrina's card for inspiration, all I could think of was that I had taken a foolish risk for nothing. If she really was missing, why hadn't one of her friends or colleagues reported it? Why didn't the woman in charge of her calendar know where she was? Did she have a history of no-shows? Could she have called in sick at the last minute? Maybe she had a family emergency and forgot to tell anyone. It was possible I'd get a call-back from her and that would be the end of that. I just had to be patient. On the other hand, I desperately wanted closure.

I turned my attention to the post-it I had unintentionally confiscated. The purloined post-it—it had a nice ring. There were two names written on the small yellow square, the writing slanted to the right with no breaks between the letters. Very precise. Gerald, no last name. And Harold, no last name. Gerald and Harold. Cute. There were telephone numbers next to their names. Two mystery men who didn't rate inclusion on her official list of telephone numbers. Unless they were recent acquaintances and she hadn't had time to add them. Or maybe their names were code for something. Although why would she bother with any kind of code on a post-it tucked in her private appointment book in her private office? They could be anybody. Pet sitters. Gardeners. Relatives. Men met through an online dating app. Anybody. But it was all I had, so it screamed *CLUE* to me.

I was acutely aware that snooping in Sabrina's address book had been an invasion of privacy bordering on the illegal. Although I doubted there was a statute citing the reading of someone's address book as a crime, sneaking into a secure building and using a false name undoubtedly put me on shaky legal ground. Nevertheless, I was willing to defend my transgressions on the grounds that my intentions had been honorable.

Gerald and Harold. And two phone numbers. It would be very unfair if the post-it was dead-end.

I got out my cell and stared at the dial screen, reluctant to take the next step. It's hard to be vague about who you are when your name and number pops up on someone's caller ID. It had been much easier to make anonymous calls when there were public phones everywhere. Even though half the time the black payphones had been battered and inoperable, their receivers dangling from useless cords. The telephone book ripped apart or missing. And the booth itself vandalized and desecrated in a variety of disgusting ways. Now you rarely saw one, except for an occasional appearance in a movie scene where someone is shot and slowly slides down the side of the glass-sided enclosure. Maybe that's one of the reasons pay phones have gone the way of the Pinto sedan; they were too dangerous.

So, a pay phone wasn't an option. But using a burner phone was—if I'd had one. Or I could do a reverse cell phone lookup. On the other hand, the fast and easy thing to do was to simply call the numbers. Maybe I would get a company name. Or, if the number went straight through to an individual, I might get a message that gave me a full name. The downside of dialing the number was the possibility of getting a real person. Of course, I could say, "Do I have Gerald Henderson?" And if they played their part correctly, they might say, "No, this is Gerald so-and-so." Or, I could say, "Sorry, I must have the wrong number" as if I immediately recognized that I had the wrong voice and hang up. It wasn't really a big deal.

Just like I'd hoped, the first call put me straight through to voice mail and got me a full name: "Please leave a message for Gerald Fontaine after the tone." The same thing happened for mystery man number two: "Harold Hanson is not able to take your call at this time—"

It didn't take long after that to find out who Gerald and Harold worked for. They were both public officials. And unless they were personal friends of Sabrina's who just happened to be in professions involving oversight of potentially illegal activities, it seemed likely that Sabrina had a very specific reason for having their telephone numbers. Gerald Fontaine was with the United States Attorney's Office for the Western District of Washington. And Harold Hanson was with the State Auditor's Office.

It was too bad the post-it wasn't dated. If she had recently contacted these two men, that might mean it had something to do with her AHA assignment. And if that was the case, well, it just might be the lead I’d been hoping to find.

Chapter 6

Can I Help You?

That evening I met my long-time friend Sophie for dinner. We've been friends since grade school when I beat up a couple of kids who were bullying her. I was tall for my age back then, still hoping I was going to end up on the short side of average. Sophie, on the other hand, has always been petite. In high school we were called Mutt and Jeff. When someone first gave us those nicknames, I had to look up the reference. I was surprised to find they were characters from an old cartoon strip. That in and of itself seemed strange for kids in our age group. Although maybe the fact that they got the two characters mixed up was indicative of only a passing familiarity with the strip. I was labeled Jeff, the short one in the comic strip. And Sophie was called Mutt. No matter how hard we tried to shed the labels, they stuck. For four long years.

At the time, Sophie repeatedly insisted that it was better to be called Jeff than "red" or "beanpole." And she thought it was hilarious that they had the labels backwards. Of course, she had blossomed in high school into a shapely short girl with lovely hair that you could actually accurately describe as "chestnut," a bold mix of copper and brown tones. She was also a cheerleader, had lots of boyfriends, and when she was referred to as "Mutt" it seemed more like a term of endearment than anything. I, on the other hand, was tall and smart. Too tall and too academic to fit in with the popular set. And I wasn't particularly athletic, so that didn't serve as an outlet. Still, Sophie and I remained good friends even after we left home. Through our college years at different colleges, through my wanderings and her marriage. And through all of the rest of our ups and downs. Her miscarriage and eventual divorce. My failed relationships and mother problems. Everything life threw at us; we were there for each other.

We had dinner in a restaurant we frequented, eating in the bar so we didn't feel pressured to hurry. We talked about stories in the news, a few mutual friends, and the latest with her ex. We were finished with dinner and lingering over coffee when I brought up the visit to Zelen and Hobbs and confessed to being in possession of a *purloined post-it.*

"That's not funny, Bryn."

"Doesn't it sound like something out of Sherlock Holmes?"

Sophie frowned. "Don't you think you should tell the police?" she asked, cutting right to the chase.

"Tell them what?" I said in a tone I knew sounded guilty and defensive.

Sophie's frown deepened and one eyebrow shot upward, a disapproving look I was all too familiar with. "But what if one of these men knows something about her disappearance?"

"First of all, I don't know for sure that she has disappeared. Second, I have no reason to believe that either Gerald or Harold would know anything as to her whereabouts. That post-it could have been there for months."

"Then why are you acting like you've discovered the secret to the pyramids or something?"

"I don't even know enough to call it a hunch, more like an inkling or a wild, baseless guess."

Sophie put both elbows on the small table and looked me in the eyes. "Bryn Geneva . . ."

I groaned. "No, not a lecture. I don't need a lecture. I need support and advice."

Sophie sighed. "You haven't changed."

"Since when?" I asked, trying to lighten the tone of our conversation.

"You have always had a way of getting mixed up in things and then having to dig yourself out."

"That's a mixed metaphor," I pointed out.

"You know what I mean." She frowned. "But this is serious. If something has happened to this Sabrina woman, you need to let someone know. It isn't just a question of lifting a post-it."

"Wouldn't you think that a family member, friend or a co-worker would notice if she really is missing?"

"You'd think so, but the question is what are *you* going to do with what *you* know?"

"That's what I wanted to talk to you about."

"Okay, so let's talk."

After several rounds of coffee, listing the pros and cons of each potential action on a pile of napkins, and arguing our conclusions back and forth half a dozen times, we came up with a four-part compromise plan. First, since I had Sabrina's address from my online research, I was going to drive by her house on my way home to see if there were any lights on. Although it was getting a little late for anyone's lights to be on and having a light on wouldn't prove she was there, it still seemed like it might be worth the extra few minutes to check. Maybe I would catch a glimpse of her and my search would be over. If not, tomorrow morning I would try her office again, and if she wasn't there, I would go by her house during the day. If I still wasn't satisfied, I would call Ben, a homicide detective I know, and ask him for advice.

Some time ago Ben and I'd had one romantic evening followed by . . . nothing. Not long after that, we'd ended up working together to put a bad guy away. When the case was resolved, he had given me a silver chimera on a chain to commemorate the event. A thoughtful but strange gift . . . followed by . . . nothing. I wasn't sure if I'd wanted *something,* but his lack of follow-through still bothered me. It was partly an ego thing and partly curiosity as to why he hadn't stayed in touch.

I finished off my coffee, said goodbye to Sophie and made a pit stop before heading home via Sabrina's. It was a bit out of my way, but traffic was light and my GPS found the shortest route. She lived in a townhouse in the middle of a row of townhouses, all connected to each other, with tiny, fenced yards in front. They may have been slightly different colors during the day, but at night they all looked alike. According to my GPS I had arrived, but the address I had for her didn't quite match up with the address on the townhouse identified as my destination. Apparently, they all looked alike to my GPS too. Fortunately, every townhouse had its porch lights on, illuminating the standardized, black address numbers. I wondered if that was a community requirement or just something considered a good safety measure. Whatever the reason, it only took a few minutes to locate the right townhouse, even without the aid of technology.

I sat in my car in front of her place, staring at the windows. There were no lights on. But, I told, myself, that didn't mean anything at 11:30 on a Monday evening. Most working people were either in bed or thinking about it by now. Like I should have been.

I had my hand on the door handle and was about to get out of the car to walk around to the back of the row of townhouses when someone tapped on the passenger side window. "Shit," I yelled, jerking around to see who was there.

A middle-aged man was bent over, peering into my car, motioning for me to roll down my window. My first impulse was to lower the window just enough to tell him not many cars have crank-style windows anymore. But even though I didn't see a weapon, I wasn't sure that was a good idea. Although he could already have pulled open my car door and attacked me if that was what he had in mind. I should have locked the damn door. Just in case I needed to make a quick exit I started the engine before pushing the down button for the window.

"Can I help you?" he asked.

"Help me?" I echoed.

"I noticed you sitting out here," he said. "Are you from the neighborhood?"

Then I got it. He was a vigilant neighbor concerned about local crime. "No, thanks," I said. "I was trying to decide whether it's too late to knock on Sabrina's door. I found myself in the neighborhood . . ." Ouch—that sounded lame. "And I just thought . . . but she doesn't have any lights on." I paused briefly. "You haven't seen her around in the last hour or so, have you?"

"You mean the dark-haired woman in this townhouse?"

"Yes." Did he think I'd be parked in front of someone else's townhouse if I really was looking for her?

"No, sorry. I haven't seen her around this evening."

"How about earlier today?" As soon as I asked, I knew the question sounded odd.

He straightened up, took a step back and stared at me as if trying to make up his mind just how strange the question really was.

"Look," I said, quickly modifying my story a bit so as not to sound like a stalker. "Sabrina and I work together and she didn't show up today. And no one heard from her. So, I decided to come by." Okay, that didn't make me sound much better. Who waits until 11:30 at night to check up on someone?

"If you were concerned about her, shouldn't you have come by earlier?" he said, as if reading my mind.

I took a breath and dug myself in a little deeper. "I should have, but I had to go over to my parents' to help them with a couple of things, and then they asked me to stay for dinner and we got to talking, and it was only when I started home that I remembered about checking on Sabrina. Yes, I should have come by earlier, but I didn't." I knew I was saying too much and talking too fast, but I couldn't stop myself.

"Have you notified the police?"

"I hope it won't come to that. But if she doesn't show up tomorrow morning, I definitely will." I hit the button to roll up the window.

"Wait," he said. "If I see her, who do I say came by?"

"Thank you," I yelled through the rapidly diminishing space. I revved my engine to indicate he should step back. He did, and I drove off, looking in my rearview mirror and seeing him standing there watching my escape. I was pretty sure he was memorizing my license plate. Damn. I should have thought of that sooner before acting like I was guilty of something more than talking too much.

I drove part way around the block trying to decide whether it was wise to get out and look around behind Sabrina's townhouse. See if there were any lights on, or doors standing open, that sort of thing. There was a very loud voice in my head telling me that it was stupid to explore the area on foot knowing the man from across the street was probably on high alert. He could even have called the police. In spite of that possibility, I slowed down and parked just out of sight, hopefully, from anyone who might notice there was a stranger in the neighborhood. Although it wasn't against the law to park on a public street, even late at night.

After a few minutes, I took a deep breath and opened the car door. Before my foot hit the ground a dog started barking. Loud, resonant barking. Probably a big mean dog. I pulled my foot back inside and closed the door. It definitely wasn't a good night to be prowling around this neighborhood. I would try again tomorrow. In the daylight.

Tuesday morning first thing I called Sabrina's home and got her voicemail. Then I called her office again and got another voicemail. When I tried going through the main desk, they told me to leave her a message. After considering briefly whether Tom Thompson would recognize my voice, I called him. He answered on the second ring.

"Hi," I said, trying for a slightly elevated pitch, not the voice of Tiffany. "I'm a friend of Sabrina's. She was supposed to meet me for coffee this morning before work and didn't show. And she isn't answering her phone. The main desk won't give me any information. Any chance you could run by her office and see if she is in?"

"What did you say your name was again?"

I could hardly lie when he could see my name on my cell. "Bryn. Sabrina mentioned you once, and for some reason I remembered your name." No surprise there.

"I'm walking toward her office as we speak, Bryn. You sound familiar. Have we met?"

"No, I don't think so." Did he ask every woman if he'd met them? My strained vocal cords were protesting. I hoped he didn't make me keep up the phony exchange for too long.

"Hold on a minute, okay?"

I heard muffled voices, then Tom Thompson came back on. "No, she isn't in today and her assistant doesn't know where she is. Is there a problem?"

"None that I know of. Well, thanks. I'll keep trying." Before he could say anything more or ask any uncomfortable questions, I abruptly ended our conversation with, "Have a good day."

Sabrina still wasn't showing up at work. Wasn't it time that someone there took notice? Maybe my call to Tom would give them the hint. Something wasn't right.

Arthur, you salacious devil. It's not looking good for you.

Step three of the plan Sophie and I had agreed on involved another drive-by of Sabrina's condo. This time I got out of the car, walked up to her front door, and rang the doorbell. Surprise—no one answered. Determined to get some answers, I brazenly walked around her townhouse, peering in windows. Based on what I was able to see, it didn't take a professional to figure out that her place had been tossed. It was time to move on to step four of the plan.

I went back to my car and called Detective Ben Peterson.

Chapter 7

Bad Housekeeping?

When Ben arrived, I couldn't help noticing that he still sported a well-trimmed mustache. It is so perfect that I imagine him spending considerable time each morning in front of a bathroom mirror, combing it, smoothing it, trimming it, making sure it is just right. That's one of the things I find off-putting about him. That and the fact that he failed to ask me out a second time.

"Bryn," he said, looking pleased to see me. Was that sincere or fake, I wondered.

"Ben, sorry to bother you."

He glanced at Sabrina's condo. "You said there's a problem?"

"The owner has been missing since Friday evening. I came by to see if she was home."

"What do you mean by missing?"

"It's a long story." I motioned for him to follow me. "If you look in this side window, you'll see why I'm concerned."

I took him to the window I knew had the best view of the disarray inside. He shaded his eyes with one hand and leaned in. "It's a mess," he said in a matter-of-fact tone.

"This doesn't look like a case of bad housekeeping to me." I knew I sounded irritable, but I'd been hoping for a more forceful reaction from him.

He turned back toward me with a smile. "I seem to remember that office of yours . . ."

I suddenly realized he was kidding me. "Okay, my point is that I know bad housekeeping when I see it . . ."

". . . and this place has been searched," he finished for me.

"That *is* what it looks like, isn't it?"

"And you say the owner has been missing since Friday. Male or female? And has anyone reported it?"

"Her name is Sabrina Valdez, and I don't know for sure, but I don't think anyone has reported her missing. Although she hasn't been showing up at work and has not been attending scheduled meetings."

"Is she a friend?"

"No . . ." I hesitated. "But I have reason to be concerned. Look, could I give you the details after we check around some more?"

"Sure." He headed toward the back of the condo and I followed, becoming increasingly concerned about what we might find.

There was an interesting metal screen with animal cutouts along one side of her tiny back yard with a row of conical cedar bushes on the other side and a low white plastic fence connecting the screen with the bushes. The gate in the middle was open.

Ben didn't even pause but went directly up to the back door. "It's not shut," he said, eyeing the partially opened door.

"Oh, oh. That isn't good, is it?"

"Under the circumstances, no. Not good." He turned back to me. "You stay here. I'm going to have a look inside."

I didn't want to hang out in her back yard while he looked around inside, but he was doing me a favor without questioning my motives, so I felt like I needed to respect his request. Although I knew it wasn't going to be easy for me to honor his directive. I've never been good at following orders.

He called out her name as he stepped through the doorway. Then he paused and announced that he was a police officer and was entering her home. There was no response.

Once he disappeared from sight, I started pacing back and forth, trying to get my mind wrapped around the idea that not only was Sabrina missing, but someone had searched her house. What did that mean? Were the two linked in some way? If Arthur was responsible for her disappearance, then what was he looking for in her home? And if not him, then perhaps I should be expanding my suspect list. Assuming Sabrina hadn't left home of her own accord, of course. That *was* still a possibility. Maybe she'd gone on a spur of the moment trip with someone, an affair she wanted to keep secret. Voluntary commitment to a drug rehab facility? An accident? She could even be in a coma in a hospital, her identification taken along with her purse by a mugger. There were lots of possibilities. And even though the word "coincidence" often gets a bad rap, there was the occasional coincidence that was just that—a coincidence.

It seemed like Ben stayed inside forever. And then some. I kept looking around, half expecting to see the neighbor from the night before heading over to see what we were up to. Apparently, he wasn't as vigilant during the day.

When Ben finally returned, I could barely contain myself. "Well?" I said, sounding suspiciously like my mother when she was grilling me about something.

"No one there. No signs of a struggle. No blood." He seemed to be going down a police procedural list. "But someone was definitely looking for something. Something they thought might be hidden."

"What makes you say that?"

"Experience," he said with a tiny grin. When I didn't acknowledge his little joke, he apologized. "Sorry, I didn't mean to be evasive. Nor to trivialize the situation. Whoever went through her condo looked under cushions, drawers, mattresses. They left clothes on the floor, took pictures off walls, pulled back rugs. Obviously went through her kitchen cupboards. Opened containers. Left the freezer door ajar. It was very thorough."

That didn't sound good. "What's next?" I asked.

"Two things. I'll call it in and get someone down here to stand guard until the police have a chance to check things out. And while we're waiting, you can tell me why you came here in the first place and why you were concerned enough to look in windows."

Two officers showed up just as I was finishing my explanation of what had happened and some of what I had done to try to track Sabrina down. I omitted a few things, a kind of unstated Fifth Amendment right. Like my midnight swim to retrieve the statue—one midnight swim seemed like enough to confess for the record. I also didn't mention Gerald and Harold or the in-person visit to Zelen and Hobbs and the purloined post-it. But I mentioned enough to let Ben know there was reason to be concerned about Sabrina not being seen since last Friday.

Ben took the two officers aside and I assume filled them in on the highlights before motioning for me to come with him. We went out front and stood on the sidewalk near my car.

"I'm going to check with the police officer you talked to on Friday evening. See if he did any follow-up. And I'll find out if anyone at her office has any idea as to her whereabouts. Their HR department should have a contact for her, and they may know the names of relatives or friends or be able to suggest someone in the company who might have some relevant information. I'll also have someone talk to the neighbors." He paused and looked me directly in the eyes. "I'm telling you this so you won't feel like you have to follow up. And I want to thank you. It was a good thing that you took the initiative you did. Especially since no one else made the effort to report her missing."

"Do you think I should have called it in right away? Would I have been taken seriously?"

"You could have called it in, but they probably wouldn't have started searching for her immediately. Not without a good reason to do so. She's an adult, after all. No, I think you did what any fearless female with a strong instinct for trouble would have done." He smiled, then seemed to reconsider. "Sorry, I keep forgetting that this is a missing person's case." He paused again. "But it is good to see you."

I felt a twinge of attraction, then my eyes went to his mustache. Maybe it was there to remind me that this relationship should remain professional.

"Well, I'm just pleased that you will be looking into Sabrina's disappearance. If you find out she's been on a beach somewhere working on her tan, I will be thrilled. Somewhat embarrassed but thrilled."

"We can always hope . . ."

When I returned to my office at the marina, I had every intention of putting Sabrina's situation—whatever it was—out of my mind. I had confidence that Ben would do everything within his power to track down the missing woman. If she turned up alive, I could relax and quit worrying about Arthur as a potential murderer. And if Ben concluded she was missing and could not be found easily, then it was definitely a job for the police.

Although I didn't feel particularly guilty about not revealing the fact that I had visited Sabrina's office as Tiffany Riddle, I did feel the weight of omission about the names on the post-it. On the one hand, I was hoping my deception wouldn't surface. On the other hand, I knew I wouldn't be able to live with myself if I later discovered I'd withheld an important piece of evidence that might have shed light on Sabrina's vanishing act. I rationalized my decision to stay quiet by arguing to myself that a connection between the two men and Sabrina's disappearance was as unlikely as winning the lottery. Then again, someone always wins eventually.

Under the circumstances, there were two courses of action I could take to vanquish my guilt. I could call Ben and say, "Hey, there was one tiny thing I left out when I talked to you earlier—" Although I might not think that what I had done rose to the level of a misdemeanor, an officer of the law might have a different opinion. That left me with the second less confrontive, possibly cowardly approach—pursue the loose end on my own. If it came to nothing, then no one needed to know about my foray into Zelen and Hobbs. But, if Gerald and/or Harold knew something relevant about what had happened to Sabrina, then I could perhaps figure out the least self-damaging way to present my findings to Ben. For my own peace of mind, I had to pursue what could be a lead. I had to know whether I was hindering the police investigation by not telling them about Gerald and Harold.

My first call was to Gerald Fontaine. Since he was with the U.S. Attorney's office, I was surprised to actually get him on the line, and even more surprised when he agreed to meet with me that afternoon at a deli that was about a block away from the large government building where he worked. I didn't even have to explain why I wanted to meet with him. Maybe he got a lot of calls from people who didn't want to talk about their concerns over the phone. Or maybe he just wanted an excuse to get out of the office for a break. Either way, I had secured a meeting with him. With a little finesse and the right questions, I just might uncover why Sabrina had his name and number on a post-it. Depending on what I learned from him, I would either report back to Ben or give Harold a call.

I arrived early. It gave me time to grab a bagel and a cup of coffee and to catch up on my email. In spite of all of the filters I've installed, and the many times I've unsubscribed to things, I still end up on far too many emails. It seems like I spend hours each day disposing of ones I didn't need to receive in the first place. I cleared the last offending message with an emphatic left-to-right swipe at exactly 2:30, just in time to see a distinguished gray-haired man enter the coffee shop as if he'd timed his entrance to the second. He looked around until our eyes met, and, without any further communication, he headed straight for me. He'd probably looked me up online. It's what I would have done in his position. And it's what I tried to do with him, but he didn't have an online presence that I was able to locate.

"Ms. Baczek," he said, landing correctly on one of the acceptable pronunciations for my surname. He didn't bow or offer to kiss my hand, but he had an old-world presence about him, a formality of dress and demeanor, like deposed royalty rather than someone who worked for the government. He glanced at my coffee and asked, "May I get you something?" His voice was well-modulated, genteel. I had to resist the urge to jump up and offer to wait on *him*, but I'd left my starched apron at home.

"No thanks."

"I shall return."

I pictured him coming back with a dainty teacup and a crustless watercress sandwich. Instead. he returned with a giant latte, a frosted cookie, and a pile of napkins. I never understand why people think they are going to use more than one napkin. It strikes me as an incredible waste.

"Sure you don't want a cookie?" he asked as he sat down. "Or a bite of mine?" Well, that was certainly friendly. I was tempted to reach over and break off a piece of cookie, but my guess was that his offer was a token gesture that he didn't expect me to accept.

"No, thank you," I said in my best mother-taught-me-manners voice.

He centered his cookie in the middle of a napkin, placed the extras off to one side, and turned his attention to me. "Well now, what can I do for you?" Most people who ask that question do so with a touch of superiority, as if they have the power to solve your piddling problem with the wave of a hand. But he sounded sincere, like he really wanted to know how he could be of help. Maybe the offer of a piece of his cookie had been sincere after all, and I'd missed out.

"I believe you've talked recently with Sabrina Valdez, an auditor with Zelen and Hobbs."

"Did I?" He suddenly seemed to be concentrating more on his cookie than on my question. It crossed my mind that was a technique he used to get people to say more without him having to give anything away.

"She had your name and number in a file she was working on." I was fudging a little, but just a little. "I'm hoping you can shed some light on her reason for contacting you."

"Why don't you ask her?"

"Because . . ." I hesitated, then decided I had no choice but to tell him the truth, or part of it, if I wanted to get answers from him. "Unfortunately, she's gone missing. My hope is that you can shed some light on what she was investigating." He probably wondered why I didn't already know what she was working on if I had access to a file with his name and number in it. He looked savvy enough to be asking himself that exact question. It took incredible self-control to hide the nervousness I was feeling.

"Missing? Like in possibly *not alive* missing?"

"We don't know."

"Who is 'we'"?

"I've notified the police," I said truthfully. "They are looking into her disappearance. Meanwhile, I'm hoping there's something that you can share with me that might point me in a particular direction." I hoped my explanation was sufficiently vague so as not to come back to bite me, yet specific enough to elicit useful information.

"I know you said my name was in a file of hers, but that doesn't explain why you decided to contact me."

"Well . . . it's hard to explain. I mean, I had a hunch—"

"A hunch?"

"Yes, a hunch."

"A guess or a premonition?"

"Does it matter?" Was he toying with me?

"Not really. I like precision."

It was time to play the emotional card. "To be honest, I'm concerned about her. No one has seen her since last Friday, and no one seems to know where she is. As I said, the police are looking for her, but they have a lot of things on their plate. I'm hoping you might be able to tell me something, anything, that suggests a lead. An organization, a person, a place, anything to follow up on, either on my own or by turning it over to the police." I sounded sincere, probably because I actually felt that way. Just because you consciously try to manipulate someone doesn't mean you aren't telling the truth, or mostly so.

He was studying my face as if he was a human lie detector. If he had kids, I bet they'd had a tough time getting away with anything when they were young. His unblinking stare was truly intimidating.

"Can you at least tell me whether she contacted you?"

He took a sip of coffee and broke off a piece of cookie. "I'm sorry, I wish I could help you. But neither her name nor the name of her company rings any bells with me. Could she have talked with someone else in the agency?"

"Oh." That wasn't what I'd expected him to say. Maybe I'd been right about him agreeing to meet with me so he could get out of the office and have a snack. "She didn't mention anyone else, but it's possible."

He was slowly nibbling his way around the rim of his cookie. It was fascinating to watch. After each bite he took a sip of coffee.

"Given the type of work you do and knowing she was an auditor who did work with nonprofits, any guesses as to what she might have wanted to contact you about?"

"I don't think it would be fair to *guess*."

"Well, any hunches, then?"

"No." His eyes told me he enjoyed sparring with me. Not as much as he was enjoying his cookie though.

"Why do people normally contact you?"

"Unfortunately, most people don't understand what we actually do and how we operate. They usually call to make a complaint, and then we try to help them determine the best way to proceed. We have limited resources and can't pursue every case people bring to us."

We chatted a little more about his division and some of the cases he had handled in the past. It was interesting but not particularly useful. I kept him talking until I was satisfied that he could finish the center of his cookie in one bite. It was like feeling compelled to see the ending of a really bad movie. Then I thanked him for his time and gave him my card in case he found that she had talked to someone else in his area.

He stood and nodded a gracious goodbye as I *took my leave*. Normally I just leave, but with him it seemed appropriate to be more formal.

Chapter 8

Crossed Wires

Back at the marina, I stopped in my office to call Harold Hanson at the State Auditor's Office and finally managed to convince his admin that scheduling a brief phone call with her boss wouldn't in any way jeopardize her standing as a negative role model for public servants.

"Fine," she conceded. Then, just when I thought I'd won the round, she added, "He will be out of the office until next Monday. Would you like to schedule a call for some time next week?"

"Since I can't talk to him until next week, can I schedule a face-to-face meeting for then?"

"It's best that you talk to him first. He's a busy man . . ."

Instead of listening to what could have turned into a lengthy explanation, I interrupted and agreed to a Monday morning telephone conversation.

After I hung up, I had an argument with myself. The good news about arguing with yourself is that you know without doubt that "you" will win. But a "win" isn't necessarily the right choice. And in this instance, there was a lot of gray area. I wouldn't be able to talk with Harold until next week—that seemed like a long time to be sitting on information that might be helpful to an investigation. Surely an official could get in touch with him before then. On the other hand, I didn't know if Sabrina had reached out to Harold or if having his number was in any way connected to AHA or her disappearance. There were pros and cons to telling Ben about my suspicions, an almost equal tally. After considerable soul-searching, I decided to give it one more day. Or maybe two.

Sabrina might show up by then. And, after all, it had already been three days, and this was a flimsy lead at best. Self-preservation is a strong motivator.

I sat down behind my computer, checked out the long list of new emails and stared at the reminder on my calendar about a report that was due by Friday. Then I looked around at my messy office, smarting as I recalled Ben's jibe about my "housekeeping." I really did need to clean the place up. The problem was that I didn't feel like tackling any of it—not the emails or the report or the mess.

After several minutes of mental self-flagellation, I ended my misery by locking up my office and heading back to the *Aspara.* It would all still be there, waiting to pounce, when I was in a better frame of mind.

Macavity wasn't home. Bubbles IV still looked puckish but had not yet gone to his maker. My refrigerator didn't yield anything appealing to eat. I'd forgotten to shop on Monday after going to Zelen and Hobbs. And I had promised to sit with the twins later that evening. An eventful if unproductive day.

I plopped myself down on my couch to reconnoiter. I'd barely had time to settle in when I heard someone step aboard. They didn't knock on the side of the cabin or call my name, just stepped into the cockpit. Most people who aren't close friends either lean down and knock on the side of the boat from the dock or call out something like, "Bryn, you there? Knock, knock."

"Who's there?" I yelled as I grabbed my cast iron fry pan off the stove.

"Bryn? Are you there, Bryn?" It sounded like Arthur.

"Is that you Arthur?"

"Yes. Can we talk?"

I reached up with my free hand and slid back the hatch. Arthur took that as an invitation to climb in, turning around to come down the steps like a boater using good boating safety practices is supposed to do. When he got to the bottom of the stairs, he noticed the fry pan I still held in a death grip.

"Am I interrupting your dinner?" he asked.

"No," I said, placing the fry pan back on the stovetop. Then, realizing I needed an explanation, I added, "I was, ah, practicing Escrima." I had recently read about Escrima when browsing a martial arts website. It looked interesting.

"Escrima?"

"It's a weapon-based form of martial arts from the Philippines," I explained. It wouldn't hurt to let him know that I was physically capable of defending myself. Even if Sabrina was okay, the way he had argued with her suggested he wasn't as easy going as his previous mild-mannered neighbor deportment had indicated.

He surprised me by saying, "I thought they used sticks or blades in Escrima."

"Well, I don't like practicing with knives in a small space." I thought that sounded reasonable, at least as reasonable as the idea that I might be practicing *any* kind of martial arts in the tiny floor space of my sailboat.

"Oh." He looked at the settee as if trying to decide whether to remain standing or to sit down. When I remained standing and didn't invite him to take a seat, he hesitated. "I want to talk about Sabrina," he said. "You being a woman and all."

I had to agree with the woman part, but that didn't explain what he wanted from me.

"You see," he continued. "I need some advice, and I . . . I don't know who else to ask." He shifted from one foot to the other, like a small boy about to confess to something. Or someone who needed a bathroom. "Ah, do you mind?" He nodded toward the couch. When I didn't say no, he wedged himself between the table and the pile of pillows on the settee.

"Advice?" I prompted, still standing.

Arthur hesitated, as if expecting me to sit down for a man-to-woman tete-a-tete. When it became clear that wasn't going to happen, he went ahead anyway. "Yes. As I've told you, she got really mad at me about the statue. And since then, she won't even answer her phone when I call." Was he trying to trick me? Was this a ploy to get me to believe he had nothing to do with Sabrina's disappearance? Or was he just incredibly pathetic?

"Have you tried contacting her at the office?" I could be just as tricky as him. "I mean, you still intend to use her as an auditor, right?"

He looked down at the table. "I'm not sure she's willing to continue with the audit. I've left messages, trying to make it clear that I will keep our relationship strictly professional going forward. But she hasn't returned my calls." He sounded like a broken-hearted suitor. But then, he had also seemed believable the night he lied to us about Sabrina not being on his boat. He wasn't going to get any sympathy from me.

"Then you need to contact Zelen and Hobbs. That is, if you want her or someone in that firm to continue with the audit."

"I'd prefer it if she continues with the audit. Otherwise, I'll have to explain to my boss, well, you know. That would be awkward, but I could manage it. It's more than that though. I'm trying to figure out whether there's something I can do to, ah, smooth over things with her. And I thought maybe you could help me . . ."

"Because I'm a woman . . ."

"Yes." He looked at me with puppy dog eyes. "What do you think I can do to get her to forgive me?"

"Tell me again why she came by that night."

"I didn't suggest it, if that's what you're implying. She asked if I would be willing to discuss the audit outside of the office. And I thought . . . well . . . I thought . . ."

"You thought she was coming on to you?" I tried not to sound too incredulous.

"Well, yes." On some level he must have suspected that Sabrina had a non-personal, ulterior motive for wanting to see him outside of the office, but we can all be delusional when something we want seems within our grasp. What I still couldn't get my mind around was what she could possibly have thought he knew that she couldn't find in the materials and data she was privy to at the organization's office.

"That night, before her, ah, departure, did you get *any* idea about what kind of information she wanted from you?"

"Not really. She did ask a few questions, but I wasn't thinking about . . . I mean . . ."

"I know what you mean. But what kind of questions did she ask?"

"Well . . ." He blinked a few times and squeezed his lips together as if trying hard to recall their conversation. Or else he was experiencing gas pains. Finally, he said, "She mentioned something about how we handle pass-through grants and asked how much oversight AHA provides. She also wanted to know how our bidding process works. And if we've ever had any trouble with any of our contractors. That sort of thing."

"And none of those questions came across as red flags to you?"

"I just thought she was making small talk. I mean, she also asked about our board members."

Financial foreplay? Could he possibly be as dense as he seemed? "Arthur, you hired her to look into the organization's finances, and she was asking you questions about possible wrongdoing. What part of that didn't you get?"

He looked stunned. If it was an act, he was definitely Oscar material. "What . . . what do you mean?"

"Sorry to be so blunt, but she's an auditor. She was asking detailed auditor questions. The kind you ask if you're suspicious about something. There was no come-on involved."

"You're saying I misread her intentions?"

It was like punishing a puppy for wheedling on the carpet, but I felt like I had to do it. "Yes, that's what I'm saying." I paused to let it sink in. "Did she seem particularly interested in any specific documents?"

"Not that I recall, and we got, ah, distracted by the statue. She hadn't commented on it even though it was right there on the table. So, I pointed to it and asked her what she thought. She stared at it but didn't say anything, until I picked it up and, ah, called out its, ah, attributes. That's when she became upset." Arthur leaned back against the pillows and stared up at the ceiling, suddenly mute. Perhaps reliving the encounter with Sabrina, maybe even seeing the exchange from a new perspective. I didn't know what else to say or to ask, so I just waited.

After a long, uncomfortable minute or two, he straightened up and started to pull himself out of the settee. "I need to go."

"To the bathroom?" I instinctively asked.

"No, home." In his haste to leave he caught a foot on the metal post that holds the table in place and sat abruptly back down. That seemed to break his resolve. He lurched forward and put his head in his hands. Was it possible he was just a lovesick schmuck who dreamed about making it with someone totally out of his league? Even so, that didn't explain why Sabrina had gone missing.

"Can I get you some water?" I asked.

He looked up at me. "A little water would be good."

I got a bottle of water out of the fridge and handed it to him. He sat upright and contemplated the bottle as though he had forgotten how to twist the lid off. "I thought she liked me."

I noted the past tense but told myself that it might only apply to our discussion about personal versus professional relationships. "Tell me again what happened with the statue." I reached over and twisted the cap off for him. He obediently picked up the bottle, lifted it to his mouth and took a swig, choking as if some of the water had gone down the wrong way. Like the realization that Sabrina may have been using him.

"She didn't like how I was, ah, touching the statue." He mumbled the words, as if reluctant to talk about the incident while trying to answer my question honestly.

"So, you were feeling up the statue while you talked about its *artistic* attributes?" Bizarre, but I could, unfortunately, picture it. And it was going to be hard to get that image out of my head.

"I thought she liked me," he repeated.

"Okay, I think I have the idea. She came to talk business, you wanted to shag her, and it went downhill from there."

"There's no need to be crude."

The man with a statue fetish was calling *me* crude? "Sorry, Arthur, but the way I see it is that Sabrina intended to pump you for information, and when she realized you didn't have anything to add to what she already knew, there was nothing more to be said. End of story." Except for letting him know that she thought he was a creep. I remembered her calling him a "twisted S.O.B."

Arthur looked devasted. "So, should I apologize?"

"An apology never hurts. But don't expect forgiveness."

"You don't think she will give me a second chance?"

Really? I thought I'd made it clear he never had a *first* chance. "Since you've asked, no, I don't." Perhaps that was a bit blunt. Dear Abby, I'm not.

"Well, thanks." This time he managed to get up and out from the settee without incident. It isn't easy to squeeze past the table with the side flap in the up position. When I'm expecting company, I put the flap down. But he wasn't company. "It's just so hard," he muttered. Then, without saying goodbye or so long or thanks, he climbed up the stairs and stepped over the slats onto the back deck. I didn't follow, but I heard him push back the tarp and felt him get off the boat, the *Aspara* rocking slightly in place. I heard faint footfalls on the cement and imagined him slowly making his way back to the *Knotty Lady*, crestfallen, his dream of conquest smashed by my womanly words of discouragement.

I poured his water down the sink and put the container in my recycle bag. Sometimes being right doesn't feel all that good.

Later that evening, Logan came by to accompany me to my brother's house. Although I adore my niece and nephew, I'm not particularly good at entertaining kids, and he is. Besides, he likes the twins. And I had thrown in the added incentive of a pizza and beer.

Noah and Emma were waiting for us just inside the door. They hadn't realized Logan was coming, and although he's one of their favorite people, they were momentarily disappointed. When I'm alone with them they run roughshod over me. I end up allowing them to do practically anything they want as long as they promise not to tell their parents. We've eaten ice cream for dinner, built forts out of furniture and sheets, watched movies their parents wouldn't allow them to watch—you get the idea. Anything. But with Logan there, the voice of reason always prevails. He seems to instinctively know how to get them to behave. It's like that British woman who uses "the voice" to command dogs. Well, almost.

After consuming our pizza in record time, we settled the kids in with a parent-approved movie. We watched with them for a while, then retired to the kitchen to chat. Logan wanted to complain about a student evaluation he had received. Online evaluations were public, so not being able to explain the circumstances was galling to him.

"Hey, didn't you get a high 'hot' rating last year?" I said to distract him.

"They did away with those."

"And don't you usually score above a 4.5?"

"That's not the point."

"You know you can't please everyone."

He sighed. "I know, but that doesn't make me feel better."

"Hey, Speaking of people who don't rate high on the hot scale . . ."

"I didn't know we were."

"Well, let me tell you about the chat I had with Arthur."

When I finished telling him what Arthur had to say about the statue and the exchange between him and Sabrina, I expected Logan to accuse Arthur of being a smarmy chump. Instead, he said, "Poor guy. I know how he feels."

"You *do*?"

"Rejection is rejection whether it comes from a babe or a hunk."

"But you're attractive . . .," I began.

"Thank you." Logan reached over and gave my shoulder a squeeze. "So are you." Then he laughed. "We red-heads have to stick together."

"I'm a strawberry blond," I countered.

"In your dreams. Although we could add some highlights—" He picked up a strand of my hair and studied it. "Actually, it's not a bad color. Although definitely not strawberry blond. I say we leave it as it is, and you get over your fantasies."

"Okay, okay. But you know what I mean. He's a sad little person who fooled himself into thinking she was attracted to him."

"Seriously, I feel for the guy. But his self-deception is not *your* problem."

"Unless it turned violent. The bottom line is that Sabrina hasn't been seen since she visited Arthur on the *Knotty Lady*. And she's still not picking up her phone."

"You haven't heard anything from Ben yet?"

"No."

"You need to tell him that you suspect Sabrina may have been looking into something illegal going on at AHA. Otherwise, they may miss some important leads."

"But they know she was doing an audit. And I don't have any evidence to back up my suspicions."

"You can tell him enough to at least make sure they look into possible links between the audit and her disappearance. Like what Arthur told you she asked about. You don't have to incriminate yourself. Or . . ." He gave me a suggestive smile. ". . . Tiffany.""

"I knew I shouldn't have told you about that."

"Hey, we don't have any secrets, do we?"

"Sometimes I think I'd be wise to keep my mouth shut occasionally."

"I'm not saying that you did anything intentionally wrong or potentially criminal." He paused for effect. "Other than impersonating a woman named Tiffany, sneaking into a restricted-entry office building, rifling through someone's desk without authorization and . . . ta da . . . walking off with something from said desk."

"Other than that."

"As the Irish say, *hindsight is the best insight to foresight.*"

"Huh?"

"Learn from your mistakes so you don't repeat them."

"Really! *And what mistakes might you be talkin' about*?" I'd been trying for an Irish lilt but it came out like I was talking under water.

"Until the point where you removed something from her appointment book, I think you were only on shaky ground, not hovering over a black hole."

"So, you agree that I need to either fess up or continue poking around?"

"What you just did was present a false dilemma, a choice between two mutually exclusive options, implying these are the only options. What you're really asking is if I approve of you withholding what could possibly be evidence and investigating on your own."

"When you put it that way . . ."

"Bryn, I helped pull you out of the water at 2:00 a.m. I know you do some weird things for the right reasons."

"Does that mean you're willing to help?"

"That goes without saying. What I'm confused about is whether you do or don't consider Arthur the prime suspect . . . assuming something bad has happened to Sabrina."

"I don't care for him, that's for sure. But I'm not convinced he's guilty of anything more than being a jerk."

"Then, are you doing all this to help Arthur?"

"Even losers deserve a fair hearing."

"And you don't think the police will be fair?"

"Okay, you've made your point. Even if I don't come up with something worth turning over to Ben, I'll think of some way to at least hint at what could be a potentially productive line of inquiry."

"Oooh. That sounds like a sidestep."

"I really, really don't want Ben to know about the post-it. Or Tiffany."

"For professional or personal reasons?"

"There's no 'personal' involved."

"I could call out another sidestep, but don't worry, we'll either find some evidence or figure out a somewhat honest if slightly deceptive way to put Ben on the right scent. Assuming they aren't already aware of potential lines of inquiry related to her audit investigation."

"Thank you. I think. And if you ever need someone to pull you out of the lake, feel free to swim by."

When the movie ended, we put Noah and Emma to bed with a minimum of resistance. Logan read to them while I cleaned up what little mess we'd made. By the time Dylan and Angelina returned from their "date," everything was back to tidy perfection. Angelina's housekeeping skills would never be a source of ridicule.

I left Logan at the head of my dock. It was a beautiful evening, clear and quiet. A few stars overhead competed for attention with city lights. Looking at the myriad of lights always made me long to take off on my boat for less populated areas. But the older I get the harder it is to get away for any length of time. I love my work but regret some of the necessary trade-offs between earning enough money to live on and simply enjoying life.

As I turned the corner toward the Aspara I thought I heard a sound coming from one of the nearby finger floats. I paused and took a few steps back to get a clear view of the dock. There was no one there. Since no one lived aboard the boat between the *Aspara* and the *Knotty Lady*, it seemed unlikely the noise had come from there. Besides, it had sounded further away. I slowly headed back toward the *Knotty Lady*'s finger float, then stopped short, questioning whether going to check out if there was an intruder nearby was a smart move.

It crossed my mind that if this had been a scene from a horror movie, the music would have turned eerie and viewers would be silently screaming, "Don't go!" There could be something dangerous lurking in the shadows next to the *Knotty Lady*. A burglar surprised in the act. A creature from the depths. Perhaps even a crazed Arthur looking for victim #2.

Don't be ridiculous, I told myself. This wasn't a scene from a horror movie, there was no music, eerie or otherwise; this was the same marina where I'd lived for years. Except for a couple of minor thefts, a dinghy used for a joy ride by some junior high kids, and the occasional party that got a bit loud, nothing bad had ever happened here.

Still, there was always a first time.

I turned back toward the *Aspara* and then paused as I changed my mind a second time. Even if it was only a couple of kids trying to break into a boat, they should be stopped. I got out my phone and called Logan, keeping one eye on the *Knotty Lady*.

When he answered I put my hand over my mouth and whispered, "I think there's someone prowling around Arthur's boat."

"What? What's that you said?"

"A prowler," I said a little louder, moving further away toward the small building on the cement dock that had once been an office for the former fuel dock and now served as a storage space for our landlord.

"It's a bad connection," Logan said loudly. "Let me call you back." He hung up before I could protest. I scurried around to the other side of the building as my phone started to do its frog noises. Too late I put it on vibrate.

"Dammit, Logan," I hissed. "You and Judd need to come over ASAP. Someone may be on Arthur's boat."

"Got it." He hung up. Seconds later I saw him and Judd start up the dock. I went to meet them, scurrying past the *Knotty Lady* as quickly and quietly as I could. I noticed that Logan was carrying pepper spray.

"That doesn't work against a gun," I observed in a whisper.

"Someone has a gun?" Judd asked, keeping his voice low, sounding and looking like he was sorry he had come. "Then let's call the police."

"I'm not sure that there's anyone there," I admitted.

"Then what are we doing here?" Judd asked.

"I want you to check it out with me."

"If there's someone nearby, they undoubtedly know we're here," Logan said. "You've gone past that finger float twice already."

"Maybe it was your cat," Judd offered. He insists he dislikes cats, but sometimes I think his dislike isn't as strong as he claims.

"Just one quick peek," I said. I hadn't thought of a small animal. Like a real rat. Or a cat. I hated to admit that was a possibility. Sabrina's disappearance had me spooked.

The two men and I silently crept up to the finger float and worked our way to the back of the *Knotty Lady*. There was no one there. The cabin door was shut. Everything looked shipshape.

"Should we knock?" I asked. "To see if everything is okay?"

"He's probably asleep."

"I say we call it a night," Judd said.

Macavity took that as his cue. He suddenly appeared on the cabin roof, jumped down into the cockpit, leapt off the boat at Judd's feet and proceeded to rub up against him.

"Damn cat" was the last thing Judd said as he and Logan disappeared down the dock.

Macavity and I headed for home. "Nice kitty," I said as we climbed aboard the *Aspara*.

Chapter 9

Not Normal

Wednesday morning I was in a bad mood. Sabrina still wasn't answering her phone. Ben hadn't called to tell me what was happening with the investigation into Sabrina's disappearance. And Bubbles IV was on his last fin.

As I stared out my office window at the marina below and the lake beyond, my mind started to wander to more pleasant things. Maybe I needed to take some time off and go for a sail. The *Aspara* was out there waiting for action. In just a few minutes I could be untied and on my way. It was a beautiful day. There was a light breeze. Just enough for a lazy hour or two away from . . .

A loud two-fingered rap on the door interrupted my reverie. Not again, I thought. My sanctuary was becoming far too popular. The person knocked a second time before I got to the door, a little louder, probably using four fingers balled into a fist. Impatient, I thought. Maybe I should yell *hold your horses* or *cool your jets*. But does anyone really say that anymore? *Patience, grasshopper,* I murmured to myself as I opened the door. There was a man in a uniform standing there, with his fist raised to bang on my door again.

"Hey," I said. "Officer Dodd, isn't it?"

"I was beginning to think you weren't here." He glanced at a notepad. "Bryn Backzeek, right?"

"That's Ba-check," I corrected. My parents usually say "bay-sick," but I've found that if I say "ba-check" the person hearing my name for the first time has a better chance of being able to spell it, or to at least come close. Then again, maybe I shouldn't be encouraging a police officer to spell my name correctly.

"Baa-check," he said, repeating it the way he apparently thought I'd said it. He sounded like a sheep with a sore throat. When it came to pronouncing my last name, it could be hard to tell the difference between a tin ear and rudeness.

"Close enough," I said. "How can I help you?"

"Any chance Arthur Stanton is here?" Officer Dodd asked, although it was pretty obvious there was no one else in the room.

"No, no one here but me." I stepped aside so he could take in the entire catastrophe that was my office.

"Any idea where he is?"

"How about at his office? Have you tried him there?" I knew my question dripped with sarcasm, but I didn't care.

"I checked. He didn't show up this morning."

"What made you think he was here in *my* office?" I was truly puzzled.

"There doesn't seem to be anyone else around."

"So, you're just knocking on random doors." It sounded like I was accusing him of being lazy; I didn't mean it that way, but from the unattractive moue pulling the sides of his mouth down, that was the way he'd heard it. "Have you checked his boat?"

His frown transformed into a wrinkle of distress, like he'd just swallowed a bug. "Can you point it out to me?"

So that was it—he didn't remember which boat Arthur lived on. To me each boat is distinctive, but to a non-boater, they probably resembled indistinguishable variations on large floating objects. No problem, I was looking for a distraction. "I'll be happy to show you." I stepped past him, pulled the door shut behind me, and started down the stairs with Officer Dodd in tow. "Maybe he slept in or is sick or something."

"Could be."

"Arthur isn't in any kind of trouble, is he?"

"I couldn't say."

I wanted to ask if this had anything to do with Sabrina's disappearance, but Officer Dodd didn't seem to be in a chatty mood. That made me even more irritated with Ben for not checking in with me. Even though I'd been kinda hoping he wouldn't so I could put off telling him about Harold Hanson a little longer.

When we arrived at the *Knotty Lady*, Officer Dodd stepped aboard and knocked. I stayed on the finger float and listened. There was no sound from inside. He knocked a second time, this time harder than before. He had the loud knocking bit down pat.

When there was still no answer he stepped off to the side, as if he was afraid someone was going to shoot at him through the door from the inside. Then he gingerly turned the doorknob and tested to see if the door was locked. It wasn't. He eased the door open a few inches and yelled: "Police. If you're in there, Arthur Stanton, please come out."

Please? It couldn't be too serious if he was asking politely.

"Stand back," he said to me, even though I wasn't even on the boat. "I'm going in." To my surprise, he drew his weapon before pushing the door open. I involuntarily took a step back. Fortunately, I wasn't near the edge of the float or I would have ended up in the water.

It isn't easy entering most small power boats without exposing yourself. And on a 38-foot Uniflight, once you open the door into the main salon you can see all the way to the bow, unless the door between the main cabin and the forward stateroom is shut. Although I couldn't imagine Arthur waiting inside with a weapon, Officer Dodd was clearly visible to anyone inside. And, since he had his gun out, there was obviously something he wasn't telling me about the situation. Unless he just wanted an excuse to act like a TV cop.

Officer Dodd had to duck to get through the doorway. No shots were fired. No one shouted from inside the boat. Everything was quiet. Either Arthur wasn't there or he really was sick, too sick to get up and protest someone coming aboard his boat without permission.

Hoping that the chance of a gunfight was past, I climbed aboard and peeked around the corner. I couldn't see anything other than Officer Dodd's broad back. He was up front, in the stateroom. I could hear a faint moaning sound.

"Get up. Get up *now*," I heard Officer Dodd order. "Get up, I said. *Now*." Obviously, Arthur—or whoever it was—wasn't being cooperative. I went inside and peeked around Officer Dodd's looming presence. Arthur was in his bunk, his body twisted, one foot over the edge, as if he was trying unsuccessfully to get up.

"Arthur, are you okay?" I asked.

Officer Dodd turned to glare at me. "You should leave."

"No, I don't think so." I looked at Arthur again. "Did he hit you?" I asked. There was definitely something wrong with him.

"No, no one hit anyone," Officer Dodd said firmly. "Now if you wouldn't mind, I need to talk with him." He pointed at the door. "And you need to leave."

"I'm not leaving until I know he's okay." My mother always tells me that I can be stubborn, and in this instance, I fully intended to stay until I had a handle on what was going on.

Arthur seemed to be disoriented and appeared to be having difficulty holding his head upright. Suddenly his eyes focused on me. "Bryn? What are you doing here?"

"I just want to make sure that you're okay before I leave you with this police officer. Are you okay?"

He looked at Officer Dodd and blinked hard as if trying to make sure of what he was seeing. "What's going on?" he asked, his speech slightly slurred. Officer Dodd reached down and attempted to pull Arthur off his bunk. Arthur resisted at first, then gave in and let the officer help him stand up.

"I'm here to take you down to the station to answer a few questions." He gripped Arthur's arm firmly and steered him toward the main cabin, motioning for me to move aside. It looked to me like if he let go, Arthur would collapse.

"Down to the station? What station?"

Not the *train* station, I said under my breath. Get a grip, Arthur.

Officer Dodd shook his head like he'd seen it all before and wasn't fooled by the act. Then he turned to me. "You really do need to leave. I'm going to give him a chance to get dressed. Then I'll take him in. You can talk to him later."

Arthur was in his Captain America PJs. The way Dodd was acting, I had the feeling he was going to need a real superhero to save himself. "Just tell me what this is all about and I'll go."

Officer Dodd seemed ready to pick me up and throw me bodily off the boat, but then he paused and apparently decided that the easiest way to get rid of me was to tell me what I wanted to know. "We need to question your friend about the disappearance of Sabrina Valdez." Then he motioned toward the door. "Now, if you'd give him some privacy—"

My *friend*? Did they think I was Arthur's friend? I was just a nosy neighbor who was interfering with police business. It was time to take a hint.

I headed toward my office, then stopped. Something wasn't right. I called Logan and got his voicemail. Then I tried Sophie. No luck there either. I spotted Hudson, our landlord, just pulling into the parking area and ran up to meet him. "They are taking Arthur in for questioning," I said, out of breath from running so quickly up the steps. I really did need to get more exercise.

"*Our* Arthur?" Hudson asked.

I didn't know how to answer that. He wasn't "mine," but then we did both know him. "*Knotty Lady* Arthur," I said.

"What did he do?" Hudson asked.

"I'm not sure he did anything. But someone he knows has disappeared."

Hudson is in his early 60s and had retired from a high-pressure job to buy and manage the marina. He often said it was that change that kept him alive. These days he is always calm, which is usually pleasant and reassuring. But, in this instance, I wanted action, or high energy commiseration, or at least something more than a measured response. On the other hand, why would I expect him to get excited just because there was a police officer hauling Arthur off to the station? I had to be more specific about my concerns.

"The problem is that I think something is wrong with Arthur. He doesn't seem to be fully functioning, and I'm afraid the police will take advantage of that to . . . well, to . . ." I paused when I realized that I wasn't sure what I was afraid of. Or what I wanted someone to help me do.

Hudson is as conservative as I am liberal, so if I'd been thinking clearly, I wouldn't have started with that line of argument. "Oh, I'm sure everything will be fine," he assured me. "The police don't railroad innocent people these days."

"It's just that Sabrina is missing. And Arthur may have been the last person to see her alive."

"A friend of his is missing? And you think what—that she could be dead?" Hudson seemed genuinely alarmed at the thought.

"Well, I don't know. But if she is, and if they suspect Arthur, well, I don't think he's guilty of anything other than bad judgement." I believed what I was saying, didn't I?

At that moment we heard Officer Dodd and Arthur coming down the dock. The officer had his hand on Arthur's elbow, either steadying him or propelling him forward, or both. Arthur still looked confused and appeared to be having difficulty walking.

When they reached the foot of the steps, Officer Dodd answered his cell. I heard snatches of the conversation as they started up the stairs.

"Bringing him in now . . . no problem . . ." He didn't acknowledge the two of us when they reached the top. Nor did Arthur. I wanted to say something, but couldn't decide what was appropriate under the circumstances, so I remained silent. So did Hudson.

We continued watching as Officer Dodd helped Arthur into the police car and drove off.

"I think he once told me something about being a heavy sleeper," Hudson offered. "I remember trying to rouse him one time when I'd been warned to keep on the lookout for a couple of runaways."

"He's had plenty of time to get fully awake. You agree he didn't look normal?"

Hudson considered my question a minute before answering. "I guess I have to agree. Definitely not normal. Even for Arthur."

Chapter 10

No Body Becomes Some Body

I tried to settle down to work on a client project, but I couldn't get Arthur out of my mind. Especially when I saw two officers heading down the dock toward his boat. What was that all about? They had to know he wasn't there. Had he really been taken in for questioning, or was there more to it? Maybe Arthur had forgotten to lock up before and they were kindly coming by to do that for him. But that wouldn't require *two* officers. It was more likely that they were there to search his boat. Didn't they need a warrant for that? And what would they be looking for? So many questions. It was all I could do to keep myself from racing down the dock after them. But one thing was fairly certain—it was unlikely they would tell me what they were up to if I asked. So, I might as well not bother.

It was about a half hour later when I saw one of the two officers coming back down the dock. Macavity came around the corner just as he reached the foot of the steps, stopping in front of him, his tail flicking back and forth. Go ahead, I silently urged, ask him what they're doing on Arthur's boat.

The officer smiled and knelt down, rubbing the top of Macavity's head. Macavity tolerated it for about five seconds, then shook his head and slowly turned and walked off. I liked seeing the officer kneel down to pet a cat. Most cats would have appreciated the gesture. But Macavity has high standards when it comes to petting.

The officer was only gone about five minutes. He returned carrying a duffle bag and once again disappeared down the dock.

I tried to focus but couldn't stop myself from getting up every few minutes to look out the window. When I couldn't stand it any longer, I called Ben. His phone started ringing just as someone knocked on the door. My office was becoming a popular stop. Maybe I should sell coffee.

"Hello." Ben's voice sounded like it was coming at me from two directions. I opened the door and there he was, answering my phone call. When we simultaneously realized what was happening, we both laughed and hung up.

He came in and sat in the chair across from my desk, sitting down gingerly, as if afraid it would collapse. "Where's Bubbles?" he asked.

"It's Bubbles IV now. I have him on my boat. He's not looking good."

"Number four! I'm sorry."

"Is this a social call?"

Ben smiled. He had a very nice smile if you ignored the mustache. It started with his mouth and extended to a slight crinkling at the corners of his eyes. Then he suddenly got serious. "No, I'm afraid I have some bad news."

"She's dead, isn't she?" That's why they had taken Arthur in for questioning. And that was why they were searching his boat. It was the only thing that made sense.

"Yes, her body was spotted this morning, on a small patch of uncultivated lakefront not far from here."

"That's sad, really sad." I hadn't known her, but I still felt a sense of loss. No more bright red high heels clacking down the dock. Her immaculate desk would belong to someone else, maybe even a person as messy as me. And Arthur could say goodbye to the second chance that had never existed in the first place.

"Dealing with death, even of those you don't know, is difficult." Ben said, sounding both thoughtful and empathetic.

"But that's part of your job, isn't it?"

"It doesn't mean I don't have feelings."

"Sorry, that's not what I meant. Although I would think that over time you would become, well, used to it. Not callous, but accepting of the finality of death, even ugly deaths."

"You may be right. The 'edge' is off. But I hope I never feel 'ho hum' about someone dying. 'That it will never come again is what makes life so sweet.'"

"Are you quoting Emily Dickinson?"

He smiled. "You recognize it."

"Quotation is a serviceable substitute for wit." I'm not sure why I popped off with that Oscar Wilde comment, but Ben wasn't offended. He laughed, a good-natured sound accompanied by a flash of white teeth.

"Touché."

"That may have come out wrong."

"I believe Wilde also said, 'Life is far too important a thing ever to talk seriously about.'"

"Do you like poetry or quotations?"

"Some poetry and all Oscar Wilde quotations. What about you?"

I couldn't help smiling at this insight into Ben. "The same is true for me."

We shared what in romance novels might be referred to as "a moment," but it quickly faded. Like a fog bow making way for the sun, our "moment" was overtaken by the more pressing topic of Sabrina's unfortunate death.

"So, what do you know about Sabrina's death at this point?" I asked.

"Off the record?"

"For my ears only." And, of course, for Logan's and Sophie's, but I wasn't going to admit that.

"Looked like blunt force trauma to the back of the head. Not sure how long she's been in the water yet. But there were also marks on her wrists, like she may have been tied up at some point."

"So not accidental drowning."

"Doubtful. We'll know the exact cause of death in a couple of days."

"Any sign of a murder weapon?"

"Nothing near where the body showed up."

"Is that why they're searching Arthur's boat?"

Ben smiled again. "You're observant."

"I take it that's a 'yes.'"

"That's a 'no comment.'"

Ben's phone rang. He answered and indicated he was going to step outside to take the call. I sat there and waited, wishing I could eavesdrop on the conversation without being obvious. A few minutes later he poked his head in and said that he had to go down to Arthur's boat. He would check back again later.

"Did they find something?" I didn't really expect an answer, but I had to try.

"Can't say. But I advise you to stay here. As soon as I can tell you something, I will."

"Thanks." The door closed and I turned to the window to watch him hurry off down the dock.

What kind of incriminating evidence could they have found? The night Arthur and Sabrina argued, I'd been willing to accept that Arthur had murdered Sabrina in a crime of passion. But when we'd confronted him, he'd appeared calm. Wouldn't he have seemed at least somewhat nervous if he'd had her trussed up somewhere on his boat? The fact that he had lied so convincingly about her not being there that evening gave me pause. Still, his actions since then did not seem like those of a murderer. More of a love-sick schmuck than a killer. But that was just my gut talking. I would have to withhold judgement until I heard from Ben about what they found on the Knotty Lady.

Unless . . . unless there was a specific reason for how groggy Arthur had been this morning. What if he'd been suffering from remorse and taken an overdose? It was possible. But how likely?

Another knock on the door, but this time I recognized the knock. "Come in, Hudson," I called.

Hudson came in and sat down. "Have you seen the police on Arthur's boat?"

"I saw them heading in that direction."

"I went down to see what was going on. I am, after all, the marina owner. I have an obligation to look out for my tenants."

Hudson was indeed a good landlord, but he was also someone who liked to keep tabs on what was going on in his tiny kingdom. "Did you hear anything?"

"Only that they found 'it.' Whatever 'it' is."

Ohmygod. "You don't suppose . . .?"

"You don't think . . .?"

"Do I think he killed Sabrina? No." I didn't, did I? "But what if they found something incriminating?"

"Like what?"

"Well, he lied about her being on his boat. At least he did initially. I don't know what he's told them today. Maybe they found something of hers there."

"I hate to think about what first came to my mind—"

"The murder weapon?" It had crossed my mind too.

We sat there a moment, both of us trying to process the fragmented information we had, filling in the gaps with imagination. Finally, Hudson stood up. "You'll let me know if you hear anything?"

"And if *you* hear anything . . .?"

Somehow, I managed to do some work on a facilitation plan for a strategic planning retreat I had scheduled for a local nonprofit. I was almost finished when the frogs on my cell phone announced I had a call. It was from Arthur.

"Bryn, I need your help."

"Okay, what do you need?" I hoped I wasn't his one call because that would make me feel very guilty if I decided not to respond positively to his request.

"They've arrested me." He sounded like he was fully awake. Awake and panicked.

"Have they charged you with anything specific yet?" I was pretty sure I knew what was coming, but I wanted to hear it from him.

"They say they're going to charge me with Sabrina's murder. Bryn, they think I killed her." His voice rose several octaves at the end, and I could hear uneven breathing, like he was struggling just to take in air.

"Stay calm, Arthur." Should I assure him everything was going to be okay when I highly doubted it would be? "Tell me what you need."

"I need a lawyer."

"And . . .?"

"Your friend Judd, do you think he'd represent me?"

"Judd isn't a criminal lawyer, Arthur."

"Oh."

"I'll ask him if he knows a criminal lawyer he'd recommend, okay?" That much I could do.

"I . . . I want someone who can prove I'm innocent."

"I'm sure you do."

"No, you don't understand. I *am* innocent. But they don't believe me. I need someone who can convince them that I'm telling the truth."

"Arthur, I'll call Judd right away and get back to you as soon as I have a couple of names, okay? Meanwhile, try to stay calm, and don't make any statements without a lawyer." I sounded like a TV character advising a client. "Okay?"

"Okay."

I hung up and called Judd's office. His admin asked me if it was important. Since I couldn't remember the last time I'd called him at work, I felt like saying, no, just calling to shoot the breeze. Instead I said, "I need a few minutes to ask him something, ah, important." To my surprise, she put me through.

I quickly explained the situation and asked if he had any recommendations I could pass along to Arthur.

"I know who I'd want defending me if I were innocent," he said.

"And if you weren't?" I couldn't help but ask.

"I'd still want one of two local criminal attorneys." He gave me their names and contact information. I thanked him and called Arthur back. He didn't answer, so I left the information on his voicemail. If he was being held on a murder charge, did they let him keep his phone or only let him use it under supervision? I should have asked. Or he should have told me. Either he'd get the names from his voicemail or he'd call back when he got the chance.

Later that evening I joined Logan and Judd for a glass of wine. When the local news came on, we huddled together on the couch in front of Judd's computer, waiting to see if they mentioned Sabrina's death. Logan kept Googling her name every five minutes or so but hadn't come up with anything yet.

It was almost anti-climactic to hear one of the home-grown newscasters refer to the breaking story about "a local woman brutally murdered and her body dumped in the lake." They flashed to the front of Sabrina's townhouse that now was rimmed with crime scene tape. Several neighbors and a few gawkers were milling about, along with a couple of kids mugging for the cameras behind the reporter who was providing "live" the same information that we had just heard. The attractive blond reporter looked and sounded like what she was saying was both incredibly newsworthy and urgent. Then she paused, lowered her pitch and her volume, and announced that there was a suspect in custody. It was like she was sharing a secret with her audience. She didn't, however, name Arthur. Maybe she didn't know the name of the suspect yet. I doubted the police would stay mum to protect the rights of the accused, but they could be waiting for a formal charge before making his name public.

"Do we know whether she was killed at her home or near the lake?" Judd asked.

"Any chance Arthur offed her here at the marina?" Logan interrupted before I could answer Judd's question.

"We don't know that he killed her," I pointed out.

"We don't know that he didn't either," Logan said. "But we do know that her body ended up near here."

"And whatever they found on his boat; it was apparently sufficient to charge him."

"The phrase 'brutally' murdered suggests a weapon of some sort," Judd said. "But it seems unlikely he would have kept that on his boat."

"Too easy to simply toss it overboard," Logan added.

My mind went to the statue. No, it couldn't be the murder weapon. If he had used it to kill Sabrina, he wouldn't have told me where it was. Or, where it used to be.

We speculated a bit longer while finishing off a bottle of a very nice Cabernet. Judd likes good wine. I was about to leave when Macavity appeared in the entrance.

"No," Judd said in a military command voice. "No."

For a moment I thought that was going to cause Macavity to race over and jump on Judd's lap. There was something about the way he was looking at Judd, like he considered the word "no" an invitation. Instead, Macavity remained in the entrance and made a yowling sound that I interpreted as, "You forgot to feed me before you left."

"Okay, let's go home," I said to my pushy cat. "Thanks for the wine," I called back over my shoulder as Macavity and I headed to the *Aspara*.

The first thing I saw as I climbed down the hatch was Bubbles IV, floating belly up in his bowl. Damn. Another body. For an instant I thought maybe that was what Macavity had come to tell me. His friend and my ward had died. Then I realized he was standing next to his food dish and glaring at me.

As soon as I'd fed my pushy cat, I took Bubbles' bowl outside and walked to the end of the dock. Saying a few words over a dead goldfish struck me as appropriate if somewhat overly sentimental. We hadn't, after all, exactly bonded during our time together.

"Bubbles the fourth. Died on a Wednesday after a short illness, cause unknown. He will be missed by Emma. And by me since I'll be responsible for replacing him . . . again. May he rest in peace." Then I dumped the contents over the side, imagining Bubbles suddenly coming to life as he—or she—hit the cold water, swimming off into the sunset, a free fish at last.

The friend who gave me the original fish said they are good companions because they listen and are never demanding. And, according to pet experts, goldfish can live as long as 45 years. None of Bubbles' predecessors had made it beyond a few months, although I had no way of knowing how old any of them were at the time of purchase. They could have been ancient when they came into my possession, ancient by fish standards, that is. Quadragenarians, gender unknown, ready to move on into the afterlife after spending a brief time with me. Or, each of them could have died before their time because of something to do with how I'd taken care of them. I'd read that a goldfish's lifespan is linked to the size of the container they are kept in. But, if that's the case, then why do pet stores sell small bowls filled with tacky accessories? To encourage on-going business?

If only Emma hadn't insisted on naming that first fish. That had made it family in a weird sort of way. And since I didn't want to be the one to explain to Emma about how pets died, I kept pretending I'd only owned one fish. Like some dog owner obsessed with a particular breed who keeps replacing expired pets with another who looks exactly the same. Sometimes even resorting to cloned replicas. I assume dog owners who did that at least came up with a new name for each new pet generation. Next to die in my possession would be Bubbles V.

Chapter 11

Goddess of Love or Death?

Thursday morning I woke up early. I think having a large cat on my chest had something to do with it. When he's hungry in the morning and I'm not up yet, he nuzzles my chin with the top of his head. I like to think it's an expression of affection, but it never lasts for long, and it is always followed by a race to his food dish. If I could teach him to serve himself and make my coffee, I'd be a happy camper.

I rubbed him behind the ears the way he likes and said, "Okay, I'll get up." Macavity jumped down and lingered long enough to make sure I'd meant what I said before heading for the main cabin.

After putting on my usual uniform of jeans and a wrinkled T-shirt, I headed for my Keurig. Macavity glared at me to let me know he should be served first, but I figured he owed me that slight indulgence for getting me up so early.

He gulped down his breakfast before my coffee was ready and looked up at me as if to ask, "Where's the rest?" That was fast even for him. Then he settled in next to me on the settee while I drank my coffee and thought about how nice it would be if someone would fix me breakfast. A real breakfast. Unfortunately, that wasn't going to happen. I'd have to settle for whatever was in my refrigerator. I was almost afraid to look.

Someone stepped aboard my boat. "Bryn, you up?"

It was Logan.

I pulled back the hatch. "Isn't it a bit early to come calling?"

"Is that what I'm doing?"

"Want coffee?"

"No, I want you to go to breakfast with me. No classes today and I woke up early."

"You're a saint. Let me grab my wallet."

Over a full, standard breakfast at Beth's we rehashed everything we'd already covered about Arthur's arrest and the death of Sabrina. Then we rehashed it again, trying our best to come up with new perspectives by testing each assumption and making a list of what we didn't know. I was so intent on our conversation I was surprised when I looked down and found my plate empty. All I had left was a half cup of cold coffee. And a scintilla of guilt.

"I can't help but feel like I'm letting Sabrina down by even considering that Arthur might be innocent," I said.

"You really think he is? I mean, initially you were convinced he chucked her overboard."

"I know what I thought then, but now I'm leaning toward a different theory."

"Related to possible illegal activities at AHA?"

"Yes, I know I don't have anything concrete yet, but I can feel it coming on."

"Like a migraine."

I couldn't resist. I leaned forward and softly sang a few words from Something's Coming from *West Side Story.* It's hard not to stand up and dance when singing lyrics from *West Side Story*, but I kept it under control so as not to disturb other customers.

Logan leaned forward and joined in with the next line.

Another voice suddenly chimed in from above, a fairly strong baritone but in hushed tones.

We looked up to see Ben leaning over us. The three of us finished together.

By then other customers were looking at us sideways, like we were a little crazy. Maybe we were. But I was pleasantly surprised that Ben knew some of the words to one of my favorite show tunes.

"Thought I might find you here," Ben said. "Mind if I join you?"

Logan raised his eyebrows slightly as I nodded for him to sit. "I hope this means you have some news you're willing to share."

"I may have. What's it worth to you?"

It took me a moment to realize he was kidding. It's hard to see someone with a pencil mustache as a kidder. But he could quote Oscar Wilde and had joined us in song. Maybe I needed to give him a chance. On the other hand, he was the one who hadn't given me a second chance.

"Breakfast on us?" Logan said.

"Can't accept bribes." Ben smiled. "But I do have a few questions you might be able to help me out with." He took a picture out of his breast pocket and placed it in front of me. It was Arthur's Aphrodite statue. He was lucky I'd just swallowed a sip of coffee or I would have spit it all over. As it was, the liquid suddenly seemed to go down the wrong way. I gasped for air and coughed.

"You okay?" Ben asked.

"Just swallowed wrong," I said, taking a deep breath. As soon as I had myself under control, I pointed at the base of the statue and asked, "What's that dark stain?"

"Forensics is working on that."

"Is it blood?" Logan asked.

"Could be."

"Where did you get this?" I asked. I didn't think Arthur's Aphrodite was a one-of-a-kind piece of art, but this seemed way too coincidental.

"Is this the statue you think they could have been arguing about?"

"Yes."

"Are you sure? I mean, you never actually saw it, did you?"

He had me there. "Actually . . . I have seen it."

Ben looked surprised. Logan was frowning and flashing me SOS warnings with his eyes.

"Where did you get this?" I asked again.

Ben hesitated. "Okay, let's do an exchange of information. I'll tell you why I have this picture, and you'll tell me where you saw it, okay?"

I nodded. What choice did I have?

"We think it's the murder weapon. The officers found it on the *Knotty Lady*." He paused. "Your turn."

"That isn't possible," I said. Logan was sending me subliminal messages again, but I didn't see any way I could avoid sharing what I had done at this point.

"And why is that?" Ben was sounding less like someone about to burst into song and more like a badass detective.

"Because the original statue is in my locker." Logan rolled his eyes and slumped in defeat. He was obviously convinced that nothing good could come from the confession I was about to make. I also had misgivings. But keeping the statue from Arthur was not the same as withholding evidence in a murder investigation.

I quickly explained to Ben that I had wanted to verify Arthur's story and had found the statue right where he'd said it had been dropped overboard by Sabrina.

"You retrieved it from the lake?"

"Yes. I have diving gear. It wasn't hard." That wasn't entirely true, but close enough. And I didn't have to mention that I did it in the dead of night. That didn't seem like an important fact. I just hoped he didn't ask for more details.

"So, you dove down, picked up the statue, and, instead of giving it back to Arthur, you hid it in your locker?"

"Well, I didn't exactly hide it . . ."

"But you didn't return it to its owner. What were you planning on doing with it?"

"I was going to give it back. I just hadn't decided when yet. Then Sabrina didn't show up, so I held onto it. I'm not sure why, I just did." I also didn't need to tell him I was considering holding onto it until Christmas. As a joke. He might not think that was funny.

Ben was staring at me. I couldn't read his expression, but I didn't think he was having romantic thoughts. "Why don't you finish your . . . " He glanced at the dregs on Logan's plate. "breakfast. Then we'll go to your locker."

Logan picked up a crust of toast and bit into it, apparently sensing my need to process what Ben had just shown us. I sipped my remaining coffee, struggling to come up with some theory to explain Ben's bombshell. Only two people knew about my midnight dive—Logan and Sophie. Arthur's statue had to still be in my locker . . . didn't it?

Ten minutes later we were standing in front of my locker. It was the third one to the right at the bottom of the stairs. My name was printed in felt pen on a piece of wood nailed to the top of the door. I hadn't opened my locker since the night I put the statue inside. Most of what was in there was probably not worth keeping, but I kept putting off going through everything and getting rid of stuff I no longer needed. At any rate, I seldom opened the locker.

The lock was intact. Not that it was anything fancy, just something I'd picked up at the hardware store. Someone could probably have picked it, but if they had, they had also locked it back up.

When I opened the door, my first thought was that everything looked exactly like I had left it. With one exception . . . the statue was gone.

"It's not here," I said, hardly believing what I was seeing, or, in this case, not seeing.

"How is that possible?" Logan said, echoing my disbelief.

"You didn't tell anyone, did you?" I asked Logan.

"Not even Judd." He might have said, "Especially not Judd," since Judd would have disapproved of everything I'd done related to the statue.

"Who else did *you* tell?" Ben asked me.

"My friend, Sophie. But she wouldn't have told anyone."

"It might be best if you talk with her about this. I'll follow up with her later."

"You don't think Arthur saw you hauling up the statue, do you?" Logan asked, still struggling to come up with a plausible explanation. Fortunately, he didn't add, "at that hour."

"Unlikely, but not impossible. But why would he use the statue to kill her and then leave it on his boat?"

Ben shook his head. "I admit, it doesn't make any sense."

"Unless someone is framing Arthur," I said.

"But that doesn't explain how they got the statue from your locker," Logan pointed out.

"Okay," Ben said, sounding very official. "You check with your friend, and I'll talk to the two officers who found the statue and see what forensics has discovered."

He started to leave, then turned back after about two steps. "I don't need to remind you that you shouldn't say anything to anyone about this, right?"

Admit my midnight dive and losing a key piece of evidence in a murder investigation? Very unlikely.

"You don't think Sophie would have told anyone, do you?" I asked Logan as we headed for my office. "I mean, what reason would she have for doing that?"

"Maybe she said something unwittingly to someone . . ."

"How can you accidentally tell someone something that complicated?"

"That's why I think someone may have seen you with the statue—either when you first hauled it up or when you put it in your locker."

"But that *someone* could only have been Arthur. I mean, no one else would have known why it was significant."

"You need to call Sophie. We have to know what she may have done before worrying about other possibilities."

I unlocked my office and we went inside. I sat behind my desk, and Logan took the chair across from it. With a feeling of dread, I punched in her number. She answered on the second ring.

"Can I call you back?" she asked.

"*No*," I said a bit too loud. I lowered my voice and continued. "I have a question that can't wait."

She asked me to hold and came back just seconds later. "Something wrong?"

"No, well, yes. The police have what they think is the murder weapon."

"And . . .?"

"It's the statue of Aphrodite."

"Really? But I thought . . ."

"Someone took it from my locker."

"But who . . .?"

For once Sophie was at a loss for words. Of course, I'd felt the same way when Ben showed me the picture of the statue. "That's the question, Sophie. I only told you and Logan about it, so, I have to ask . . ." I hesitated a moment, then blurted it out: "Did you tell anyone about me retrieving the statue?"

There was silence at the other end of the line. An uncomfortable, telling silence.

"Seriously? You told someone?!" My voice became a bit screechy, definitely in the rude range, but I was incredulous. Incredulous and furious.

"I'm sorry, Bryn. You have to understand . . ."

"Understand what?"

"Well . . . how can I explain . . . it was a good story."

"A good story?! It was something personal that I told you in confidence, one friend to another."

"I am sorry, truly sorry. But I didn't name you or get specific about anything. Besides, at the time we didn't know that Sabrina had been killed."

"So, who is this person you told this *good story* to?" I get sarcastic when I'm upset, and I was very upset. I felt embarrassed and betrayed.

"Someone I met at a party. I was trying to impress him by being, you know, interesting."

"You shared something I did—that I'm aware was borderline strange—because you hoped it would be *interesting* to some man?"

"Not strange. *Unconventional* perhaps. But definitely an interesting story, yes."

"Okay. We can talk more about this later." I took a deep breath to calm myself. "For now, just give me his name."

"You're not going to talk with him about this, are you?"

"Sophie, someone stole the statue out of my locker and now Arthur has been charged with murder because it was found on his boat. I need to give the names of anyone who knew about the statue to Ben." I took another deep breath. "He'll be contacting you by the way."

"Well, you can't suspect Dane of breaking into your locker."

"Maybe not. But we don't know for sure, do we? Or maybe he had someone he wanted to impress with a 'good story,' someone who decided to steal the statue." My anger was ebbing, slowly, but I wasn't about to let Sophie off the hook completely. If she had one weakness it was her obsessive desire to meet and mate the love of her life. I did understand the urge to find someone to share your life with, but this time it seemed to me that she had gone a little too far.

"Oh. I suppose it's possible—" I could tell by her tone that the implications of what she had done were sinking in. Good.

"So, tell me Dane's last name, his number, and where he works. I'll take it from there. Do *not* call him and warn him about this. I want to ask him in person who he told."

"Why don't I set up a meeting for drinks tonight. I'd like to hear what he has to say too."

I couldn't think of any reason why not, so I agreed. "Just don't tell him anything in advance to suggest the real purpose for our meeting, okay?"

When I hung up Logan asked, "Shouldn't you tell Ben right away about this Dane guy?" He'd obviously pieced together the storyline from listening to my side of the conversation.

"Maybe. But I'd like to find out if Dane told anyone first. Once Ben takes this over, I won't hear any more about it until he's good and ready to tell me."

"But you'll call him tonight after the meeting, right?"

"Yes, of course."

Logan smiled. "For the record, it *is* an amusing story."

"About a kooky friend."

"Nothing wrong with kooky."

"Point taken. Okay. I'll let Sophie make it up to me."

"That's borderline blackmail, you know."

"So?"

The empty space on the middle bookshelf suddenly intruded on my consciousness. Reluctantly I stood up and said, "I guess it's time to deal with another body. Want to go with me to the pet store?"

Logan glanced at the bookshelf and groaned. "Not again!"

Chapter 12

Poker Talk

I ended up buying a new fishbowl, a larger one, and several new decorations, including the treasure chest I'd promised Bubbles III. I also bought a pirate skeleton with an eye patch, holding onto a steering wheel. A bit macabre, but I liked it. With the lava rock pass-through I already had, Bubbles V and his companion would hopefully be entertained enough to hang around for a while. I had purchased two goldfish this time with the idea that if one died and the other didn't, maybe I could talk to Emma about pets and death with the consolation that we still had one fish. It wasn't as if goldfish were expensive. In fact, their purchase price ought to tell prospective buyers everything they needed to know about life expectancy issues. I wondered how many other adults bought replacement fish for children without telling them about the death of their pet. The practice might be as common as lying about the Easter bunny and Santa Claus. No doubt it was a solid line of business for the pet sales industry.

After clearing a space for Bubbles V and Friend on my bookshelf, I considered doing something with the pile of books I'd removed to make way for the larger bowl, other than leaving them in a heap on the floor, that is. In my professional life I pride myself on getting things done in a timely and efficient manner. I'm also committed to regular boat maintenance, for both practical and cosmetic reasons. But there are some things that beg to be on a procrastination list. Straightening up is one of them. Why try to hide things away when you just have to find them again when needed? Cleaning is another. You can spend hours wiping off surfaces only to have dust reproduce itself from nothing in less time than it took to remove it in the first place. I left the pile of dusty books on the floor and went back to work.

I got in a couple hours of work before Sophie called with the time and place for our meeting with Dane. She apologized again for telling him about my midnight swim in the first place, and I forgave her, a little bit. The fact that she found something I'd done "entertaining" still stung. Although I had to admit that, if she had done something like what I'd done, I might have passed along the story under the right circumstances. But she wouldn't have done something like that, so the comparison was moot.

Ben hadn't called since I made the arrangement to talk with Dane, which was a relief. Maybe I could tell him about Dane and Harold at the same time, camouflaging the significance of the latter. No, he would see through that ploy. I would be better off to delay the second conversation, depending on how the first conversation went.

Sophie had requested that I tread lightly with Dane so as not to ruin her budding relationship with him, even though he was just the latest in a long line of potential prospects. I gave him three months tops. That seemed to be Sophie's average before she decided whoever she was dating wasn't "the" one. Sometimes I felt like she enjoyed the hunt more than the catch. From my point of view, it would either happen or it wouldn't. And there was a lot to be said for being single. In truth, Macavity was more than enough commitment and responsibility for me.

Sophie was at the coffee shop when I arrived. She and Dane were scheduled to go out to dinner afterwards. I was just the hors d oeuvre.

We hugged—even though I'm not a hugger—me hunching over to get down to her level. It was an A-frame hug, and not particularly comfortable for me, but Sophie has always felt like that's the only appropriate greeting between friends. Once I sat down, she pushed a cup of coffee toward me. "I got you your drip."

She said it with all the distain of someone who prefers a more exotic cup of coffee.

"Thanks. Don't worry—you're forgiven."

"You do know that I didn't think it would ever come up."

"You didn't intend on introducing Dane to me?"

"Well, I didn't tell him it was you, just that it was a friend."

"A friend who just happens to live on a boat. Duh."

Dane picked that moment to appear. He was tall and professional looking with dark, styled hair and no five o'clock shadow. He bent down and kissed Sophie on the cheek before holding out a hand and saying, "You must be Bryn. Sophie's told me a lot about you."

More than you might imagine, I said to myself. We would get to that soon enough. "It's good to meet you." I used my well-behaved voice. "I understand you're in real estate."

"And I understand that you are a consultant." There seemed to be more than enough understanding to go around. But I didn't really care what he did for a living, just whether he was a thief and possibly a killer, or if he'd passed along my story to someone else who was one or both. Somehow, he didn't look like a killer. But then, killers come in all shapes and sizes and are sometimes real charmers.

We made small talk for a few minutes, me assessing him while he mainly tried to impress me with a vocal resume of sorts. Maybe it was more for Sophie's benefit than mine, but the more he talked about himself and his business dealings, the less impressed I was. If by some miracle he made it past the three-month mark with Sophie, I'd have to learn to like him. But at this point I didn't have to exert much real effort, and I was free to be judgmental, as long as I kept those judgements to myself.

When we reached a lull in his self-aggrandizement phase, I finally got around to asking the question that was the reason for this awkward coffee klatch. "Well, Dane, since I know the two of you are headed out for dinner, let me ask you something before you have to leave." He looked at me with eyebrows raised, poised to enlighten me, perhaps thinking I was going to ask for real estate advice. "Remember the story Sophie told you the other night about the person who retrieved a statue from the lake in the middle of the night?"

After a brief look of surprise, he smiled and glanced at Sophie. She was looking down at her coffee. "Sure. Why?"

"Well, I was wondering if you repeated the story to anyone."

Now he looked puzzled. "Why would you ask that?"

"The story was about me."

Dane laughed. "*You* went diving for a statue you thought might be a body in the middle of the night?"

"Yes." I wasn't wild about the tone that accompanied his characterization of the facts, but I wasn't going to be sidetracked. "Now, can you tell me if you repeated the story to anyone?"

"I don't understand. Sophie didn't attach a name to the story, and neither did I. So what does it matter if I told a few guys about it?"

"You told 'a few guys' about it?" I could feel the muscles tighten in my neck. A *few* guys? I didn't like the potential number of suspects that conjured up, nor the all-male bonhomie depicted by his use of the phrase "a few guys."

"I play poker with some guys once a month."

"So how many *guys* were there?" He either ignored or missed my sarcasm, but I saw Sophie's mouth tighten.

"There's six regulars."

"Long-time friends?"

"Not really. More like business acquaintances. I manage mostly large building projects, so I have contacts throughout the industry. In our group there are two realtors, two in construction and a home inspector. We drink a little, talk about sports, exchange a little money. It's all in good fun." He gave me a big grin. "They loved the story about the letch and the naked lady."

"Sounds like you may have embellished details a little."

"Well, I may have too," Sophie said softly. "You know how stories get exaggerated. I mean, it wasn't as if I was telling a story about *you*."

"Actually, you were." I was getting mad again. But deep down I know a *good* story sometimes needs a little puffery to be a *great* story. "Okay, what's done is done." I took out my phone and pulled up my email. "Just give me their names and any contact information you have for them."

"Why?"

"Because I'm going to contact them."

"Why?" he repeated, sounding both confused and irritated. "What's this all about?"

"Sorry. I forgot to mention that the statue was stolen from my locker, and I'm trying to figure out who took it. Unless you want to confess—?"

He laughed. Then he realized that I was serious. "Don't be ridiculous. I wouldn't do that. And no one in my poker group would either. Besides, they had no way of knowing you were the one the story was about, since even I didn't know."

"Did anyone ask where you heard the story?"

Dane blinked and sat very still for a moment. "Now that you mention it—" He stared straight ahead as if trying to read the answer on the far wall. "I can't say for sure, but I think someone did. We weren't concentrating on conversation, you understand."

"And you mentioned Sophie?"

"Well, they already knew I'm dating her."

I could see that he was trying to figure out where my line of inquiry was going. Even I wasn't sure. How could any of those men have connected Sophie to me? And, even if one of them had, where did the statue of Aphrodite and Sabrina's murder fit into the picture? If I had blabbed the story to anyone else, I might not be so certain that one of Dane's poker buddies stole the statue out of my locker. However, under the circumstances, the odds were that it was either one of them or someone they told. And the only way to find out for certain was to follow up with each of the poker players. Of course, Ben would take charge of that, but having the names, I could poke around a bit too.

"Will you give me their names?"

"Of course. But I can't believe—"

"Look, I know this is difficult for you, and I appreciate your help. I would also appreciate it if you didn't contact any of them and give them a head's up."

He took out his phone and frowned at it as he started to punch in the names. "I suppose they have to know it was me that gave you their contact information."

"Not necessarily. Although they will guess that someone at the game did. If I were you, the next time you play poker with them, I'd admit you told me about it. Only the thief will be ticked."

When Sophie and Dane left, neither of them was too happy. I stayed behind, ostensibly to finish my coffee, but the real reason I hung back was that I didn't want to be forced to make small talk walking out with them. Things had been strained enough without prolonging the conversation. And I definitely didn't want to find myself saying something that would alert Dane to the fact that I intended to turn over the names he had given me to the police. He would figure that out soon enough. As would Sophie. She was sure to be peeved with me. I was counting on her practical side recognizing that I had no choice.

Back at the marina I stopped by my office to check on Bubbles V and Friend. They were swimming around and around, both in the same direction, as if one was chasing the other. I wondered if they ever swam past each other coming from opposite directions, smiling as they passed by. Did goldfish smile? Maybe they had a special tail wave for friends.

Macavity was waiting for me on the dock next to the *Aspara.* Like an impatient parent marking time until a teenager returned from a date. "Hey, Macavity. I have a right to a life, you know." He cocked his head to one side as if questioning my statement. "Okay, so I don't have much of a life, but it's still a life." Macavity rubbed up against me as I unlocked the hatch, tearing down ahead of me, stopping by his treat drawer.

"Let me throw something in the microwave first, okay?"

From his yowled response, it wasn't okay, but I did it anyway. Then I got out a couple of bite-sized pieces of Seafood Medley and fed them to him one at a time. They were supposedly *scrumptious tasting with an enticing texture*. He gobbled them down, glared at my empty hands gesture when I ran out of goodies and jumped up on the couch, waiting to see if my dinner would have anything interesting in it for him. I always insisted he wasn't supposed to have any people food, but we both knew I didn't mean it. Although I was careful about what and how much I gave him out of concern for his health.

"You'll have to wait until I call Ben," I explained. Why I bother telling him anything is beyond me; he doesn't really listen. But it's a habit I can't seem to break. I hit Ben's number on my phone and was pleased that he answered. I was anxious for him to start working on the list of names I was going to give him.

"You're clairvoyant," Ben said.

"Not that I know of . . ."

"Well, I just heard back from forensics. You may be surprised to find that your fingerprints were not on the statue we recovered from Arthur's boat. But guess whose were?"

"Arthur's?"

"See, you *are* clairvoyant."

"I thought they might fade from being in the water."

"You fortunately pulled it up before that happened."

"But why weren't mine on the statue?"

"Maybe he wiped the statue down before using it as a murder weapon."

"Anything else?"

"Like blood?"

"Like blood."

"Yes. There hadn't been any attempt to clean it off."

"So, the statue was the murder weapon."

"Looks that way."

"Estimated time of death?"

"That's a bit problematic. He must have waited a few days before killing her."

"If you're referring to Arthur, where would he have kept her? On his boat? That seems unlikely."

"He may have a locker somewhere. Or he could have rented a room. We're working on that."

"What does he say?"

"That he's innocent. What else?"

"You are truly cynical, aren't you?"

"In my line of work, you have to be."

"Don't you have hunches though? I mean, don't you sometimes sense when someone is telling the truth?"

"Hunches are for amateurs. Professionals deal in facts."

"Not innocent until proven guilty?"

"In theory."

"Well, I think you could be looking at the wrong person for Sabrina's murder."

"Is that a hunch, or do you have some facts to back up your theory?"

Was he teasing me? "I do have one fact, well several, depending on how you look at it. I talked with Sophie, and she did mention me retrieving the statue to someone. I asked him about it, and he claims he didn't know it was me specifically, but he passed along the story to five of his poker buddies."

"So, Logan, Sophie and six poker playing men knew about the statue."

"Any one of the men could have taken it out of my locker and framed Arthur."

"Unless Arthur figured out that you had it and stole it from your locker himself," Ben countered.

"That's possible too. But I'm leaning toward one of the six men as the thief. Well, I've mostly ruled out one of them. Sophie's friend doesn't strike me as a likely suspect. He seemed truly surprised when I admitted I was the one who had, ah, found the statue. That leaves five. And any of them could have told someone else. That's something you'll have to figure out."

"Enlighten me. Why did Sophie tell her friend about the statue?"

"She thought it was an amusing story."

"Hmmm." I could tell he was holding back a laugh.

"You don't have to comment. I know how it looks."

"You're lucky I know you; otherwise, you'd be on the suspect list."

"Thanks. The names are on their way—I just hit send."

"Arthur's lucky to have a friend like you."

"I am NOT Arthur's friend. I don't even like him. But everyone deserves a fair hearing."

"And you think the police aren't being fair?"

"I didn't say that. But as Mortimer Adler said, '*The telephone book is full of facts, but it doesn't contain a single idea.*'"

"Well, Aldous Huxley said that '*facts do not cease to exist because they are ignored.*'"

"I'm not asking you to ignore the facts, just think outside the box."

"Hey, you're using telephone books to prove your point. Do they even exist anymore?"

"You win. But remember, Martin Luther King said, that "'*The moral arc of the universe bends at the elbow of justice.*'"

"Now *you* win. I don't even know what that means."

"But it's eloquent, isn't it?"

Ben laughed. "We need to do this again sometime. When I'm not investigating a homicide."

Chapter 13

The Ex-Boyfriend

Friday arrived on tiny streams of sunlight through a porthole, mellow and copacetic. Macavity let me wake up naturally instead of sitting on my chest. It was early enough that I had time to luxuriate in the comfort of my bunk, until nature called. I found a clean T-shirt at the top of a pile of clothes that needed sorting. After getting dressed, I had my usual three cups of coffee from my one-cup Keurig. Life was good.

When I got to my office Bubbles V and Friend were happily swimming around and around in their bowl. No one had invaded my space; the mess was exactly as I had left it. And there was nothing to distract me from the work I needed to do for a client. Except for the questions chasing themselves around my head, that is.

There was one thing in particular that bothered me. Why had Arthur been so groggy the other morning? Had he taken a sleeping pill? Was he always slow to awaken in the morning? Was it possible? No, it wasn't. Well, maybe . . . someone could have drugged him. But that was pretty far-fetched.

Actually, there were two things that bothered me. Not only was I puzzled by his grogginess, but I couldn't figure out why the murder weapon was on his boat in the first place. If he had stashed Sabrina somewhere for several days before ending her life, why would he bring the murder weapon back? Was he really so smitten with his precious Aphrodite that he failed to consider that the police might come looking for it? And, most important, what possible motive could he have had for doing in someone he so obviously had a thing for? Was he really some monster hidden in the body of a nerdy, sex obsessed Captain America wanna-be? That sounded like the plot for a very bad made-for-TV original movie.

I wasn't surprised when there was a knock on my door. Maybe I should consider washing the coffee cup I reserved for the occasional rare guest.

"Come in," I yelled.

The door opened slowly, gradually revealing the head of a young woman as she peeked around the corner. "Are you Bryn Baczek?" she asked with perfect pronunciation.

I stood up. "Please, come in."

She pushed the door open and stepped inside. She was average height with shiny brown hair that framed her face and ended neatly tucked in at her chin line. She was wearing a blue pantsuit and a white blouse. Nothing flashy, but definitely not casual Friday attire. "I'm Lilly Blaine, Arthur Stanton's assistant. He said you would help me."

"Ah, it depends. What do you need?"

"If you could show me his boat and perhaps stay while I remove some files he left there—I feel uncomfortable being there by myself under the circumstances. I wouldn't want anyone to think I'd removed something I wasn't supposed to take."

"Of course." I moved toward the door and she backed out onto the deck.

"I appreciate this. I probably should have called ahead. Sorry."

"No problem." I wanted to add that the police had already searched the boat; there was nothing she could remove that hadn't already been vetted. But it might be interesting to chat with her, so I was more than willing to be helpful.

We headed down the dock toward the *Knotty Lady*. "Arthur told me that you helped him find a lawyer," Lilly said.

"Yes, I have a friend who is a lawyer, and he made a couple of recommendations. I hope one of them worked out."

"Oh, yes. Arthur has a lot of confidence in the lawyer he hired. Even though he didn't manage to convince the court that Arthur should get bail. I think it had to do with him living on a boat."

"How's he holding up?"

"As well as can be expected."

I wanted to ask if she thought he was innocent. But I decided a little more chitchat might be in order first. "Had you met the deceased, Sabrina Valdez?"

"Oh, yes. I had the pleasure of being the one to make our records available to her."

Was that a sarcastic remark coming from this sweet seeming young woman? A *pleasure*? Or was that corporate speak for *I was fulfilling my responsibilities with the positive attitude required by our mission statement?*

"What was she like?"

"Oh, competent, not overly friendly."

"I gather Arthur was under the impression that she was, ah, friendly." I turned to see her reaction. She looked at me and shook her head.

"He can be such a putz at times."

"I've noticed that myself."

"He thinks he's a real lady's man."

"Really? Did he ever come on to you?"

"He tried a couple of times. But I made it clear I wasn't interested. After that, he was fine."

So, he had a history of misjudging cues from women he flirted with. Not too socially astute, but that didn't make him a murderer. And if he was used to being turned down, then wasn't he less likely to have flipped out over Sabrina's rejection?

When we arrived at the Knotty Lady. I climbed aboard first, and Lilly followed. Then she stepped around me, reached under the dinghy on the cabin roof, and searched around until she found a small bag with a key in it. I moved to the side while she unlocked the door and went inside.

At that point, I decided to up the game a little. "You did hear that the police found the murder weapon on the boat, didn't you?"

"Um hum," she said as she started going through the files on the table. "Arthur is stupid about some things, but I can't believe he would have killed someone and kept the murder weapon around. I mean, he could simply have tossed it over the side, right?"

"So you think he's innocent." There, that was big question. What did someone who knew him think about his potential for violence and the likelihood that he was a murderer?

Lilly paused, still holding the corner of a file, but looking directly at me. "Look, Sabrina wanted something from Arthur. That was fairly obvious. I don't know what it was, but it wasn't sex."

"You think she had a hidden agenda?"

"It didn't have to be very well hidden for Arthur to not see it. He was clearly smitten."

Smitten? She did have a way with words. "But you don't have any idea what she might have been after?"

"No. But these files are what she asked for."

We both looked at the files on the table. I hesitated, then asked, "Can you tell me the kind of information that's in them?" I wanted to ask to look through them myself, before she took them away, but I didn't think she would go along with that.

She sifted through a couple of the folders. "They seem to be straightforward financial files. I can't understand why she would need to look through them here and not at the office."

"You're sure there's nothing unusual in them?"

She thumbed through the files, glancing inside a couple, scanning pages quickly, like she was familiar enough with the data to understand the significance of the information.

"Looks like straightforward stuff to me."

"I wonder if the police went through them." I said the words out loud, but I was really just trying to process the thought.

"Nonprofits don't have financial secrets. The police probably assumed that the information in these files has no relation to what happened to Sabrina."

"What about you? Do you think they could be connected in some way?"

She pursed her lips and seemed to give my question some serious thought. "I don't see how. But I'll make copies of these files in case the police want to take a closer look."

And obviously to make sure nothing happens to them. Smart woman.

"We both assume that Sabrina wasn't at all interested in Arthur as a, ah, man. But how can we be sure? I mean, some women have strange tastes." Although from what I'd overheard during their argument, the possibility that she'd been attracted to him seemed highly unlikely.

"Well, for one thing, she had a boyfriend. One day when Arthur was late for a meeting, Sabrina and I chatted a bit. She was complaining that her boyfriend was jealous. Didn't like it when other men looked at her."

"Interesting. You don't know his name, do you?"

"She may have said, but I can't recall."

Lilly put the pile of folders she had collected into a bag. "Well, I think that's everything. Thanks for coming out here with me."

As we walked back down the dock, she asked a few questions about what it was like to live aboard a boat. I said I liked it but that it wasn't for everybody. Too little space, upkeep takes effort, you have to walk down the dock in all kinds of weather to get to your home, and it's hard to entertain friends. What I didn't say was that, for me, it was a relief not to be expected to invite guests over, and I like having an excuse to walk around wearing functional clothes rather than trying to live up to current fashion trends.

When I returned to my office, I was even less focused than I had been before. I swiveled my chair around so I could look out at the boats. Then I turned toward Bubbles V and Friend and watched them circle their bowl. Another few inches and I was staring at the door. No one knocked; it remained silent. Like Bubbles and Friend.

I couldn't get Sabrina's jealous boyfriend out of my mind. Surely the police knew about him. Why wasn't he a suspect? Oh, that's right, they'd found the murder weapon on the *Knotty Lady*. But, what if—?

Finally, I called Ben and didn't bother with small talk. "Hey, I just wondered if Sabrina's boyfriend is on the suspect list."

Ben laughed. "You think investigation details are public information? Or are you under the impression you are a consultant for the police department?"

"I would like that. We could do a TV series. I could be a famous writer of mysteries—"

"Been done."

"Or . . ."

"Or I could just tell you that I can't tell you."

"Could you at least tell me his last name?"

"No."

"You know I can find out on my own."

Ben laughed again. "I have no doubt that you can. But at least I can honestly say you didn't get his name from me."

"You're no fun."

"You haven't given me a chance—" He suddenly sounded serious. Did I need to remind him that in our current culture it was he who should have taken the initiative about a second date. Not that, as a liberated female, I couldn't have followed up. But he hadn't; and I hadn't. Maybe it was time to take charge.

"Want to have dinner some time?" I blurted out.

"Yeah, good idea."

I paused, waiting for him to say a little more. When he failed to take my invitation to the next level, like suggesting an actual evening for our dinner, I thanked him for taking my call and hung up. No name. No dinner. No nothing. Other than the embarrassment of being brushed off.

Perhaps I would have finally brought up Harold Hanson if our conversation hadn't taken a wrong turn. And if Ben had been more open about the boyfriend's role in the investigation, I might have moved on. But I couldn't help but feel that if I discovered something the police hadn't found out on their own, I could somehow get back at him for what I perceived as a slight. Petty, but motivating, nonetheless.

I called Lilly and asked if there was anyone she knew who could give me the name of Sabrina's boyfriend. She offered to call someone she thought might know. "You going to check him out?"

"Thought I might."

"In my opinion, the police are so focused on Arthur they aren't looking at anyone else."

"That's what I think too."

"Okay, I'll get back to you with his name."

I was just about to call it a day when the frogs started singing or complaining, whatever. It was Lilly. "Well, I got an earful," she began. "I talked with a colleague who didn't have anything good at all to say about Butch Jones, Sabrina's *ex*-boyfriend."

"Did you say 'ex'?"

"Yes."

"And did you say Butch Jones?" Well, well, well. Somehow, I didn't think it was a coincidence that Sabrina's ex had been one of the poker players to hear the story about my midnight swim. And I assumed that Ben must have noticed the connection too.

"Yes, to both. Apparently, she'd finally broken up with him after almost a year of physical and emotional abuse."

I hated it when women let themselves become victims. I couldn't understand why they didn't either end the relationship or fight back. "That's sad."

"Her colleague said that Sabrina was a strong woman in so many ways, but for some reason she kept going back to Butch."

"I can't say that his name makes him sound attractive. More like a Mafiosi."

"Ha. Well, he does work for a construction company, BluSky Construction. She also said he's a hunk, but full of himself."

"Narcissistic and abusive—nice combination."

"One more thing. Sabrina's memorial service is Sunday. I can send you the details if you're interested in going."

"That soon?"

"Her family wants a small funeral but decided to do a variation on a wake or celebration of life right away. I don't think it's any particular religious practice. But they are apparently active church members and the minister agreed to do it."

"They didn't notice she was missing, but now they want to hurry up and celebrate her life?"

"What can I say? Families are like that."

Yes, I knew all too well how strange families could be. But a service to start the healing process did make sense, especially given the circumstances of her death. Why not attend? If it was a large enough crowd, I could easily stay low profile. Maybe Butch would be there. It would be a chance to check him out.

Chapter 14

The Game is Afoot

It was Saturday, and I still hadn't told Ben about Harold and my growing suspicion that Sabrina had been going beyond her usual audit duties by looking for evidence of wrongdoing at AHA. In some ways it seemed like still another piece of evidence pointing at Arthur. And although it was a chance to broaden the suspect list, that would only happen if I made a convincing argument for pursuing it as a lead. It seemed to me that I needed to know more about the players and the possibilities before voicing my suspicions. Starting with the possibilities. Once I had a handle on the ways in which a nonprofit could be susceptible to fraud, then I could speculate about who had motive and access. What I needed was a quick course from an expert. Fortunately, I knew just the person. Unfortunately, he wore a three-piece suit and a vest when invited to a family dinner. Was I really desperate enough to call him?

Apparently, I was.

John was sitting at a small table near the front windows of the coffee shop. He wasn't wearing a three-piece suit, but he did have on a sweater vest. A vest and khaki Dockers. Functional if not fashionable. When I walked in, he looked so pleased to see me that I had to suppress the urge to run away by reminding myself that I wasn't meeting him under false pretenses. I'd been up front about the reason I wanted to get together. Still, it crossed my mind when I saw his face light up that he may have thought my stated reason *was* the false pretense.

We shook hands, like business acquaintances. Then, as we headed toward the counter to get something to drink, I said, "This is on me. What would you like?"

"Oh, that isn't necessary," he said awkwardly.

"I insist. You're doing me a favor."

He looked like he was struggling to figure out how to respond to the idea that he was there to do me a favor when his good manners finally kicked in. "A soy latte, please."

"Pastry?"

"No, thank you."

"Okay. Why don't you save us a table?" The coffee shop was filling up, and people were rapidly staking out their claims to seating before getting in line.

He seemed reluctant to leave me alone in line but did as I suggested. I was pleased not to have to make small talk while waiting for our coffee. And, as I stood there, it occurred to me that I would have to make sure that my mother didn't get wind of us having coffee together. She would probably start planning the wedding.

When I sat down and handed him his latte, he seemed subdued. "You said you wanted to know about the nature and scope of financial fraud an audit could uncover, correct?" I assumed that was his way of saying he understood and accepted the purpose of our coffee get-together. I appreciated that; maybe there was some way other than dating him that I could repay him for the favor.

"Yes. I'm looking into an organization's finances and suspect there are some issues, possibly criminal, and I'm not sure what I should focus on."

"Well, first let me say that an audit is more likely to discover errors than fraud. Fraud schemes are purposely covert. They exploit whatever weaknesses there are in the accounting system and controls. An auditor can only offer 'reasonable' assurance that an organization's financial statements are in order."

It sounded like a lecture he had given before. "But wouldn't an auditor notice if there were weak controls?" I didn't know exactly what I was asking, but I assumed there were standard controls for an organization's finances. Just like there were standardized processes for almost any work done repeatedly. Establishing workplace procedures for individuals and teams was one of the things I did as part of my consulting practice. You couldn't reach strategic goals if you didn't have effective systems in place to get the work done.

"Auditors use sampling techniques to test performance. It would be too expensive to examine every single transaction."

"So, you're saying that a clever criminal could fool an auditor."

"It's been known to happen."

"But it's also possible that a smart and conscientious auditor might discover something incriminating."

"Of course."

It seemed to me that Sabrina could have been smart enough and conscientious enough. If so, the question was what issue was she probing when she came across something irregular?

"In your typical organization, who would have the knowledge and position to pull off some type of fraud?" I asked.

"Anyone with on-going access to financial records. Or, depending on the type of fraud, it could be someone in billing or purchasing. Or it could be a simple matter of check tampering or padding expense reimbursements. There are lots of possibilities."

He paused and took a sip of latte. "It would be helpful if you could be more specific. For example, what type of organization are you looking into? And do you have any particular suspicions about the nature of the crime?"

"Well . . ." I hesitated. Then I decided he was right; I needed to be more specific if I was going to get useful information from him. "It's a medium sized nonprofit with a fairly hands-on, large board with lots of connections and partnerships with other nonprofits doing similar work. I know the auditor was asking questions about pass-through grants, oversight, and the bidding process. But there could be more. Does that help?"

"Yes, that gives me some context." He thought a moment before continuing. "Unfortunately, fraud is a fairly common problem in nonprofits. It's estimated that forty to fifty billion dollars are lost to fraud each year. Usually in organizations with fewer than a hundred employees. There are lists of safeguards to adopt for just that reason, but especially if an organization started small and grew quickly, those safeguards may not be in place. The fraud is usually committed by the founder, the treasurer, the bookkeeper, or the signer of checks. They often create fraudulent financial documents and fail to share bank statements with board members."

"You seem to know a lot about fraud in nonprofits."

He nodded his head in acknowledgement of my compliment, as if it were his due. "I train other accountants," he said.

"Well, I certainly came to the right person then." I gave him a smile of appreciation, trying not to make it more than that.

"Thank you," he said with a tone of formality that indicated he was totally aware of the smile's limitations. "In my experience, the person committing the crime is someone you wouldn't suspect. The most typical theft in charities, for example, is committed by a female employee with no criminal record. Someone who has been with the organization for at least three years. Someone between the ages of thirty-five and fifty who needs money."

"How are most irregularities discovered? I mean, if not through annual audits, how does an organization find out they have a potential case of fraud on their hands?"

"Sometimes a new board member who takes their fiduciary responsibilities seriously asks the right questions to initiate an investigation. Sometimes the perpetrator gets greedy and exposes their activities by overplaying their hand. But usually, it's through a tip. Some employee who suspects something isn't quite the way it should be."

"Hmmm." I wondered if Sabrina had received a tip. That might be worth following up on. Would she have shared that with a colleague?

"There are a couple of things about nonprofits that makes them vulnerable. For one thing, there is usually an atmosphere of trust created by common purpose. In addition, there is a reliance on volunteer boards who may or may not have business or financial expertise."

John took a sip of latte and asked, "This have something to do with the murder committed by your marina neighbor?"

I was obviously underestimating John based on stereotyping and resistance to my mother's matchmaking efforts. Shame on me. "Yes. I probably should have told you up front. But I'm not part of any investigation. I'm just curious."

"I can understand. I would be too."

But would you have taken a midnight swim? Even without the stereotyping, I couldn't imagine that. "And I don't think my neighbor is the killer."

"Because he's a good guy?"

"No, nothing like that. He's a loser in a lot of ways. It's just that the facts don't add up."

"But the police think they do?"

"Yes, but . . ."

"Do you know something they don't?" He had lasered in on the relevant question.

"Not exactly. Well, maybe. I mean, they know the victim was hired by my neighbor to audit the nonprofit he works for, the Affordable Housing Association. And they know she went by his boat to grill him about some files related to the audit. But they left the files on the boat after searching it, as if they weren't important."

"I'm familiar with AHA. They do good work and are highly respected in the nonprofit world."

"That's my impression too. But I still suspect the victim may have come across something illegal." I was on the verge of mentioning Gerald and Harold, but I couldn't think of how to do it without confessing to the post-it. "I keep in touch with one of the detectives on the case. The police don't have the time or resources to follow up on an unsubstantiated lead. But if I come up with something that seems worth pursuing, I know he will take a look at it."

"That makes sense to me. Given the pressure officials are under to solve crimes quickly, seeking closure without actively considering all of the possibilities is probably almost irresistible. Even though I believe most officers care about both the truth and justice. In spite of the bad apples that make the news."

"I agree."

"But if you come up with something, you'll take it to your detective, ah, the detective you know?"

He was obviously wondering about my relationship with "*your* detective," but I wasn't about to enlighten him. Not that I was at all sure about the nature of our relationship myself. And the fact that he wanted reassurance on this point reinforced my initial impressions of him. Knowledgeable, yes. But a rule bender—no way.

"To be fair, there's a lot of evidence to suggest my neighbor did it. For instance, they found the murder weapon on his boat."

"But if you're right and your neighbor is innocent, and you go poking around, won't you be putting yourself in jeopardy?" His tone suggested he was torn between wanting to encourage me and wanting to warn me off.

"I'll keep whatever I do discreet. And I don't plan on taking any action on my own, if that's what you're asking. I won't hesitate to call the detective I know if I find anything at all worth looking into."

"That's good. I wouldn't want you to do anything dangerous. Well, you know what I mean." His cheeks flushed slightly. It was apparently more of a personal than a professional concern. He quickly covered up the awkwardness by adding, "Please call me if you have any questions about anything you come across. I would be happy to help out in any way I can."

"I appreciate that. Thank you."

It was too bad I couldn't picture him as the Watson to my Sherlock, but I was thankful that he had given me enough information to get me in the game. Because based on what I now knew, the game was definitely afoot.

Chapter 15

Memorials and Mental Floss

Sunday, I slept in. Macavity crawled up on my bunk and stretched before settling in, legs tucked under this body, his breathing slowly transformed into purring, a gentle comforting sound. He likes it best when things are calm. And consistent. If he'd had a chance to choose his owner instead of the other way around, he probably wouldn't have chosen me. But in spite of my flaws, he hangs around. Perhaps for moments like these.

Macavity's purring was mesmerizing. Trance-like. Although I was awake, I felt completely relaxed. My mind at ease. Suspended in time. It was a moment of mental flossing, the plaque of random thoughts slowly dissolving until I was cleansed of all the clutter and useless information that usually chases itself around in my head. Now, thanks to Macavity, there was space to form new thoughts and allow fresh perspectives to creep in.

Slowly, very slowly, ideas began to take form, with analytic sharpness that made me feel like I was within seconds of solving Sabrina's murder. Unfortunately, the feeling of mental clarity vanished as quickly as a fog bow when the sun breaks through and chases away the thin layer of gray. But instead of a brilliant aha, like discovering the pot at the end of the rainbow, my thoughts were still encased in dense grayness. Nevertheless, I forced myself to slog on, hoping I could recapture that fleeting moment of heightened awareness before it slipped away forever.

Arthur and Butch seemed like the most likely suspects, but perhaps there was a link between one of the other poker players and Sabrina, a connection that could be discovered with a little effort. Or maybe one of the poker players blabbed about Aphrodite to someone else who wanted Sabrina out of the way. If no one pursued those potential connections, they would undoubtedly remain hidden. Especially since the police were focused on tightening the net around Arthur.

There were several reasons Arthur was no longer at the top of my suspect list. My gut said he wasn't the murderer, and it seemed to me that he could easily have been framed with the statue I'd retrieved. Unfortunately, if he had been framed because of me hanging onto that statue, that meant I shared some responsibility for him being under arrest for murder. It also meant that Sabrina's death wasn't an act of passion or a random killing. Someone had gone to a lot of effort to cover their own tracks and point the finger of guilt at Arthur. Unless my gut was wrong, and Arthur had killed Sabrina.

If, however, you started from the assumption that Arthur was innocent, there were a fair number of facts that pointed to Butch as the likely murderer. At the same time, "the butler did it" cliché almost ruled him out for me. Unless he *did* do it. Sometimes the butler *is* the guilty party. And it could even have been an accident. Butch may indeed have cared for Sabrina in his own warped way, but he could have taken using her for a punching bag a little too far. Once she was dead, he either had to confess or cover his tracks. Under those circumstances, hearing my story told at the poker game would have been fortuitous good fortune. It would have suggested exactly who to frame and how.

Since the police had Arthur under arrest and knew all about Butch, the loose end that needed some tidying was determining whether one of the other poker players—or someone they told about Aphrodite—knew Sabrina personally or was involved with the AHA and whatever it was Sabrina was investigating. Surely Ben had considered there might be a trail to follow there. But maybe not: why look for new clues when you think you have the case solved?

Given my updated understanding of how nonprofits functioned financially, it seemed to me the most likely people in the AHA financial food chain that Sabrina might have been focusing on during her audit would be either board members or some AHA administrator. A fairly limited but not small group of suspects. Then again, maybe someone involved with AHA's finances was too obvious. Surely with all of the safeguards AHA had surrounding its fundraising and spending it would be next to impossible for any of these individuals to embezzle enough to make it worth the risk.

Macavity apparently decided our idyllic moment was over. He leapt off the bunk and went in search of more interesting activities. I appreciated how he'd help me focus my thinking about Sabrina's death, but it would have been even more helpful if he'd been able to contribute a few ideas of his own. He was, after all, a pretty good judge of people.

My timing had to be just right, early enough to be able to check people out as they arrived at Sabrina's memorial service, but late enough so as not to call attention to my presence. And it would have worked. *If* Ben hadn't been on the same timetable. We both started up the wide stretch of cement steps to the church at the same time. He from the north; me from the south. We met at the top of the steps, outside a pair of ornate wooden doors.

"I'm not surprised to see you here," he said, extending his hand.

"I was actually hoping you wouldn't see me."

"Your hair does give you away."

"It's been a curse for as long as I can remember."

He looked at me thoughtfully. "I'm surprised that you feel that way." Before he could say more, several people swept past us into the church.

"I'd better let you do your job," I said, hurrying after them. Over my shoulder I added, "You might want to check out whether Sabrina's ex-boyfriend, Butch Jones, is here." I paused long enough to blast him with a toothy smile.

"Someone's been busy." He smiled back and let me take the lead.

There was a person handing out memorial service programs just inside the entrance next to a table with stand-up panels covered in pictures of the deceased at various ages. I accepted a program and paused to look at the pictures. Based on the display, Sabrina had always been a good-looking girlie type. She had also apparently liked to swim and dance and party with friends. I hadn't known her but seeing the snapshots of her looking so engaged with life gave me pause. You never know what's going to happen next. When you may find your life cut short and its story told in a collage of photos on a table in the lobby of a church.

"I can't believe she's gone," a young woman's voice next to me said. Just as I turned toward her, she started sobbing. I reached into my purse and handed her a Kleenex.

"I'm sorry for your loss," I said automatically, the perfunctory words softly stated. Then, before she could ask about my relationship to Sabrina, I moved on.

Small groups of people were forming in the lobby. Some looked like they could be relatives, clutching tissues and handkerchiefs, faces streaked with tears, publicly mourning their loss. There was also a cluster of men and women that looked like work colleagues. Dressed in dark, professional suits, with stylish haircuts and polished shoes. They were chatting and smiling at each other. No tears in that group. A few young children ran around between the adults, blissfully unaware of the solemnity of the occasion. Meanwhile, more and more people were arriving. Some stopped to talk to people they recognized, but most were going directly inside. It was going to be a large gathering.

Organ music piped over a raspy sound system to signal that the service was about to begin. Just as I turned to go inside, someone grabbed my arm. And not gently.

"You that woman who's been asking questions about me?" Keeping his voice low, he practically hissed the words at me, like an angry gander.

"It depends on who you are." I had no doubt who he was, but I wanted to hear him say it. He wasn't as good looking as I'd expected given Sabrina's classy attractiveness. Barely as tall as me, but with muscled shoulders and arms that bulged inside the material of his navy-blue jacket. His dark hair was combed straight back, one loose strand hanging alongside his face. His dark eyes were his best feature, deep vats of molten chocolate.

"I think you know who I am." He squeezed my arm.

"Please remove your hand," I said firmly. When he didn't, I added, "There's a police officer just a few feet away who would welcome the excuse to arm wrestle with you. Maybe you would like to be in the evening news for accosting a mourner at your ex-girlfriend's memorial service."

He glanced nervously around and slowly released me.

"Let's get one thing straight," I added. "I have not been asking around about you. Your name was mentioned in connection with a poker game where the murder weapon was discussed. But as Sabrina's ex-boyfriend, your name was bound to come up in the investigation of her murder." I emphasized the words "ex" and "murder."

"You're not with the police," he said, although he sounded uncertain.

"No, I'm not." I let silence hang between us. Well, silence except for the sizzling sounds from the lousy sound system that was playing something that sounded like a recording of the Song of the Volga Boatmen.

"I loved her, you know." He sounded more like he was trying to convince himself than me.

"But you didn't mind roughing her up a bit from time to time. Strange way to show your love." I probably shouldn't have brought that up, but I find that kind of behavior contemptible, and I wanted to heap disapproval on him. Bury him in disdain.

His voice transformed to gangster rasp. "None of your business." Then he turned and walked away.

I quickly followed the remaining stranglers into the sanctuary and took a seat in the last row, noting that Ben was on the opposite side of the church in the same back row. Butch had taken a seat on the aisle a few rows ahead of where I was seated. His dark hair glistened with whatever was holding it in place.

The unpleasant music ceased and a wave of murmuring flowed over the crowd. Then everyone fell silent and the service began.

The remarks by the minister were fairly brief, but the ceremonial speeches that followed seemed endless. Each time another person got up to say a "few words" about Sabrina I mentally groaned. Sometimes I enjoy stories told by friends and family about the deceased, but there was something about the tone of this service that felt staged and artificial. It wasn't until her brother got up that I sensed any real emotion. He made her sound warm and caring and described her as part of a close-knit family. Someone who had managed to overcome a lot to make it in the business world. Her colleagues may have seen her as tough and competitive, but her brother remembered her as the carefree and fun-loving child and woman in the pictures in the foyer.

I lingered after the service was over, watching people file out, scanning faces, speculating about relationships. When I saw Butch approach Sabrina's brother, I wasn't surprised to see her brother frown and turn away without saying anything. Butch looked around to see who had noticed, saw me watching, scowled, and quickly left.

Ben was nowhere in sight when I finally left the church. I'd almost expected him to be waiting for me, to compare notes about the memorial service attendees. And perhaps to apologize for not telling me that one of Dane's poker buddies was Sabrina's ex-boyfriend. Maybe even to suggest we get together for coffee or a drink. But no such luck.

Chapter 16

Financial Sleuthing

Monday morning I forced myself to get up early and make my way in the cool morning air down the dock to my office. The day was overcast, not cloudy exactly, but more like there was a thin layer of grey gauze blanketing the sky, the sun more ghost than presence. The water also was a lifeless gray, completing the circle of environmental gloom.

The omnipresent gray reminded me of the first time I saw a fog bow. I was at anchor in Squirrel Cove in the Canadian San Juans. As I stepped out onto the deck with my morning coffee, I found myself staring at a white arc in the distance, refracted sunlight from tiny water droplets in the air. If the droplets had been larger, there might have been color, a rainbow. Instead, there was a streak of white against an ashen backdrop. The moment felt special, as if the fog bow was a promise that the sun would come out, but for a short time, I could enjoy the soothing calm of a monochrome world.

When I opened the door to my office, my eyes were immediately drawn to two bright spots of color, orange in motion, swimming around and around. I wondered if they stopped and floated when there was no one there to observe them. Like small kids who only cried over a scraped knee if there was someone there to give them sympathy.

"Good morning, Bubbles and Friend. I see you haven't gone belly up yet." Oops. Maybe I shouldn't have mentioned that possibility. "Ah, change that to *good day to be inside*." I'm not sure why I bothered; they continued doing their own thing as if I wasn't even there.

Trying to be a responsible pet owner, I sprinkled some granules of goldfish food over the surface of their watery home. It was described as a variety blend for enhancing vitality. Although since all they did was swim around, I wasn't sure how they would make use of extra energy. Maybe they could race each other from one end of the bowl to the other or leap out of the water occasionally like a breaching whale. One of the goldfish, I couldn't tell which, grabbed a couple of granules from below as the rest of their meal slowly became waterlogged and started to sink at an almost imperceptible rate.

"Breakfast. Get it while you can." My warning skipped like a flat rock over the water in their bowl home. Fish number two apparently got the message though because he—or she—dutifully slurped up several granules. Not exactly *fast food*, but definitely food on the move. "Come on, I've got my stopwatch on." Supposedly whatever they ate in two minutes was the right amount to feed them daily. I'd been warned not to overfeed them, but to make sure they got fed an appropriate portion each day. If I didn't get the servings just right, how was I supposed to vacuum up leftovers?

I stood there and watched while the granules continued to sink, slowly disappearing into the pebbles at the bottom of the bowl. The goldfish continued to nip at their food, not at all enthusiastically, following it as it descended. Maybe I needed to toss in a few greens. Was there such a thing as a goldfish that was a finicky eater? I'd also purchased some 7-day feeder blocks in case I needed to be away and didn't want to bother Hudson to fish sit. What I didn't understand was how you kept them from eating the whole block on day one and starving the rest of the week. Whatever it took, this time I fully intended to do everything within my power to keep my golden friends alive until Emma was more interested in boys than in pets.

My call to Harold Hanson at the State Auditor's office was scheduled for 9:00 am. I sat down at my computer and opened a blank Word document to put together a list of questions so I wouldn't waste his or my time, since it was doubtful that I would get his protective assistant to schedule a second call without a knock-your-socks-off reason. When the empty screen appeared, I found myself formatting the page rather than getting straight to substance. There's something about typing notes on a computer that makes it feel official rather than simply informal brainstorming. Sometimes I think I'm better off making lists on the back of used envelopes.

I decided on two lines of inquiry, depending on whether he'd actually communicated with Sabrina. If he had, it was just a matter of how much he would be willing to share with me. If it sounded like he knew something but was unwilling to talk about it, I would have to call Ben and come up with a reason why he needed to get in touch with Harold. Preferably without mentioning the post-it. On the other hand, if Sabrina hadn't gotten around to contacting him, then we would end up talking in hypotheticals. I decided that I would be as honest as possible in order to get any helpful information he had to offer about why people usually got in touch with him. The main stumbling block in either scenario was trying to explain why I was involved in the first place.

Meanwhile, I was considering calling Lilly to see if she would introduce me to someone in accounting at AHA and also put me in touch with the board treasurer. Or maybe she could introduce me to a friend of Sabrina's, someone she might have shared confidences with. I could, of course, approach a family member, although it seemed too soon to intrude on their grief. As a last resort I could try to find someone at Zelen and Hobbs who might be willing to talk with me. Although based on what I'd overheard at her office and seen at her memorial service, my guess was that Sabrina didn't confide in the people she worked with. Besides, I had already made an appearance there under another name. That might prove awkward. Maybe I could claim that I'm a wanna-be writer and Tiffany Riddle is my *nom de plume.*

At 9:00 o'clock on the dime, I punched in Hanson's number and put my phone on speaker. While I waited for someone to pick up, I placed my list of questions next to a fresh notepad to the right of my computer and got out a backup pen in case the one I had chosen ran out of ink. I felt super prepared to take notes, less so about how to approach the conversation.

The same female voice answered his phone, but this time I didn't need to persuade her to put me through to her boss; she said she was transferring me as soon as I identified myself. There were no unnecessary words, no chitchat. She apparently didn't want to add me to her friends list on Facebook or anywhere else.

"Harold Hanson." The voice was commanding and a bit too loud. I lowered the volume level on my phone.

"Thank you for agreeing to talk with me, Mr. Hanson. My name is Bryn Baczek. I'm following up on a call you got from Sabrina Valdez about two weeks ago." I paused, giving him a chance to either deny or verify that he'd received a call from her. How he responded would determine which line of questioning I took.

"Yes."

Yes?! That was all he was going to give me? "I assume you remember the call." Hint, hint.

"Yes, I do."

Okay, I would go with first set of questions. "Well, I'm sorry to ask you to repeat what you told her, but as you may know, Sabrina died unexpectedly. I'm trying to make sense out of her notes." That wasn't completely dishonest in that it would have been true if I'd had access to her notes.

"I'm sorry to hear about her death." He was silent for a moment, as if processing new information and trying to come to a decision. It was possible he hadn't read about her murder in the papers. Then, "What would you like to know?" I was relieved he wasn't going to ask me right away about my relationship to Sabrina. Without specifically claiming to be a colleague of hers, I was banking on him assuming that I was. My back-up story was a bit weak, grounded in squishy reality and plumped up with fiction. It might not pass the smell test.

"She was investigating a potential fraud case, and I believe she called you because the organization receives some state funds. From what I can tell from her notes, it looks like you were unaware of any problems but told her what to do if she came across evidence to back up her suspicions." It was a guess. But if the organization was already under scrutiny there would have been no reason to do away with Sabrina. Unless the killer didn't know they were already close to being discovered by an official agency.

"Let me refer to my notes. Hold a moment, please."

How I wished that no one had ever mentioned that it takes 20 seconds to sing Happy Birthday twice. Now I find myself measuring every wait in 20 second intervals. And it's an annoying ditty. Harold took four choruses of two each before he came back.

"Ms. Baczek?"

"Yes?"

"Your website says you are a consultant."

Oh, oh. "Yes, that's correct. I'm a management consultant. I do a lot of work with nonprofits." Just not with AHA.

"I believe you did some work for one of our local offices."

He was good. That had been several years ago. "That's right. Leadership and strategic planning. It was a good group."

"You understand that I can't share details over the phone."

"I do. We're trying to put the main pieces of her investigation together." *We?!* Had I really said *we*? "I don't need any specifics from you. But it would be helpful to know if more than one agency was looking into possible fraud allegations with AHA." Go ahead, Harold, verify she was asking about fraud or embezzlement, any sort of criminal activity associated with AHA. Do it, please. Now.

"Not that I know of. At least not at the state level."

Surely he would have corrected me if it hadn't been AHA that she had called him about. I would accept his non-denial as confirmation that Sabrina had suspected something wasn't quite right at AHA. "Thank you. That tells me where to focus my efforts. I appreciate you taking the time to talk with me."

"You're welcome. And if you find anything that impacts state funding, you'll let me know." It wasn't a question.

"Absolutely."

After hanging up, I took a deep breath and tried to calm my heartbeat. I hadn't lied, but I had definitely been misleading about my involvement with AHA. And he knew who I was. With luck, he wouldn't give it a second thought. But if he discovered I'd been deceptive, there could be consequences. I didn't think I'd committed any crime that I could be charged with, but I could be barred from doing more consulting gigs for the state. On the other hand, if a government agency refused to hire anyone who'd ever taken a few liberties with the truth, that would severely limit their applicant pool.

I had advanced a few baby steps in my theory about where Sabrina's investigation had been pointing her, but I still felt like I needed to do a little more sleuthing before calling Ben. There was nothing that screamed *clue* that would guarantee he would follow up. And he would probably warn me against pursing it further. Maybe with good reason. I was aware that there might be risks in following up on Sabrina's probe into AHA finances. After all, it hadn't ended too well for her. Still, my curiosity was like an itch that had to be scratched. I promised myself that after one quick dive into the financial abyss of the AHA I would turn over what I learned to the police and immediately distance myself from any further investigation. Find out as much as possible while minimizing my involvement. Get in and get out. Before Sabrina's killer had me on his, or her, radar.

Once I had rationalized probing a little more, I called Lilly to ask whether I could look at the financial records Sabrina had been viewing, the ones she'd retrieved from the *Knotty Lady*, and any others that she knew Sabrina had reviewed. The nonprofit's financials were of public record but starting from scratch wouldn't help me much.

"That's a little unusual," Lilly said hesitantly.

"I know. But so is the situation. And it doesn't seem like the police think there's a link between Sabrina's audit investigation and her death."

There was a moment of silence. "And *you* think there is?"

"Seems like a possibility, doesn't it?"

There was another moment of silence. "This has to be between the two of us."

"That works for me. And since I don't have any official status, if there is anything proprietary, you can pull it out or maybe summarize it for me. If I see anything that I think could be significant, I'll have to let the police know. We can talk about the best way to do that when and if I find something. Okay?"

"I *do* want to see her murderer caught," Lilly said slowly as if talking to herself rather than to me. "And I think Arthur has been treated unfairly." She paused before announcing her decision: "So, yes, I guess I'm okay with that."

The other thing I wanted from Lilly was an introduction to their accountant and to the board treasurer. But those requests might be better made in person. Too much all at once could result in her shying away from helping me.

The AHA was located in an older brick building near the waterfront. Several other nonprofits were located there, not because the accommodations were all that great, but because the rent was cheaper than in other parts of the city. I parked at an outlying parking lot and took the light rail the rest of the way. The station was only two blocks and one bakery stop away from AHA. I grabbed a couple snickerdoodles and a cup of coffee, ate one of the cookies while walking and saved one for later.

According to Lilly's directions, once inside AHA's third floor headquarters, I would find her office on the left, past a block of cubicles. I took the elevator up, worrying a little about the creaking and squeaking sounds it made. I'm always leery of elevators. I imagine getting stranded between floors, a cable breaking, the doors not opening, getting trapped with a claustrophobic who freaks out when the elevator stalls, all sorts of horror movie scenes. I read once that the odds of getting stuck in an elevator were 1 in every 100,000 elevator rides. I wasn't sure if those were personal odds or the odds for the elevator riding population in general. If the latter, I could easily be number 100,000 in the not-too-distant future. I needed to start taking the stairs.

The third floor had an aisle down the middle with offices on both sides. AHA was across from RRH, whatever that was. I wondered if using initials instead of full names was a money-saving effort or if you had to be in the know to be welcome.

There was no one at the high counter just inside the door for AHA, but I could hear a hum of activity from the cubicles that were clearly visible from the entrance. I made my way past them, glancing around at the cubicle dwellers, all of whom seemed to be busy, most of them focused on their computers.

Lilly came out into the hall as I drew near, by accident or because she sensed me coming, I wasn't sure. I noted that her shiny brown hair was perfectly coifed, just like the first time we'd met. I wondered what happened when she got caught by breeze from a fan or an open window. Did her hair stay messed or simply fall back into perfection? Like a model shaking her head to show off her hair in a shampoo commercial—hair swirling around before returning to its original not-one-hair-out-of-place glory.

She was wearing a different pants suit today, but with the same cut as the one she had worn to the marina. I had a vision of a row of suits lined up in her closet, all the same style but in different colors. I was quite certain her white blouse had never seen a coffee stain.

"Please come on in." She motioned me into her office and waited until I had crossed over to the chair in front of her desk before closing the door. "I would offer you coffee, but I have a meeting I have to go to shortly."

"No problem, just had some. And I don't want to take up much of your time. But . . . I would like one more favor."

She actually took a step back as if trying to ward off another request.

"I would really like to talk to your accountant. And maybe to the board treasurer. I know that means my interest won't remain between you and me, but I will undoubtedly have questions that only they can answer. Also, I would like to see the last few annual financial reports. I know there's a process for requesting to see them, but I assume your accountant would have hard copies that I could browse on site without making a formal request."

Her mouth looked like there was a "no" forming, so I was surprised when the rounded mouth started with an "o" and widened into a "kay." "Okay. That makes sense." She sat down at her desk and picked up her phone. "Earl Grey, our accountant, has been here at least fifteen years, maybe more. He can answer any questions you have about our finances. His office is just down the hall."

"Earl Grey?"

Lilly smiled. "Don't go there. He's very sensitive about his name. And there are a few immature employees who don't appreciate his gloomy demeanor, so they give him a bad time about it. 'Would you like a cup of Earl Gray, Earl Grey?' 'I think we're out of Earl Gray, Earl Gray.' I hear a lot of that sort of thing in the lunchroom."

She punched in a number and got a response right away. Although I couldn't make out the words coming from the low voice on the other end of the line, it was obvious that Earl Grey was not happy about the request. Lilly's expression quickly changed from sunny to determined. She ended the conversation with a statement that did not allow for push-back. "She'll be there in about a half hour, so please have everything set up for her. Thank you."

"The problem with a cell phone is that you can't slam down the receiver," I commented.

"He was definitely a bit bent out of shape about taking the time to get the documents together, but he said he would." She added, "As if he is just overwhelmed with work."

"You didn't give him much choice. Professional and firm. I admire your ability to do that without sounding peeved."

She laughed. "Glad I didn't sound like I felt." She moved a stack of files to the middle of her desk. "You can use my office to review these files I retrieved from Arthur's before your meeting with Earl. My only request is that you be discreet if someone drops by. That probably won't happen, but you never know."

"Don't worry. I'll be vague, say I'm working on something for you and expect you back after your meeting."

"And if I'm not here when you're finished, just put them in my in-box."

"No problem."

"Now, about our board treasurer, Jan Benson. She works at an engineering firm just two blocks away. I can call her if you'd like."

"That would be good of you." I hesitated, then asked, "And if you could also give me the name of someone close to Sabrina, someone she might have confided in . . .?"

Lilly frowned. "As I said before, I didn't really know her. You may need to talk to someone she worked with. Sorry." Another professional yet firm response. But I couldn't complain; she was already doing more for me than I had any right to expect from her.

Lilly made the call to Jan and set up an appointment for me to meet with her at 2:00 in her office. Before leaving for her meeting she made sure I had everything I needed, wished me luck in finding something that might be helpful to Arthur's case, and explained how to get to Earl's office. Now, all I had to do was study the evidence and come up with a theory. Easy-peasy, as my niece would say. Emma loved the sound of those two words together and would sometimes repeat them over and over in a singsong voice. Easy-peasy. Easy-peasy.

I took a deep breath and opened the first file.

A half hour later I was none the wiser. Not so easy-peasy after all. A bit of a bummer, in fact. I had known that whatever secrets were in those files wouldn't be that easy to find. But if the files were important enough for Sabrina to ask Arthur to let her peruse them outside of the office, there had to be something in them she felt was worth a second look. If only Arthur had kept Aphrodite out of sight, perhaps she would have revealed her concerns through questions she asked him.

I didn't relish being late for my meeting with Earl, but it seemed worth the time to take a few pictures of some key documents from the files I'd just perused. Maybe by going over them again once I was back in my office and not feeling any pressure to hurry, I would see something I'd missed this first time around. Or maybe John would be willing to take a look and find something I hadn't. In any case, it seemed worth a try, so I snapped away before stacking the files in Lilly's in-box and heading down the hall to meet with the AHA accountant.

My first impression of Earl Grey was not favorable. For one thing, he had an obvious comb-over. One long hank of his gray-streaked hair was dangling about a half inch from his head as he leaned over his desk. For another, although I was sure he was aware of me standing in his open doorway, he didn't look up until I knocked. Then he made a point of glancing at his watch before getting to his feet. "Yes?" he said as though he wasn't expecting me.

"I'm Bryn Baczek." I studied him as I waited for him to respond. He was in his mid-forties with a downtrodden air that said to me that he'd been in low-level jobs for far too long. His pants and shirt were complementary shades of gray that seemed to blend with his overall neutral appearance. A living stereotype from a Dicken's novel. Although I'd considered the possibility that the "accountant did it," it was difficult picturing him revving up enough passion to kill someone. But I was willing to reserve final judgement until after I'd reviewed all of AHA's financials.

"Lilly said you'd be here . . ." He looked at his watch again, letting me know I had been a few minutes later than he'd expected. Then he stood up and seemed to be considering whether he was going to help me or not. I had the feeling that his assessment of me was even less flattering than mine of him. When he finally came out from behind his desk, I noted that he was quite a bit shorter than me. He must have noticed our height difference at about the same time because he squared his shoulders and stretched his neck, as if trying to extract every centimeter of elevation he could muster. "I've set things up for you in the conference room." He motioned for me to step out of his office. Maybe he wanted to give me space and privacy, or perhaps he didn't want to be readily available for questions. In the long run it was probably a better arrangement. I would be able to take my time and not feel like he was begrudging me every second spent on the reports.

Once out of his office he took the lead, walking ahead of me down the narrow hall. "I may have some questions," I said to his back.

"Um."

"I assume you'll be in your office."

"Um." Was that a "yes-um" or a "no-um"? I couldn't tell.

"If I have questions, I'll come and find you." My tone was firm, as if to say, I'll even wait for you outside of the men's room if necessary.

Glancing back, he asked, "What are you looking for anyway?"

"I'm not sure," I admitted, angry with myself for not anticipating that question.

He paused at the door to what I assumed was the conference room. "You an accountant?"

"No." He waited for me to say something more, but I didn't add anything.

"Do you work for . . . another agency?"

"No." I could have ended his guessing game but decided not to. Just to see what he came up with. He obviously hadn't Googled me.

"A friend of Sabrina's?"

"No."

"Associated with the police?"

Did he sound nervous? "No."

Obviously annoyed by my evasiveness, he finally got blunt: "So, what's your interest in our finances?"

He had me there. "I'm a consultant. I'm searching for . . ." I looked him in the eye and paused before finishing my sentence ". . . a motive for murder."

If I'd been trying to shock him into saying something incriminating, I could have saved my breath. He didn't miss a beat. "Good luck with that." He opened the door and stood aside for me to enter. As soon as I stepped across the threshold, he left without explaining what he had set out for me. Earl Grey, the butt of colleagues' teasing was neither as soothing nor as distinctive as the tea with which he shared a name. Nor had his "good luck with that" response to my wild assertion about looking for a motive for murder given me reason to absolve or accuse. Just in case, I put a virtual red dot next to his name.

I settled in at the desk and started looking through the AHA's financials he had provided. Although I'm not an accountant, I know how to read a balance sheet and a cash-flow statement, and I've done enough work on nonprofit financials as part of the strategic planning I've done with them that I'm able to grasp the big picture of how an organization is doing. But because AHA was an alliance of organizations with multiple joint projects going on at the same time, as well as blended sources of financing, it was a quite a bit more complex than anything I was used to reviewing. Still, it was clear they were solvent. And they seemed to have the kinds of controls in place that John had told me about. At least they had guidelines they were supposed to follow as described in a 17-page handout for board members. And it appeared that the person who signed the checks, Jan Benson, didn't issue them. Earl did that. According to John, that was the way it was supposed to be.

Although I had agreed with Lilly not to remove any documents, neither she nor Earl had instructed me not to take pictures of pages of interest. And after all, I was looking at public documents. Even so, I checked to make certain no one was looking before I added more pictures to the ones I'd taken earlier. I included quarterly reports as well as pages that listed donor gifts and invoices. Anything I thought might contain clues about potential opportunities for fraud. There was *something* that had thrown up a red flag to Sabrina. Something that made her ask to see the files Arthur had taken home with him. Although, as clever as she was, there may have been only one or two specific items she was interested in. The rest could have been decoys. And that was assuming I was looking at *all* of the reports and documents Sabrina had examined, and that none had been "corrected" to better conceal misappropriations.

On my way out, I stopped by Earl's office. Once again, he made me knock to get his attention, as if he was so absorbed in whatever he was reading that he was totally unaware of his surroundings. To be fair, perhaps to an accountant numbers are as captivating as a page-turning thriller. Still, he made me knock to get him to look up, and then he once again had to glance at his watch to let me know he was a busy man. Ignoring his visual cues, I sat down in the only other chair in his office.

It was too bad I actually had a few serious questions to ask. His attitude made me want to introduce a few tea factoids into our conversation just to annoy him. Like, Ireland drinks more tea with milk per person than Britain. I wouldn't have to reference the fact that Earl Grey was a popular tea in Ireland, just the comment would be enough. Or maybe he'd appreciate a joke my niece had told me: What do teapots wear to a party? A T-shirt.

Instead, I said, "I assume you talked to Sabrina when she was here."

"Of course. It's my job to support audits."

"Could you tell me a little about what her concerns were?"

"Why would she be concerned about anything?"

"Most audits find a few things that need to be cleared up or fine-tuned. I thought she might have discussed this with you."

"No, there wasn't anything to discuss."

"So, she didn't mention to you the recommendations she was making in her report?"

That fabricated, in-the-moment question caught him off guard. "What recommendations?"

I stood up. "Sorry, if she didn't discuss her concerns with you, then I'm not authorized to say more." If he *was* the killer, it probably wasn't wise to provoke him, but at the same time, I could understand why colleagues teased him. It was as if he had a "kick me" sign taped to his back. But that didn't mean I had to kick him. He might only be guilty of having an unappealing personality. And everyone deserves to be treated with respect. "Thank you for organizing the reports for me. I appreciate it."

He nodded but didn't say anything. Either he'd been temporarily stunned by my comment or he didn't really care if he'd been helpful. It was rather a lame way to end our exchange. But the only thing left for me to do was to leave. So I did.

I had just enough time to grab a sandwich and an iced tea before heading off on foot to my meeting with Jan Benson, the treasurer of the board. Although I'd intended to hold off eating my sandwich until after the meeting, my stomach was making so much noise I finally broke off a corner of the panini vegetarian special and managed some chewing while walking. Chewing, walking, and thinking about the upcoming interview. True multitasking.

Given how little I'd learned from the documents I'd reviewed, I wasn't entirely sure what I was going to ask her. Maybe I'd just try to get a sense of whether she had any general concerns about AHA's finances. Or whether she had talked with Sabrina, and if so, about what. I didn't have enough information to articulate specific suspicions. Although one thing I could find out from her was whether AHA adhered to the recommended controls listed in their 17-page document. Or if the document was seldom read or referred to but simply paid lip service. From what John had said, a lot of nonprofits skimped on following procedures, not necessarily because there was something dishonest going on but because of the lack of experience of staff and board members or because everyone trusted and believed in the nonprofit's good intentions. Finding out more about AHA's attitude toward their guidelines might give me some ideas about where to look further.

Of course, another reason for meeting with the treasurer was to decide if I thought she was potentially clever enough to come up with a scheme to embezzle money, dishonest enough to follow through, and evil enough to commit murder. Too bad I had to rely on intuition and guesswork instead of clairvoyance. Clairvoyance would be a handy superpower.

Unfortunately, I immediately liked Jan. I say *unfortunately* because I'd been hoping to come up with a viable suspect. Instead,

I seemed to be eliminating all of the individuals who had started out at the top of my alternative suspects list.

Jan was a few years older than me, but not by much. She had clear skin, bright blue eyes, and the blond hair I have always wanted. She invited me into a conference room to chat, offered me coffee which I accepted, and then settled in as if prepared to stay as long as I had questions that needed answering.

"I've been at AHA," I explained. "It has been suggested that Sabrina might have discovered some irregularities in their finances, so I took a look at the documents she reviewed." I didn't say suggested by whom. Nor did I let on that I was not authorized to look at any AHA documents.

"I didn't know that," Jan said. "What kind of irregularities?" She seemed sincerely concerned.

"You never talked with Sabrina about AHA's finances?"

"Actually, she reached out to me, but we didn't get a chance to meet in person before she, ah, before she died."

If you can't say the word *murder* did that disqualify you as a *murderer*? "Did she indicate what she wanted to discuss with you?"

"I didn't get the impression it was anything important. I mean, the auditor always seems to have a few questions. It wasn't an unusual request." She sat up in her chair. "It was just something insignificant, wasn't it?"

If she was faking surprise at the thought that there might be something wrong with AHA's finances, she ought to try out for a part in a Broadway play. On the other hand, successful criminals most likely succeed because they are good at faking it.

"That's what I'm trying to find out."

She didn't hesitate. "Well, how can I help you?"

John had mentioned that most financial irregularities were discovered through tips. Although Jan had already indicated she was totally unaware of any problems, I had to ask. "As the treasurer, has anyone come to you with any concerns about something that might be amiss? Even something minor?"

"No. No one. In fact, we're financially very sound. I mean, no nonprofit ever has enough money to do everything they want to do, but we have some major donors who have been very generous, and we have funding from several grants and state programs."

"Do you mind if I ask how involved you are in keeping track of financial records?"

"I leave the day-to-day work to Earl, but I have absolute faith in him. He's been with the organization for years."

"Do you or the board as a whole monitor your list of financial safeguards on a regular basis?" I hoped that wasn't an insulting question.

"Earl makes a report at each board meeting. And AHA has good processes and safeguards spelled out in detail." That sounded suspiciously like an "I didn't know we were supposed to do that" but we have lengthy documentation that proves we know what we're doing.

"What about some of the contractors you employ for the low-income housing you're building. Do you think the controls you have in place keep them from padding their costs?"

"BluSky Construction came highly recommended. And I don't think they have exceeded their estimates by much. You always expect final costs to be slightly higher than the original bid."

"BluSky?" How had I missed that when reviewing AHA's financials?

"Yes. We've used them before for smaller projects, I believe."

"Are you aware that Sabrina's ex-boyfriend is employed by them?"

"No. I didn't know that. Maybe that was what she wanted to talk with me about. It could look like a conflict of interest, with her auditing a company her boyfriend works for."

Plausible, but, in my opinion, not likely. I decided to try a different tack. "Do you know why she was hired instead of the auditors you've used in the past?"

"No, I just assumed Arthur had his reasons for switching firms."

Perhaps he *did* have his reasons. And maybe they weren't all prurient. There was always the possibility that I had been too quick to dismiss him as the murderer. That I was expending time and energy trying to clear the name of a killer. Not a pleasant thought.

I asked a few more questions and came to the conclusion that there was no need to prolong our meeting. She was a smart professional woman, but it didn't seem as though she had been intimately engaged in the details of AHA's finances. She saw her role as big picture oversight, and she would have been even less likely to uncover fraud than your average auditor. Unless she had me completely fooled and was a master criminal. I mentally put her in the "highly unlikely" category, thanked her for her time and left.

As a result of my financial sleuthing, I had come full circle—back to Arthur. I wondered if Earl knew why Arthur had decided to go with a different auditing firm. I could give him a call and ask, although I anticipated that he would say it wasn't up to him to make those kinds of decisions. After all, it was *his* work that was being audited. And Zelen and Hobbs was a reputable local firm. But I would also like his take on how well AHA followed established safeguards. *If* he would be willing to talk to me about that, which I doubted.

I could also call AHA's former auditors and see what they had to say. Although my guess was that they would be pretty tight-lipped. If they had done something to warrant the change, they weren't going to admit it. And even if they hadn't, it was doubtful they would share any client information with me.

It was time to turn the financial sleuthing over to Ben. He had the authority to ask the tough questions and insist on answers. Although I still didn't feel as if I had enough information to jumpstart his interest in this line of inquiry. I needed to make one last stop.

Chapter 17

Tiffany Riddle Redux

Zelen and Hobbs was an energetic walk and one short light rail ride away. Later, I would retrace my journey to pick up my car. That was easier than trying to park downtown. And cheaper. On the way I called Sophie to see if she wanted to meet for drinks and maybe dinner. We lost contact for a full rendition of Happy Birthday as the train went through a tunnel but managed to make plans to meet before the next tunnel cut us off a second time.

Tom was in, and he agreed to have Tiffany Riddle come to his office for a brief chat. He didn't even ask what she wanted to chat about. He met me at the elevator on the 3rd floor and gave me a warm handshake and a quick onceover. He was still too young for me to be interested in him in a romantic way, but he was wearing another attractive green shirt, this one trending toward something in the mint plant family. I wondered if he had minty breath.

He took me to the coffee room and poured two cups of coffee without asking whether I wanted coffee or how I took it. I couldn't decide whether that was good or bad, polite, or misogynistic. Not that it mattered. I was just there for information.

"So, what can I do for you?" he asked as we took chairs opposite each other at a tiny table that wobbled when I put my elbows on it. I quickly sat up straight, thankful I hadn't slopped coffee all over.

"First, I have a confession to make."

"A confession. How intriguing." He was smiling, like I was engaging in some sort of flirtatious ploy.

"Yes. My name isn't Tiffany."

The smile faded somewhat, replaced by a slight puckering between his eyes. "So, you just go by 'Tiffany,' right?"

"No, I go by the name on my birth certificate—Bryn Baczek."

The pucker between his eyes deepened, and the smile disappeared completely. "Then why did you tell me your name was Tiffany Riddle?"

It was tempting to say my reason for calling myself Tiffany was a riddle, but it didn't seem like the right time to be flip. "When we met in Sabrina's office, I wasn't there because she'd agreed to meet me for lunch. I was there because I was worried about her. She wasn't answering her phone and she wasn't at home. I was searching her office for some clue that would tell me where to look for her."

"This was before she died, wasn't it?"

"It was probably right around the time she was *murdered*." Dying and being murdered aren't the same in my book but getting snarky about it was probably uncalled for. "But of course, at that time, all I knew was that she was missing."

"I still don't understand. If you were a friend concerned about her whereabouts, why didn't you use your own name?"

"Because I wasn't supposed to be in her office." He sounded like someone who thought jaywalking was a crime.

"But . . ."

"I didn't sign in." When he still seemed confused, I added, "It was a spur-of-the-moment thing, okay? I didn't want anyone to know I was investigating her disappearance. No one else was concerned, so I didn't want to make a big deal about it. But now, that seems irrelevant. She's dead. And someone is responsible for her death. That's why I wanted to talk with you."

"Why me?"

"Ironically, you are the only person at Zelen and Hobbs that I know well enough to contact."

"That *is* ironic." He actually smiled at the thought. "And a bit pathetic."

"I'm sorry I gave you a phony name."

"Forgiven. Now please tell me what this is all about." Apparently, he didn't hold grudges.

"Well, first of all, Sabrina wasn't a friend. But I happen to know someone who was." Well, Arthur wasn't actually a "friend," but that was as close as I could come to the truth without explanations getting complicated. "He thinks Sabrina may have been on the trail of some illegal activity, possible fraud. But I haven't been able to verify any details. I was hoping that maybe she mentioned what she was investigating to you."

He shook his head. "No, she didn't say anything to me. But she was pretty close to the vest when it came to the projects she was working on. Nor was she one to meet up with colleagues after work or sit around gossiping over coffee."

Even though it had been a longshot, I was disappointed. "Is there *anyone* in the office that she might have confided in?"

He shook his head again. "I can't think of anyone. As I said, she kept her professional distance." He leaned forward as if not wanting to be overheard. "There's a lot of competition for clients. And Sabrina was an ambitious woman."

"Were you surprised when she was hired to audit AHA? I mean, they had used the same firm for a number of years."

"Not really. We're always interested in finding new clients. Sabrina was an aggressive salesperson and, well, a very attractive woman. That helped bring in clients."

"If she was onto something, wouldn't she have left notes somewhere? Has anyone checked her computer?"

He gave me a hard stare. "Are you some kind of undercover cop?"

I couldn't help but smile. "No, afraid not. Just a consultant who can't let go of an idea once I'm convinced there's something there."

He leaned forward again, this time as if to encourage confidential sharing. "Okay. Let me get this straight. You think Sabrina came across something illegal while auditing a client. And to avoid getting caught, they did her in. That about it?"

"That's my theory. Unless the ex-boyfriend did it. You ever meet him?"

"No, like I said, she kept to herself."

"So, what about her computer. Anyone check it?"

"I would think the police took a look. But I'll tell you what, if it's still here, I think I can get her admin to give me access. And I'll do some asking around."

"Maybe I should just contact the police at this point." If he got in trouble, then I would be in trouble.

"And spoil my chance to play detective?"

"You realize that it could be dangerous to snoop around. After all, someone felt threatened enough to go after Sabrina."

"I could point out that's what *you* are doing. Besides, I'll be discreet." His confident grin was probably intended to let me know he was a macho male who could take care of himself. It was the equivalent of chest beating.

"Just promise me that if you come across anything suspicious that you won't pursue it. You'll tell me right away so I can take everything to the police."

"I promise. That is, *if* you—or Tiffany—will have a drink with me some time. Maybe dinner."

"Sorry, but . . ."

"I know, let me guess—you're in a committed relationship." He didn't wait for me to answer. "Story of my life. Okay, I'll work for the satisfaction of discovery."

I didn't correct him about my relationship status. He'd been so quick to accept a "no" that I doubted he was even serious about wanting to get together. Although Sophie would say I should have encouraged him. He was eligible, employed, and not bad looking. Still, as nice as his shirts were, I couldn't picture us together. Why waste time on a non-starter?

I took the light rail back, walked to my car and drove to the restaurant where I was going to meet Sophie for drinks and dinner. I was early, so I called Logan, but got his voice mail. Other than Sophie and Logan, I don't have many close friends. In my consulting business I meet a lot of people I think it would be nice to get to know better, but there are only so many hours in the day, and I have pets to take care of. Then there's my family. I don't see them as much as they'd like and more than I prefer. Except for my twin niece and nephew. They are right up there at the top of my priority list. And I wouldn't mind seeing more of Catrin, although she's at that age where separation from family is important. Maybe in the future—

I'd already had one glass of wine when Sophie arrived. That's usually my limit when I'm driving, but I ordered another to be sociable.

"Hard day?" Sophie asked.

"Frustrating."

"Tell me about it."

That's all she needed to say to get me to pour out the details of my unproductive investigation. I ended by complaining about my lack of progress and how I felt partly responsible for getting Arthur arrested.

"How do you figure?"

"Well, if I hadn't retrieved the statue, then the murder weapon might not have implicated him."

"Or, if I hadn't told Dane . . ."

"I've already gotten past that," I interrupted.

"You sure?"

"Yes, I'm sure."

Sophie reached across the table and put her hand over mine. "You have nothing to blame yourself for."

"Besides, given what I've told you, Arthur may have done it."

"I agree. Although the thing that bothers me the most is what you said about how groggy he was when the police searched his boat. Did they do a drug screen?"

"No, at the time they assumed he'd taken a sleeping pill. And he was too foggy to demand a test."

"That screams frame-up to me. Someone drugged him."

"It's too late to test for it; we'll never know."

Our meal came and we were momentarily distracted by our food. I'd ordered a French dip with fries. Sophie was having her usual chopped chicken salad. The only thing she varied was the type of salad dressing. I was just starting in on the second half of my sandwich when Sophie surprised me with a question about something I hadn't considered.

"What if Sabrina had gone after the AHA contract because she knew in advance there was something fishy going on? Maybe she'd heard something through the ex-boyfriend."

"Well, I definitely think Blu-Sky is worth looking into."

"But not by you," Sophie said emphatically.

"I'm just a conduit, not an investigator."

"Do you mean that in the metaphysical sense?"

"I was just thinking how nice it would be to be clairvoyant."

"I think you'll have to settle for being smart. And a smart person knows when to step away from something."

"Point. Game. Match."

"It is, however, like reading only part of a book. So many unanswered questions. Like whether there was anything on her computer to suggest what she had been looking into."

"Even if Tom gets a look at her computer, I doubt there will be anything on it. Sabrina was pretty secretive. I'll ask Ben if they looked at her computer when I talk to him, even though he won't be able to tell me anything."

"Then why ask?"

"Because I'm curious, and because I can't help myself."

Maybe it was the Tiffany Riddle in me that made me step over the line. But I did know better. And I really did need to make sure Tom didn't do anything to put himself in danger. Tomorrow I would call him off and tell Ben what I had learned so far.

Tiffany Riddle RIP.

Chapter 18

Before the Storm

Storms have a way of sneaking up on you. I've been out on the water when it was glassy calm. No breeze. No storm clouds on the horizon. Then suddenly there's a ripple on the water and the sky turns a shade darker. It doesn't take long for ripples to become whitecaps and the sky to transform into a menacing swirl of unrest. Sails are furled, the engine turned on at full speed, and you head for harbor. If you're lucky, you make a safe haven before the storm reaches its peak.

The phrase "calm before the storm" applies to so many situations. The eerie silence before a monster attacks in a movie. The twins sleeping so soundly you almost forget the chaos of their waking hours. The hush that falls on a crowd when they know something is about to happen. The anticipation when a conductor of an orchestra raises her or his hands. A speaker approaching a podium. Runners crouching for the starting gun.

Tuesday morning I was slowly coming awake, aware of Macavity on the bunk next to mine. His rib cage rising and falling rhythmically. I tried mimicking his breathing, but it was a little too fast for me. Not much, just a little. I remembered reading that cats take as many as 30 breaths per minute while sleeping whereas humans take from 12 to 20. By my estimates, we were both breathing normally.

My mind was drifting in and out of consciousness when there was a loud *bam, bam, bam* that reverberated throughout the boat as someone pounded on my hatch.

Macavity leapt straight up into the air as if he'd been hoisted by invisible wires. Still half asleep, I swung my feet over the side of the bunk and grabbed my robe.

Bam, bam, bam.

"Just a minute," I yelled. Was the marina on fire?

I was about to unlock the hatch when it occurred to me that it might be a good idea to find out who was pounding on my boat before I opened up. "Who's there?" I shouted.

"I know you're in there!" The voice was loud and male. He sounded vaguely familiar. And really angry. I was fairly certain it was Butch, Sabrina's ex-boyfriend.

I grabbed my cell and called Logan just as the pounding resumed, even louder than before, if that was possible.

BAM! BAM! BAM! Like a thunderstorm and an earthquake at the same time. The boat bounced against the side of the dock.

"Bryn? What's going on?"

"I've got a situation."

"Situation?"

"Butch, Sabrina's ex-boyfriend, is on my boat, pounding on my hatch. And he sounds really mad."

"Don't let him in. Judd and I will be right over. Okay?"

I was about to say I had no intention of letting him in, but the phone had already gone dead.

"Open up!" His booming voice was probably carrying to the far corners of the marina. The image of Godzilla coming up from the depths to wreak revenge came to mind. I pictured him standing there with one fist in the air, primordial ooze dripping on my deck.

"Give me a minute," I shouted back. I ran up forward and grabbed a pair of jeans and a shirt. How long would it take Logan and Judd to get over here? And what on earth could they do if Butch was as out of control as I feared. Would they think to bring pepper spray?

Macavity was making a low hissing sound and pacing back and forth, clearly upset and almost as angry as Butch.

The pounding ceased, but I could still sense his presence on my boat. I wondered if he was trying to come up with a way to break in. Maybe he had a weapon.

I slipped on a pair of Top-siders. They were my one concession to nautical fashion trends. They really are great deck shoes.

When I heard Judd's voice say, "Get off that boat and stand back," I felt like the cavalry had arrived, although on foot rather than horseback. If it came to a physical showdown, could one physically fit lawyer, even with his professor sidekick, win out over a buff construction worker? I had my doubts. Maybe I should call Hudson. If there were enough witnesses present, Butch might back off.

"Stay out of this." Butch did a good impression of a snarling predator about to attack.

"Don't make me call the police." Logan sounded more confident than I guessed he felt at the moment.

"Just get off the boat and stand back," Judd repeated. "Then we can talk about what you want. Okay?"

"She called you, didn't she?" Butch hit the word "she" like I was some sort of female demon out of an original Grimm's fairy tale.

"Are you going to get off the boat?" I could picture Logan holding out his phone as if ready to hit speed dial for backup. I decided not to call Hudson. Butch would either calm down or Logan would call the police.

My boat has tiny portholes that are about at eye level with the dock. All I could see were shoes. Judd was standing with his feet slightly apart, ready for the attack. Logan had on his favorite tennis shoes with a bright blue strip running parallel to the sole and matching shoestrings. I give him a hard time about his taste in tennis shoes, but they looked great from that angle. Although given the way he was standing, moving back and forth from one foot to the other. suggested he was ready to run at the slightest provocation.

The boat had stopped rocking. But Butch did not step off. It was an old-fashioned Western stand-off.

"Well?" Judd said. "Your call."

The *Aspara* suddenly bounced up and down as Butch apparently leapt off onto the dock. I unlocked the hatch, slid it open and peeked out, prepared to help out the best I could if there was a fight. Maybe I should grab my cast iron fry pan.

All three men were on the dock. They were staring each other down. Like animals about to pounce. As I stepped out into the cockpit, three pair of eyes turned to look at me. Judd and Logan were standing next to the *Aspara* to my left. Butch was less than a broad jump away, about three feet from the edge of the dock and four feet to my right. For a moment no one moved or spoke. Then Macavity broke the spell by whipping past me, bounding off the boat and disappearing down the dock. So much for loyalty.

"So, what's this all about, Butch?" I asked.

He took a step toward me, glanced at Judd and Logan who had also taken a step forward, and stopped where he was. It was like they were on a chess board trying to anticipate the competition's next move.

"I just want to talk." He sounded almost reasonable. Was he deterred by the presence of the two men, the threat of police involvement, or by the large bear pepper spray canister that Logan had poised to use on him? He had been prepared to stand his ground, after all.

"About what?" I asked.

"About the rumors you're spreading." The reasonable tone was leaking out of his voice, traces of anger creeping back in.

"What do you think I've been saying?"

"That I had something to do with Sabrina's death." He was definitely angry again, but he seemed in control. For the moment.

"Come off it, Butch. All of her friends and colleagues knew that you hit her from time to time. Even the police are aware of that. So, what could I tell anyone that they didn't already know?"

"You admit you've talked to people about me. And to the police." He had me there.

"But I haven't been going around bad-mouthing you. I've been looking into the audit Sabrina was working on, that's all."

"That's not what I've heard."

"I don't know who you've been talking to, but you're way off base."

Logan lowered the spray cannister. His arm was probably getting tired. "Why are you so hot and bothered about what people are saying anyway? Do you have something to hide?" he asked.

That's right, Logan. Poke the monster with a sharp stick and see what it does. Well, hold onto your pepper spray; I'm going to take a poke too. "Did Sabrina talk to you about problems with BluSky and the work they're doing for AHA?"

"What's that supposed to mean?" Butch sounded more puzzled than mad.

"*You* tell *me*."

He paused a moment, then started to move away. "No, I'm not telling you nothing."

"If you know something, you should go to the police with it."

Butch took a step back.

Judd moved toward him, pressing his retreat. "Just tell us why you're here and what you want from Bryn. Then I think it would be best if you left."

We all seemed to be holding our breath. The lull before the storm? I certainly hoped not.

"Go to hell," Butch said suddenly with feeling. Then he turned and stormed off down the dock, leaving us out of harm's way.

Judd, Logan, and I took a collective deep breath.

"He's a crazy man," Logan said.

"And possibly dangerous," Judd added.

"I agree." I could feel the adrenaline draining away. "Come aboard; I need to debrief."

Once below, Judd and Logan took over the settee, and I got out a folding stool I use when I have guests. It's not very comfortable, but it's an extra seat.

"You don't think he'll come back with a gun, do you?" Logan asked.

"Always the optimist," I kidded. But I, too, was worried about a return visit, with or without a gun.

"Obviously, he has a violent streak," Judd observed.

"He usually reserves that for his girlfriends," I said, trying for a little humor and failing miserably.

Logan reached across the table and put his hand on my arm. "You okay?"

I nodded.

"So, what did you do to get him so riled up?" Judd asked.

"What did *I* do?"

Logan jumped in. "He didn't mean it like that."

"Something made him come after you," Judd persisted.

"I have been asking a few questions, and his name keeps coming up. Maybe he *is* sensitive about the abuse charges. He might actually have believed no one knew. Or maybe there *is* some connection between what Sabrina was investigating and the construction company he works for. He could be in it up to his menacing eyeballs, although I've been going on the assumption that he may have alerted Sabrina to problems with BluSky, not that he's involved in criminal activities. He just doesn't seem far enough up the food chain to be involved in some kind of white-collar fraud."

"The bottom line is that you've done something that ticks him off, and he doesn't like it," Judd summarized unnecessarily.

"And he's a violent guy," Logan added.

"You should go stay with your parents for a while," Judd concluded. He obviously had no idea what a terrible suggestion *that* was. You can't go home without becoming the child again. At least not with my mother at the helm. The mere suggestion of it made me feel the urge to refuse to eat my vegetables.

"Or stay with Sophie for a few days," Logan quickly countered.

I considered their suggestions. Even though Butch was a scary guy with a bad track record of hitting women, he didn't strike me as someone smart enough to have framed Arthur. He was physical, direct. Still, I couldn't rule him out. I couldn't rule anyone out. And even if he wasn't the murderer, he seemed unstable enough to be a threat that I shouldn't ignore.

"Or . . ." Logan began, obviously still trying to come up with something I would agree to. ". . . why don't you move the *Aspara* to that space in front of the building? The boat that was there sold. There would be people around during the day, and the area is lit up at night. I'm sure Hudson would be fine with you mooring there for a few days."

"Good idea," I said. That appealed to me. Closer to people. Well lit. But not forced to abandon my home.

Macavity suddenly came aboard and jumped into my lap. I'd apparently been forgiven. He nuzzled my chin. Affectionately. Or just to let me know we hadn't had breakfast yet.

The storm was temporarily stalled.

Chapter 19

Macavity's Not There!

After I explained my situation, Hudson had no problem with me mooring in a space I wasn't paying for. He's a good landlord and a kind person. He even offered to put in a spotlight next to my official moorage spot, but I assured him my request to move to the head of the dock was as much a question of being near a hub of activity as it was to have better lighting. Besides, a spotlight would probably freak out Macavity. And usually, I kinda like the slightly overcast glow over what I call home.

There was only one drawback to my new location. We seemed to be getting more than the usual number of looky-loos. And rather than casually walking the docks like they typically did, they were stopping to read the names of boats. There must have been some local news coverage that mentioned the *Knotty Lady* and either named the marina or gave sufficient detail that people could figure it out if they tried hard enough. Their interest felt intrusive, like we were fair game for observation, animals in a zoo. I couldn't help but wonder how they would feel if I went into their residential neighborhood and peered in their windows.

The biggest advantage of mooring at the head of the dock was being right in front of my office. If I craned my neck looking out of the window behind my desk, I could see the *Aspara*. It would be much easier to keep my eye out for prowlers. Especially for muscled prowlers with loud voices. The downside was that I was tempted to turn around and look out at the dock every five minutes just to be sure everything was okay.

By the time I finally managed to get some work done that needed doing to keep my consulting practice profitable, the sun was beginning its nightly descent. As I stepped outside, I paused to admire the lovely pinkish streak hovering above the skyline. There was no wind, not even a whisper of breeze. Everything seemed peaceful. I decided to go home and feed Macavity, then take a walk around the neighborhood. Maybe I'd jog to Gasworks Park and run up the tiny hill to the sundial to watch the sun set. I needed some time to clear my head and stretch my legs.

I knew Macavity would be irritated with our new living arrangement, so I was glad I'd finally taken time to do a little shopping. I got out a can of his favorite imitation salmon meal and called out his name through the open hatch. I wasn't surprised when he didn't come running. He considered the entire marina his home and could be out wandering anywhere. And although it was technically dinner time for him, since he couldn't count on being fed at the same time every day, his stomach might be saying "dinner," but he couldn't know for sure that I would be serving it up then. It crossed my mind that he might even be watching me from a distance, waiting in the shadows to make me feel guilty for moving his home, his base of operations. He was "there" somewhere; I just didn't know where "there" was at present.

After locking up, I headed up the steps to the street level, my hand on the pepper spray in the pocket of my sweatshirt. Just in case.

There was no one on the road. Only a couple of cars drove by as I made my way past marine businesses and a few ramshackle buildings that managed to elude being torn down in spite of being within city limits. I loved the fact that the area hadn't changed much since I first moved to the marina, but I knew that it wouldn't remain the same forever. I had to enjoy it while it lasted.

The park was basically deserted. Family visitors had gone home for dinner. A handful of people were strolling near the water. A few dogs were sniffing around, perhaps hoping to scare up a squirrel to chase. A couple, pressed together in an embrace, were silhouetted against the darkening sky, oblivious to their surroundings. I couldn't help envying the lovebirds. It wasn't that I felt unfulfilled as a single person. And I didn't want to be like Sophie, constantly on the lookout for the "one" that would make my life whole. If I happened to meet someone I wanted to spend the rest of my life with, that would be great, but I was happy with the way things were. I had companionship in good friends, a family that cared about me, and a cat who stayed with me of his own free will. I was a lucky woman.

My breathing was ragged rather than regular by the time I reached the sundial. It wasn't much of an incline; I really needed to get more exercise. I sat down and took in the view of the city lights reflecting off the glassy water. A pleasant evening on the water is about as good as it gets in my book. Whether in a boat, looking down from the top of a knoll at the remains of a gas production plant, or peeking out of my tiny office window . . . *water*, that was the important element. Adventure stories, tall tales, myths, poems—people were constantly trying to capture the sight and sound of water. Lines from poems I'd read and re-read over the years came to mind as I sat there: *"glimmering and vast," "caressing waves upon the shore," "a gray mist on the sea's face," "ever changing, constant."*

As the ground grew hard and cold, I reluctantly got up and headed back. Macavity would probably have eaten by now. Maybe he would have forgiven me and be waiting on the settee, expecting an evening treat.

My feet made little crunching noises in the gravel alongside the road as I half jogged, half walked back to the marina. Occasionally I was forced onto the road by an obstacle . . . a parked car, a puddle, a container awaiting pick-up, the remain of a chicken wire fence. There were no sidewalks in the area, but there were short stretches of parking areas in front of businesses that catered to industrial marine services.

When I got to the marina, I scanned the docks for signs of life. Particularly for signs of hostile life that might be waiting for me to return to the *Aspara*. But there was no one around. The *Aspara* was spotlighted with a wavery glow from a lamp post and the waning dull glow of a sun that was on the verge of disappearing behind the house-covered hill in the distance.

Macavity wasn't in the main salon. Nor had his food been touched. I checked to make sure his porthole entry hadn't accidently closed during the move, but it was wide open. Something didn't feel right. Macavity might ignore me out of pique, even eat and leave, but to not eat his dinner?

I grabbed a flashlight and went out to search the marina, half expecting Macavity to be sitting on the dock where the *Aspara* was usually moored. Just to make a statement. But he wasn't there. I searched every nook and cranny on both docks, walked around the office building, listening at doors. Then I went back and paused at each boat, looking and listening. I was starting to panic.

Logan and Judd were out for the evening, so I couldn't enlist their help. Besides, Judd would simply point out that Macavity was, after all, just a cat. Cats disappear from time to time, doing who knows what. And it was true, Macavity had disappeared for an evening or two in the past. I had worried about him being injured and in pain, unable to drag himself back to the *Aspara*. Until he returned under his own steam. But that was then. Now there was the added fear that he could have been taken or hurt by Butch to get back at me for perceived wrongs. Butch had battered Sabrina, what would stop him from taking out his anger on a cat? Especially if he thought I was fond of the animal. Which I was.

I used to kid my friends about how attached they were to their pets, but the truth was that I couldn't imagine my life without Macavity. He had become family, no, better than family. He might yowl a bit about something he didn't like, but he never went on and on about it. And now I may have put him in danger by ticking Butch off. Rationally I knew I should give him time to come home on his own. But I couldn't get it out of my head that he could be out there somewhere, hurting and in need of help. Rational or not, I had to go look for him.

My first thought was that if he wasn't in the marina, maybe he was on one of the nearby docks. I was halfway down a long wooden pier just west of the marina when I came across a man walking a teensy, short-haired dog that resembled a large rat. I stopped him to ask if he'd seen Macavity.

"He's a large orange cat with a white stomach," I explained. "He has dark swirls on both sides."

"A ginger marmalade?" the man asked.

"You've seen an orange cat?" The ginger marmalade label wasn't' one I was familiar with, but it sounded like the right color.

"No, but I'll keep an eye out. Muffy is afraid of cats," he added.

I wasn't sure if he intended to keep an eye out on my behalf or because of Muffy's fear of cats. "Here." I handed him a card. "Please call me if you come across him. His name is Macavity."

"Strange name." Not a poetry afficionado then. He put my card in his pocket.

I continued down the pier to the end. There was no sign of Macavity.

Next, I walked along the line of businesses the other side of the wooden pier. Whenever there was a break between buildings, I entered the narrow, dimly lit spaces, calling for Macavity. His disappearance almost made me wish I had named him something different. It was hard to call out "Macavity, here kitty, kitty, Macavity." But that's what I was doing. Searching and calling out for him. "Ma . . . cav . . . ity."

I came across some undesirable heaps of smelly debris, heard the scurry of an unseen animal as it escaped around a corner, and discovered that a lot of the businesses in the area collected junk behind their buildings. There were rusty motors, battered rowboats, piles of chains, hydraulic hoses, rusty cables, stacks of unmarked boxes—all places for a wily cat to hide. But the only cat my flashlight captured in a frozen moment before he ran off wasn't Macavity.

Tired and chilled from the night air, I returned to the *Aspara*, defeated but still hopeful. When I saw that Macavity's dinner remained untouched, I felt a pang of disappointment, sharp and personal. He wasn't there.

I threw myself down on the settee and took out my cell. If Logan didn't want me to call him while he and Judd were out with friends, he didn't have to answer. It only rang twice before I heard him say, "Bryn? Are you okay?"

"Sorry to bother you, but Macavity's missing. I've looked everywhere."

"Just a minute." I could hear him saying something in the background, then, after a short pause, he said, "What did you say about Macavity?"

"He's missing."

"And you think something's happened to him?"

"I'm worried that Butch either took him or . . ." I couldn't quite bring myself to put words to my worst fear.

"He might just be punishing you for moving the boat." Logan can read my mind, and maybe Macavity's too.

"If so, he's doing a good job of it."

"We're about to leave. Stay put and I'll help you look when I get back, okay?"

The sound of Logan's voice had been reassuring. Together we would find Macavity.

I made myself a cup of coffee and sat down to wait. It was hard. I kept hoping to hear Macavity come in through his porthole. As soon as he arrived, I would scold him for making me worry. Then pamper him with his favorite food and ear rubs. Meanwhile, all I could do was wait. Wait for the sound of soft paws on the deck. Wait for the sound of Logan and Judd coming down the steps. Wait, impatiently wait.

I've never heard the marina so quiet. So unsettlingly quiet. The emptiness filled with random thoughts. Visions of Macavity trapped in a cage with a malevolent Butch standing over him. Sabrina dropping Aphrodite off the stern of the *Knotty Lady*. Arthur running his hands over the erotic stature. The empty space in my locker where I had stashed it. Then, for some reason a cartoon of Opus, the penguin from *Bloom County*, came to mind. He was flossing between his ears. It struck me that was what I needed to do. Stop worrying about Macavity and clear my mind. Make use of the silence to concentrate on why someone felt it was necessary to take Sabrina's life.

I mentally began making a list of loose ends and potential leads. Pieces missing from the larger perspective. As the list got longer, I realized I needed to write things down. I scrounged around in my junk drawer and came up with a scrap of paper and a pencil stub and began scribbling.

1) Gerald had not gotten back to me. He was probably a dead-end, but it might be worth a follow-up call.

2) I had pictures of financial documents that I should study and also that I should show John. He might see something in them that didn't jump out at me.

3) Someone should be checking out BluSky Construction. Was Ben already doing that? What was the best way to bring that up with him?

4) Had Ben questioned Butch? Had he asked whether Butch had said something to Sabrina that got her interested in BluSky's operations, either in relationship to AHA or as a stand-alone problem? Would Butch admit it if he had?

5) On the other hand, had Ben considered the possibility that Sabrina had said something to Butch about her audit, something to suggest she was looking into BluSky? If so, had Butch mentioned this to his boss?

6) Should I revisit the question of why Arthur had hired Sabrina instead of their previous auditor? Was it even remotely possible he had been trying to hide something?

7) Did I need to get back to Tom Thompson and make sure he wasn't poking around too much in something that could backfire on him?

When I heard male voices in the distance, I jumped up and climbed into the cockpit. Judd and Logan . . . at last. I stepped off the boat and rushed out on the dock to meet them.

"No sign of him yet?" Logan asked as they reached the bottom of the stairs.

"No, nothing."

"He will probably show up by tomorrow," Judd offered, not sounding entirely convinced of what he was saying. "But let's have a look around," he added quickly.

"You'll help?" I was sorry I sounded surprised, but I was. I'd expected him to say goodnight and let Logan and me conduct the search.

Logan deflected my response by asking, "Where should we start?"

"I think we need flashlights," Judd said. "And I would like to change shoes. Maybe put on a different jacket."

"Me too," Logan said. "It's chilly. We'll meet you back here in a few minutes."

"Sounds good." I also needed to get my flashlight, cell, and a warmer jacket. It was good to be taking action. It was good to have help.

I was once again waiting impatiently. This time at the foot of the stairs. When I saw Judd and Logan headed in my direction, I did a double-take.

"Macavity!" I shouted.

Logan had him cradled in one arm and was rubbing his head with his other hand. Macavity looked perfectly happy, blissfully unaware of all the anguish he had caused me. "This yours?" Logan was grinning. Judd's look was noncommittal.

"Where did you find him?"

"You want to tell her?" Logan asked Judd.

"He was on the *Carpe Diem*."

"On?"

"Inside."

"What was he doing inside?"

"Go on," Logan urged.

"He came on board when I was finishing up my breakfast this morning. I think he could smell the lox on my bagel."

"And?" What was I missing?

"Well, I put some lox out for him, then finished getting ready for work and left. Apparently, he was still on the boat. Then Logan and I went out for the evening without coming home. I'm really sorry."

"You fed Macavity lox?"

"Shouldn't he have lox?" Judd asked, sounding almost concerned.

"Well, I can't imagine he will be satisfied with his fake salmon after that," I said, struggling with the idea that Judd, self-proclaimed cat hater, had actually fed my cat an expensive delicacy.

"Hey, you two. Crisis over. Be happy." Logan handed me Macavity, and I dumped him unceremoniously on the back deck. He disappeared around the side of the *Aspara*, heading for his personal entrance.

"Thanks," I managed to say, struggling to control my emotional feelings of relief.

Judd cleared his throat. "Even so, I don't think your concern was unwarranted. Maybe you ought to keep Macavity inside for a few days."

Logan was grinning but keeping his mouth shut. I may not have solved the mystery of who killed Sabrina, but I had definitely learned one of Judd's closely held secrets.

Chapter 20

The Intruder

As soon as I pulled the hatch shut and locked it from the inside, I also closed Macavity's private porthole entrance. Judd was right, I needed to keep an eye on him for a while, for my own peace of mind as well as for his safety. How I was going to manage that during the day was not something I could envision, but at least at night I could keep him locked up.

On one other occasion I had moved my boat to another marina to avoid a dangerous situation, keeping Macavity inside in case we needed to leave in a hurry. But that was a temporary arrangement that ended as soon as the bad guys were caught. This time I wasn't even sure that I needed to be concerned. But Butch was a wild card. If he came back a second time when no one was around, I wasn't sure what to expect. It seemed to me the best I could do was to remain inside as much as possible, always have pepper spray handy, and, when I needed to be out and about, stay alert to my surroundings.

A yowling broke into my unsettling thoughts about what I needed to do to keep myself and Macavity safe. My pampered cat had apparently discovered his egress had been blocked. After chowing on his delayed dinner, he must have been planning on an evening stroll before bedtime. He raced back into the main cabin and leapt up the stairs, stopping to stare at the closed hatch as if he could will it to open with a magical scowl and a penetrating glare. When that didn't work, he jumped down on the settee next to me and whapped my arm with one paw as if to say, "Ah, come on." At least he didn't have his claws out.

"Sorry, Macavity. We're prisoners for now. You're already wearing your orange jumpsuit, so get used to it."

Macavity responded by putting both paws on my leg and flexing his nails.

"You threatening me?" I asked. "After what you put me through?" I removed his paws from my leg and he reluctantly let me pull him into my lap. Then he gave himself over to a good rub behind the ears, rolling over to show me his Purex white belly. When he started purring, I was relieved. At least for a time I was back in his good graces. He even stayed put when my cell phone started making frog noises.

It was Terry Finn. Terry was someone I knew and liked but hadn't been in touch with recently. Work and life seemed to interfere with me making an effort to maintain relationships like I knew I should. Logan and Sophie were the exceptions. Proximity and friendship combined to keep me constantly in touch with Logan. And Sophie and I had long ago created a bond that wasn't likely to be broken by neglect or distance. Cultivating a broader circle of friends was something I always intended to make a priority but never seemed to get around to doing.

"Terry, it's good to hear from you."

"Well, I wish it was under better circumstances."

"Oh, oh. What's wrong?"

"I suppose I should make small talk before jumping right in to ask a favor, but my mother is ill, and I need to go stay with her for at least a week, maybe longer. The problem is Cora. I could put her in a kennel, but she's getting old, and I hate to do that."

Cora had been with Terry since she was a puppy, a loveable Corgi with short legs, a roly-poly body, and a sweet disposition. "Are you asking if I'll dog sit?"

"It would put my mind at ease if you could. And you can use the Jacuzzi. The refrigerator and pantry are full. You can even eat the brownies I have in the freezer."

Terry knows how much I love soaking in a tub, not something I get a chance to do often. And her brownies are the best. "You know how to bait the trap, don't you?"

"Well, you're so good with Cora. And she isn't much trouble these days. She's okay being alone during the day. All you have to do is make sure she has food and give her a little attention. You don't even have to walk her, just let her out into the back yard twice a day to do her duty. What do you say? I'd owe you big time."

"Of course. I'll be happy to house sit with Cora, Terry. Sorry about your mother—I hope it isn't anything too serious."

"Just a bad case of the flu. She's too weak to take care of herself, but she doesn't want to go to the hospital. I can't blame her; I wouldn't want to either. So, I really appreciate your willingness to house sit at a moment's notice. That's above and beyond." I'd done some house-sitting for Terry in the past, and Terry had done favors for me on more than one occasion. In addition, I couldn't help thinking that the timing was perfect.

"Is it okay if I bring Macavity? I might not feel like running back and forth every day. I can work from there if that's okay with you." There was no reason I could think of to tell her how serendipitous her call was. I didn't want to add to her worries. But her house was the perfect hidey hole. Being gone for a week would give Butch time to cool down. And maybe the police would make some headway on the case. Once they'd identified the murderer, I wouldn't have to worry about being a target.

"Yes, of course. He and Cora can amuse each other."

Somehow, I doubted that it would work out quite like she envisioned. Cora might be amused by Macavity, but it would take more than a compact pooch with miniature legs and a basket full of toys to keep Macavity amused. Especially in a strange house, a larger prison than the boat, but still captivity.

"When do you leave?"

"Tomorrow mid-morning. Is that convenient?"

"No problem. I can be there at whatever time works for you."

Not only was it "no problem," it couldn't have been timed better. As soon as I hung up, I started making plans. I would leave my cell at home and use Terry's landline for calls. Although I had teased her in the past about still having a landline, at the moment I was grateful for it. I could leave my car in the marina as a decoy and have Logan drive me to Terry's. She didn't live that far away, and I could always hop a bus or take an Uber or a taxi if I needed to go someplace while staying there.

I called Logan and made arrangements for transport, put some clothes in a backpack, filled a bag with cat food, coffee, and cookies—the three "C" essentials—and set them aside for the morning. There were only two things left to do: get my landlord, Hudson, to take care of Bubbles V and Friend and pick up my computer and some client files from my office.

Macavity sensed something was up, and he was letting me know that he was pretty sure he wasn't going to like it by making noises deep down in his throat, not quite growling, but not exactly joyful burbling either. If he had known exactly what was going to happen the next day, he would have been furious. As it was, he was only at the pouting stage. Tomorrow he would rage.

Wednesday morning I got up early, put some food in Macavity's bowl and hustled up the steps while he was distracted. I barely made it out the hatch before an orange paw popped up through the space remaining between the slat inserts and the sliding hatch cover, preventing me from closing the hatch. Did he think he could flatten his full-figured cat body enough to slip through the narrow opening? Or was he making a statement, a one-pawed protest against the inevitable. We played a game of whack-a-mole, with me the whacker and his paw the mole, until I managed to poke his paw back far enough to pull the hatch closed.

I was fairly certain he was swearing at me in cat language as I got off the boat and headed for my office.

The first thing I did was feed Bubbles V and Friend. Then I grabbed the bowl and their two types of food and headed for Hudson's office. "Come in," he said when I knocked. As soon as he saw me, he started smiling. The smile stopped when he saw the fish.

"You can probably guess what I'm about to ask," I said, doing my best imitation of a helpless and needy woman. Hudson's old-fashioned chivalry usually worked to my advantage. Although I felt a little guilty using it to get what I wanted. Just a little, not all that much.

"You know what happened the last time you left one of your fish in my office."

"Don't worry. These two are healthy. And Emma doesn't even know yet that there's a back-up. And . . ." I put the fish food down on his desk. "This is a 7-day feeder block. You won't even have to bother feeding them for 7 days. Just enjoy their company. If I'm gone longer, you can use the regular fish food." I set the bowl on a side table next to a plant. "Besides, see how good that looks?"

"You plan on being gone about a week?"

"A week, maybe a little longer. I'm going to house sit for a friend who has a sick mother. And a dog. A well dog, but an old dog that needs tending."

I knew the sick mother and aging dog would soften any resistance Hudson might be experiencing. "Well, I guess I can take care of them for that long."

"You're the world's best landlord," I said. Then I paused.

"There's something else?" Hudson sounded wary.

"If anyone asks, don't tell them that I've gone away, okay? Just say you haven't seen me. That will be the truth, mostly."

"Has that guy you're worried about threatened you?" I'd given Hudson a high-level overview of why I'd wanted to tie up in plain sight for a while, but I hadn't gone into detail.

"No, but he's still angry about something I didn't even do. It's just easier if he thinks I'm here. I wouldn't want him showing up where I'm house-sitting."

Hudson nodded. "That's probably a good idea."

"If you need to get in touch, Logan will have the number. He'll also be checking on the *Aspara* from time to time. I'm taking Macavity with me." I nodded toward the fish. "Seriously, they're good company. They listen. Never talk back. And they're colorful."

Hudson smiled. "Take care of yourself."

"You too."

I organized what I needed from my office and sent copies of the files I'd taken photos of to John, with a brief explanation, and said I'd call him in a day or two to see if he'd found anything. Then I called Logan to let him know I was ready. He met me in the parking lot. After loading my office stuff in the car, I went to my locker to get my Sherpa Original Deluxe Animal Carrier. Only the best for Macavity. "With luck he'll think he's going to the vet."

"He doesn't mind going to the vet?"

"He hates it."

"Then . . .?"

"He'll hate this more."

Back at the boat, I asked, "Which do you want to carry, my bags or Macavity?"

"You're kidding, right?"

"Okay, let me go down and see if I can get him into the carrier."

Logan laughed. "Bryn the lion tamer."

"This is much worse; I think *they* use tranquilizers." I pulled the hatch back a few inches and peered inside. "Grab him if he gets past me."

I pushed back the hatch and dropped the carrier inside before hurrying down the steps. I found Macavity on his bunk, dozing almost peacefully. I set the carrier down on my bunk and opened the front flap. Then I reached over and picked him up. As soon as he realized what was happening, he started struggling. I had to shove him in and tip the carrier on end in order to zip it shut. "Good kitty." Sure.

He circled around his cage several times before throwing himself down like a kid having a tantrum. "I'm sorry. But it's for your own good." Isn't that what people always say when they are forcing you to do something they know you won't like?

I pulled back the hatch and handed my bag and pack up to Logan. He looked down at me. "I don't see any scratch marks."

"He puts up a good fight at times, but he doesn't play dirty."

Once at the car we both looked around to see if anyone was lurking nearby. As far as we could tell, the coast was clear. No potential enemies in sight. As a precaution, though, Logan took the car through several evasive maneuvers on the way to thwart anyone who might be following.

"I doubt that was necessary," I said after his third attempt to throw off any tails. "Butch isn't what I would call subtle."

"There could be someone else worried about what you've been up to."

"That has occurred to me. But I think the most pressing concern is Butch."

"In any case, I'm glad you're doing this."

"I haven't told Sophie yet. Or Ben. They are the only two I'm going to give Terry's phone number to. I told Hudson to contact you if he needs to get in touch."

"I approve."

"I'm probably overreacting."

"That's better than getting attacked by a crazy." He paused, then added, "Or a murderer."

"Or a crazed murderer."

Logan took a sudden right turn, studying his rearview mirror. I groaned. Ignoring speed limits, he raced down the residential street and made a left, pulling over to see if anyone came roaring after us. No one did.

"You're enjoying this," I said.

"Only because I don't think anyone is following us. But you have to promise that you'll call me if someone suspicious shows up at Terry's."

"What would make them suspicious?"

"You know what I mean. I'm just saying that you need to be careful. Keep your cell with you and call if you have the slightest inkling that something isn't right, okay?"

"I left my cell on the *Aspara*."

"Why did you . . . oh, so no one could trace you. Wouldn't it have been sufficient to have simply turned it off? Or temporarily removed the memory chip?"

"Too much fiddling around. Besides, Terry has a landline I can use. But, for the record, is it okay if I call the police before I call *you* if a crazed murderer appears on Terry's doorstep?" I was trying to make light of his concern.

"Only if you have them on speed dial." He laughed. "I assume you will put me in the number one spot on Terry's phone."

"Nothing is going to happen! That's why I'm doing this."

"I know. But I'm going to miss you."

"That's sweet."

"No one to wake me up in the middle of the night asking to be pulled out of the water. No one calling for help fending off a muscular and very angry construction worker. No one begging for me to search for her missing cat. No one . . ."

"I get the point."

"Let's just hope things get back to normal soon."

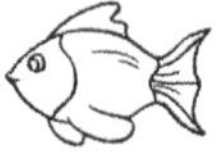

Terry was packed and ready to leave when we arrived. She stayed long enough to hand over the keys and to encourage me to make myself at home. "The stuff in the refrigerator won't keep. Please eat whatever you want."

"And the brownies are where?" I asked to make certain they were still part of the agreement. Terry laughed. "Leftovers in the freezer are labeled. I always make extra for times when I don't feel like cooking. Eat what you want."

"I'll try to leave a few scraps for your return."

We walked her out to her car and said our goodbyes. On the way back we stopped by Logan's car to pick up my stuff, including Macavity. "This is it, big guy. You're officially on vacation."

I put his cage on the floor in the living room just as Cora made her appearance. Her eyesight and sense of smell isn't the greatest, but she hesitated as though sensing there was another animal in her domain. As for Macavity, one look at Cora and he doubled in size, his fur standing straight up. He reminded me of the African puff adder I saw one time on a nature program.

"You trying to impress Cora or are you intimidated by an aging Corgi?" I asked, bending over his cage, my hand on the latch.

"You going to let him out?" Logan asked, eyeing Cora as if she was about to enter a Roman arena where the lion was waiting to attack.

"I have to some time." I pointed the opening toward Cora. "Get ready," I warned.

When I unzipped the flap of Macavity's carrier, it fell on the floor like the red carpet being rolled out for a celebrity. We were both prepared for Macavity to come racing out. But he didn't. Rather, he exited his cage like he was royalty about to take a stroll among the local peasants. Cora laid down on her side and whimpered while Macavity walked stiff legged over to her, sniffed, and then continued on into the other room. Cora got up and slowly followed like an obedient servant.

"This is interesting," Logan said.

"Let's have a cup of tea and a brownie," I suggested. "Let them get used to each other."

It felt good to relax in a cheerful kitchen and drink tea out of bone china cups. I only put out one brownie each, saving the rest for myself for later. While we sipped tea and tried to make our brownies last as long as possible, I shared my thoughts on what follow-up was needed in the investigation of Sabrina's death. I also told him about my meeting with the board treasurer and the unpleasant exchange with the unflappable and obnoxious Earl Grey.

"Have you discussed any of this with Ben?"

"Ben and I haven't had any discussions about anything lately. But, yes, I plan on telling him my thoughts."

"My money is still on Butch."

"That's just because you don't like him."

"Maybe. But he connects the dots between Sabrina, Blu-Sky and AHA."

"But I don't see how that constitutes motive. At least not without proof there was something illegal going on at Blu-Sky. And that Butch was somehow involved."

"We could be missing the obvious, maybe killing Sabrina was an accident."

"You mean he hit her one too many times? Or that he hit her and she fell on something that killed her? That kind of thing?"

"It could have happened that way."

"And the fact that she may have been investigating the company he works for is just a coincidence? And what about the time lapse between when she went missing and when she died? Oh, and have you forgotten that she may have been tied up?"

"When you put it that way—"

We were right back to where we had started our conversation.

Logan stayed a little over an hour. On his way out we were pleased to see Macavity and Cora sitting side by side on the floor next to the couch. Macavity was licking a paw. Cora was making snarfling noises but seemed okay sitting next to a cat. After all, she could have gone somewhere else. I wished I could tell Macavity it was only for a week and thank him for being such a good sport.

One crisis averted. It was time to make some calls.

Sophie was getting ready to meet Dane for drinks when I called. It seemed to me that she was doing that a lot lately. Oh well, the more she saw of him the sooner it would probably end. I gave her my contact information, warned her not to tell anybody, emphasizing the *anybody,* and said to have fun with Dane. She was nearing the two-month mark with him, so I didn't expect him to be around much longer. Although I doubted his name would quickly fade into the archival memory of past boyfriends. His role in causing me grief and making me a possible target for assault or worse, put him in a special category. His name would live on, even after he became history as far as Sophie's love life was concerned.

Ben answered his phone in spite of not recognizing the number. Or maybe because he didn't know it was me; it was hard to know for sure. I explained that I was house-sitting for a few days. It didn't seem necessary to tell him to stay mum about it, I mean, as tight-lipped as he was, who was he going to tell?

"I know you can't give me any details about the investigation, but could you at least reassure me that you are looking into BluSky Construction? I think they could be involved somehow."

"We're pursuing several lines of inquiry."

"That's definitely reassuring."

"Look, you've been helpful, and I appreciate that. I wish I could talk with you about what we've discovered so far, but I can't. And although we may not move as quickly on leads as you would like, we do get there eventually."

I wasn't willing to drop it there. "It's crossed my mind that Butch might not be the guilty party but could still be involved. What if he unwittingly said something to Sabrina that made her suspicious of BluSky? Or what if she was already looking into BluSky and said something to him that he then passed along, perhaps innocently?"

"Got it. But you do realize that it wouldn't be appropriate for me to share details of our investigation with you?"

"I understand. I do. And I'm confident you know what you're doing."

"But . . .?"

"No 'but.' I'm just anxious to see this resolved."

"As am I."

After I hung up, I realized I hadn't been entirely honest with Ben. There were several "buts." *But* I wasn't sure it was a top priority with them. *But* I wasn't convinced they were pursuing all possible suspects now that they had Arthur in custody. *But* they hadn't studied AHA's financial documents. Well, I didn't know that for sure. *But* if someone had looked at them, they may not have been as determined to find evidence of fraud as I was. My conversation with Ben left me feeling like I was reading a book, had just reached an action packed, page turning chapter, and was being forced to put the book aside. Not something I was good at.

As I sat there reflecting on my conversation with Ben, I regretted not calling Tom Thomson to warn him off. I should have done that before coming to Terry's. Maybe tomorrow I could go somewhere and buy a burner phone, or if Logan came by, I could use his cell. A week was a long time. Anything could happen. Or nothing could happen. Both were unsettling prospects.

There's something about being in someone else's home that feels a bit unnerving when it gets dark. The creaks and groans that make up the house's personality are all unfamiliar. The icemaker clunking. The electric heat coming on. Squirrels, or some other kind of critters, running across the roof. Cars pulling into driveways up and down the street. Strange dogs barking at real or imagined noises. And Cora snorting from time to time as she lapsed into some doggie dream.

I was finally getting used to some of the disquieting house noises and was about to turn in when I thought I heard something that was all too familiar and definitely not good: a door opening. Then the sound of muffled footsteps. Footsteps that were coming in my direction.

Chapter 21

The Curious Incident of the Dog in the Night-time

There was a thin stream of light coming in from a full moon, but not enough visibility to help me locate something I could use for a weapon. I hadn't thought to bring my pepper spray with me. Stupid, stupid, stupid.

The footsteps were getting closer. Why wasn't Cora barking? What good was a dog that didn't warn you when there was an intruder in the house?

I moved behind the guest room door, wishing I had street clothes and shoes on. My flimsy nightgown didn't seem like appropriate attire for fending off a burglar . . . or . . .? Whoever it was had paused just outside my door. "I have a gun and I'm not afraid to use it," I yelled. Desperately wishing that was true.

"Terry?" a hesitant male voice said. The intruder knew Terry's name?

"Who are you?" I wasn't sure that burglars used their real names, but it was worth a try.

There was a slight pause. "Who are *you*?" Then, louder, "Terry? Terry?" The footsteps headed away from the door in the direction of Terry's bedroom.

I grabbed a robe and a lamp and returned to my position behind the door.

Moments later the man came back and stopped on the other side of the door. "Where's Terry?" he asked. I wasn't sure I wanted him to know there was no one else in the house.

"Why don't you tell me who you are first. Then I'll tell you about Terry."

"I'm Blake Landau, Terry's brother. Who are you?"

Terry did have a brother, but I couldn't for the life of me remember his name. And how did I know that was really the person standing just the other side of the bedroom door? "Prove it."

"What do you want me to do?"

"Slip your driver's license under the door."

"Only after you tell me who you are and why you're in the guest room when Terry's not here."

"I'm a friend. Now slip your driver's license under the door." I was trying desperately to remember if Blake was her brother's name, but I was coming up with zilch. It seemed unlikely someone would show up at this hour claiming to be her brother if he was really a burglar or hired muscle, but I couldn't see how it would hurt to play it safe.

"Just a minute." I heard some muffled sounds of something happening, then I saw a card being pushed under the door. I reached down and picked it up, flipping on the light so I could see the picture on it. I couldn't remember the last time I'd seem Terry's brother, but there did seem to be a family resemblance. And the last name was right.

"What are you doing here? Terry didn't mention you'd be dropping by. Especially not in the middle of the night."

"Well, if you must know, my girlfriend kicked me out. There weren't any lights on, so I assumed Terry was already in bed. I remembered where she keeps a spare key outside, so I let myself in. I was planning on staying in the guest room."

"This room?"

"No problem, I'll be fine on the couch. But I'd like my driver's license back."

"Give me a minute and I'll meet you in the kitchen."

I heard him walking away. I slipped out of my nightgown and pulled on a pair of jeans and a T-shirt. I didn't bother combing my hair.

Neither Cora nor Macavity so much as opened an eye as I passed through the living room. They apparently didn't care who came into the house as long as their beauty rest wasn't interrupted. Or maybe I underestimated Cora. Perhaps, like in the Sherlock Holmes story, it was the fact that she hadn't barked that should have told me she recognized the intruder.

Blake had put on the hot water and asked if I wanted a cup of tea. "Sure." I handed him his driver's license and sat down at the table. He was a few years younger than Terry, somewhere in his late 30's, boyish looking, with sandy blond hair and blue eyes. "Sorry your girlfriend kicked you out."

"She had her reasons." He was looking at me as if he, too, was trying to reconcile vague memories with the person across from him.

"It's been a while," I acknowledged. "Someone's wedding, I think."

"I've been away; I only recently returned to the area."

"New job?"

"No, my girlfriend got a job here and I followed. Now I have no job and no girlfriend."

"Bummer." I couldn't think of anything else to say.

"So, where's Terry?"

Oh boy. On top of what he just told me, now I had to tell him about his mother. "Your mother wasn't feeling well and Terry went to help out." Please don't let him ask me what's wrong with her.

Blake collapsed on a chair and put his head in his hands, as if he was about to break down, perhaps cry. I didn't know what to do so I said something inane: "It will be okay. You have to give it time. Your mom's in good hands and as for the rest, well . . ." I'm a good listener, and that was apparently what Blake needed. When I got up to get our tea, he started telling me about what had happened and why. All I had to do was nod occasionally, and mutter a few “uh-huhs.” We went through two cups of tea each before he asked me the question I’d been dreading.

“I don’t know what to do. What do *you* think I should do?”

It’s not that I’m unsympathetic about people’s relationship problems. I’ve lived through quite a few with Sophie and Logan as well as several of my own. The one thing I’ve learned is that there are no quick fixes, no easy answers. No duct tape for relationships.

“You need to finish your tea, try to get some rest, and consider talking with her about this tomorrow.” I sounded as confident as Dr. Ruth, but the image that swept through my mind was Lucy charging a nickel for advice.

He dutifully drank down his remaining tea, thanked me for talking with him, and headed for the couch. I went back to the guest room and tried to recapture that moment when I’d felt relaxed enough to get some shuteye. I didn’t think I would ever go to sleep, but the next thing I knew sharp strands of sunshine were poking around the corners of Terry’s floral curtains.

When I got up, I found Blake and Cora curled up together on the couch. Macavity was apparently already on the prowl. I caught up with him in Terry’s office, sniffing the furniture, probably finding Cora’s scent everywhere. “Come on,” I said. “Time for breakfast.” As if he understood what I’d said, he dutifully followed me into the kitchen and waited until I opened the can that contained his equivalent of bacon and eggs, plopped it into the cat serving dish I’d brought with me and placed it on the floor next to a ceramic bowl with a dog paw print design. The two could dine together—sweet.

I had coffee made and had eaten two pieces of toast with Terry’s excellent blueberry jam when Blake came in. “Do I smell coffee?”

I poured a cup for him. “Cream or sugar?”

"A little cream, please." He sat down at the table. He hadn't changed out of his clothes, and he had a crease on the side of his face from the welting on the throw pillow on the couch. I offered him toast, but he said he wasn't hungry. I poured myself another cup of coffee and sat down across from him.

"You should call Terry," I said. "It's fine with me if you stay here, although I'd rather not leave for a couple of days. She'd probably be okay with you staying in her bedroom."

"You'd rather not leave? Do you live nearby?" He seemed genuinely interested in something other than his girlfriend for the first time since he'd arrived. The next thing I knew I was telling him *my* problems, just like he had dumped *his* on me the night before. I explained that I hadn't mentioned any of this to his sister because I hadn't wanted to worry her. But that I would prefer to give the police a few days to make some progress on the case, and Butch a few days to cool down, before heading home. That is, if he, Blake, didn't mind sharing the house and the brownies.

Blake not only didn't mind sharing house-sitting duties, he welcomed the distraction. He immediately started trying to make sense out of everything I'd told him, exploring possibilities and posing several new theories. After a lull in the conversation, he said, "There's one thing that doesn't feel right to me. I mean, I hang out with the guys, sometimes play cards. What I can't picture is why Butch's boss would take him to a poker game when the rest of the players were white collar types. From your description of Butch, it doesn't seem like he would fit in."

"Maybe they needed an extra body."

"Could be. But what if it's more than that? What if there's a connection between the two. I mean, what if Butch and his boss were into some kind of scam together? Maybe the boss felt he couldn't say 'no' if Butch wanted to play poker."

"And Butch got wind of Sabrina's investigation . . ."

". . . and one of them eliminated the threat."

"One's a murderer and the other's an accomplice." I chewed on the idea for a minute. "Given that scenario, why would Sabrina had been tied up before her death? And why would Butch go along with the murder of his girlfriend?"

"I thought you said he threatened you and that you came here in part to avoid a confrontation with him."

"True. He's an abuser and a thug, but he just doesn't strike me as a cold-blooded killer."

"Or, maybe you're right and Butch was nothing more than an extra body for the game. Maybe his boss was scamming AHA on his own, using an inside man."

"Or woman."

"Some man or woman on the inside who was cooking the books to cover the scam."

"So, Butch's boss or the inside person could be the killer. And Butch isn't even in the loop. But once his girlfriend is murdered, you'd think he would become suspicious." Was I giving Butch too much credit?

"Not necessarily. The people doing the actual work don't necessarily see the paperwork for a project. Maybe he truly didn't have a clue."

"Unless they were using substandard supplies and charging top dollar. If that was the scam, then Butch might be able to connect the dots, right?"

"Yes. But that isn't the only possible scam." After a brief pause, he said: "Then how about this. Someone on the inside has something illegal cooking and it involves BluSky. Sabrina uncovers discrepancies in their financials that make her suspicious. She mentions it to Butch, and he tells his boss."

"Wouldn't that make Butch as much of a threat as Sabrina? If he wasn't directly involved, that is."

"Maybe he'll be the next person to disappear. You never know."

"That still leaves us with the question about who framed Arthur. Assuming he's innocent."

"If Butch is upset with you because he thinks you're badmouthing him behind his back, he's undoubtedly been complaining about you, probably to anyone who will listen. Like to poker player buddies. Maybe it was his loose lips that gave one of the poker players the idea to use the statute to frame Arthur."

"That means it could be someone at the poker table other than Butch's boss who is connected to the illegal activities at AHA. Wish I could explore their connections. But that's not something I can do. That's a police thing."

"Butch is the direct link to all of this," Blake said. "I feel sure of it. Maybe you need to talk to him."

"You want me to just walk up to Butch and ask whether his boss is doing something shady? Or did any of the other poker players seem unusually interested in the statue I pulled up from the lake? Or maybe I should just ask him if he killed his girlfriend?"

"Why not? I'll go with you."

It took me a moment to realize Blake was serious. Maybe he was right. By talking to Butch I might learn something, and it would give me a chance to diffuse the situation with him. Even if the police didn't solve the murder, I wanted to go home sometime in the not-too-distant future. Of course, there was always the possibility that a chat with Butch could make things worse. I would have to try hard not to let that happen.

Without warning, Macavity jumped up into my lap. I took his orange face in my hands and asked, "What do you say, can you dog sit for a while?"

Chapter 22

A Day Without Sunshine

"This is a stupid idea," I said as Blake drove us to the construction site.

"There's two of us."

"But he's big. And mean."

"We can do this—" Blake sounded confident; but then, he hadn't met Butch . . . yet.

The construction site was huge, the partially built building still in the stage where you could see its bones and had to imagine the rest. The ground around it was uneven, mounds of dirt waiting to be leveled and landscaped once the disruptive building process was complete. No use cleaning up if more messes were going to be made.

An excavator and a backhoe loader sat idle off to the side of the building, like sleeping monsters guarding their worksite. Men in hard hats and bright-colored safety vests were scattered around the site, some working in two's and three's on various parts of the building, some standing around, perhaps planning what needed to be done next, others surveying what was in progress.

There was a chain-link fence that enclosed most of the site, but there was an opening large enough for big equipment to go through just across the street from where Blake pulled over and parked. It was probably shut at night, but it meant we could walk right in without permission. I was almost sorry there wasn't a barrier preventing us from easy access.

If Butch hadn't been at the construction site, or if he hadn't been willing to talk, things might have played out differently. But he was there, and he calmly agreed to having a conversation without displaying the slightest reluctance to do so. Maybe he didn't want to cause a fuss in front of his fellow workers. For whatever reason, he motioned us to follow him to the edge of the work area, far enough away from equipment sounds so we could talk without shouting.

On the drive to the construction site, Blake and I had strategized about what to ask Butch and in what order. We had decided to start with the issue we were convinced had something to do with Sabrina's disappearance, the possibility that BluSky was involved in something shady or criminal. We had agreed I should take the lead on this, jumping right in so as not to give him a chance to give too much thought about his answer.

"I know you have to get back to work, so I'll get right to the point." I paused just long enough to put on my "this is serious" face. "We think BluSky is skimming money from their contract with AHA and that you know all about it."

"No way," Butch responded, clearly agitated by the accusation. Was it my imagination, or could I see the corded muscles in his arms twitching? "They have plenty of business. They don't need to cheat." He added that his boss was a great guy, hard-working and a straight arrow.

"So, you never talked with Sabrina about the BluSky-AHA connection?" I said.

"No, there was nothing to talk about."

We had agreed to switch off asking question, so it was Blake's turn. He asked Butch about the poker game, what was said and if Butch repeated the story about the statue to anyone.

"Hey, you think I'm some schoolgirl passing along gossip? Sure, we drink and tell stories on poker night. But that's where it stops."

"You didn't talk to anyone at BluSky or AHA about the statue story?"

"We don't have time to stand around and tell stories at work. And who would I talk to at AHA? I don't even know anyone there."

"You don't go out for a beer after work occasionally?"

"Sure, but we have better things to talk about than some stupid statue."

My turn. "Did Sabrina say anything to you about her audit of AHA?"

"Nah. We didn't talk about her work." He puffed up a bit. "Our relationship wasn't like that. Besides, I'd broken up with her by then."

"I was under the impression that *she* broke up with you."

"No way." He gave us a toothy snicker. "She couldn't get enough of me."

Blake apparently didn't like Butch's comment. Maybe he was a little sensitive about the whole breaking up thing. For whatever reason, he suddenly became confrontive.

"You're hiding something," he said loudly and more accusative than he perhaps should have. "And I know *she* dumped *you*. But that doesn't explain why you don't seem to give a damn about who murdered her."

"Who says . . ." Butch's fist was aimed at Blake's face when I leapt in and pushed Blake aside. Then I stepped in close to Butch as he turned toward me and kneed him in the crotch like I'd been taught to do in my self-defense class. Butch doubled over in pain, but I didn't for one moment think he was down for the count.

I glanced around and saw that several other burly looking construction workers were figuring out that something wasn't quite right. All for one and one for all was probably their motto. I grabbed Blake's arm. "Come on. It's time to get out of here."

He shook off my hand, ready to stand his ground, apparently hoping to regain his dignity. Then he looked in the direction I was pointing and saw the other workers headed our way. Without another word we hotfooted it out of there.

"Sorry," Blake said as we drove off.

"Don't be. I doubt he'll go to the police. After all, he tried to throw the first punch. And he's not going to want to admit that I kneed him. The big man taken down by a woman? I think we're in the clear."

"You were right though. Trying to talk to him was a stupid idea."

"No argument there."

"Thank you, by the way. You're pretty good at that kneeing thing." I heard the compliment, but I knew what he was thinking, that *he* had been there to protect me, not the other way around.

"Hey, you might have ducked and counterpunched if I hadn't shoved you. It was just a reflex reaction."

Blake shook his head. "No, I didn't see it coming. Since my girlfriend kicked me out, I'm not myself."

Before he could sink back into ennui about his broken relationship, I suggested he pull over and let me make a couple of calls on his phone. One of the two could change where we were headed.

I called Tom Thompson first. He didn't answer, so I left him a message telling him that he should definitely not be pursuing any issues related to Sabrina's audit investigation and that I would explain everything to him later. I added that at least one person was being physically threatening and that we needed to let the police handle things from this point on. Out of the corner of my eye I caught Blake smiling at my comment about the police. When I clicked off, I turned to him and said, "I'm going to do exactly what I told him."

"Want me to head to the police station?"

"Very funny."

John answered right away and said that he'd received the documents I'd sent and had been looking at them at that very moment. He didn't question how they had come into my possession. And he was more than happy to give me his assessment.

"How soon would you be available?" I asked. Blake poked me in the ribs, pointed at himself and mouthed "include me." I rolled my eyes and mouthed back, "Of course."

"I have some time this afternoon. Why don't we meet for coffee after work, say 5:30 or 6:00?"

"Actually, I'm house-sitting for a friend. And someone else is working on this with me now. He would like to be there too. Why don't we all meet at my friend's place? I'll make us coffee."

When he agreed, I gave him Terry's address and asked that he not mention to anyone that I was staying there. He didn't sound the least bit surprised at the request and agreed to be there before 6:00. He really did have some admirable traits.

"Now what?" Blake asked.

"Now we go back to Terry's and wait." Blake looked disappointed.

"I have copies of what I sent to John. You can review them before he comes, okay? Get up to speed."

"Those documents from AHA–should I ask how you got them?"

"I was given permission to look at them. Let's leave it at that, okay?"

"No problem. Just hope we find something incriminating."

"Me too. And if we do, I'll call my police friend."

Changing topics, Blake asked, "So, what's the name of your boat?"

"The *Aspara*."

"*Aspara*. Is that short for asparagus?"

"Tacky. I didn't think *you* would go there."

"So, I'm not the first."

"It didn't cross my mind that *anyone* would think that when I named her *Aspara*."

"Where did you come up with the name?"

"It's from a book, *Islandia*. There was a boat named *Aspara* in the book. It was supposed to mean *seagull.*"

"You named your boat after a seagull?"

"They were more appealing in the novel than the ones around here."

"I would hope so. Dirty white, harsh screech, scavengers."

"They aren't that bad."

"Never liked seagulls."

"I can tell."

"You like living on a boat?"

"I do. Every time I go away, I feel like I'm abandoning her. A boat is more than a plaything or a place to live. It has a personality, an identity unique to its existence. At least an older wooden boat does. I'm not so sure about modern fiberglass boats made from cookie-cutter molds. Although sometimes I wish I didn't have all of the upkeep."

"How does your cat like living on a boat?"

"He doesn't talk about it much."

"You know what I mean."

"He likes routine and being in one place, so he might prefer a house. But he copes."

Blake and I stopped at the grocery on the way back to Terry's. Since there were two of us, we thought we needed to spring for some of the food rather than eating up all of Terry's reserves. Although her reserves were far better than anything we could whip together on our own.

Blake perused the AHA documents while I put together a late lunch. We were just finishing up our sandwiches and a shared bag of chips when John arrived. We offered him coffee and some store-bought cookies. He accepted the coffee but turned down the cookies. I couldn't help wondering if his eating habits were as fastidious as his clothes. There was no way I could picture him wolfing down a bag of Doritos in front of the TV.

He had a leather briefcase with him. He sat down across from us, put his briefcase on a chair and pulled out a file. "I printed what you sent me." When he opened the file, I noticed there were lines highlighted in yellow on the top page. Then, as he spread out a few of the pages, I could see red checkmarks and tiny stars next to some paragraphs.

"Looks like you found a few things," Blake observed. He commented while chewing a cookie, his mouth opening and closing as he spoke. John's eye flicked in his direction, but if he disapproved of talking with your mouth full, he didn't make it more obvious than that one subtle glance.

"I wish I could tell you definitively what Sabrina was looking into. But I can't. She didn't make any notes or leave any marks on these pages. But . . ."

"But . . .?" Blake and I said in unison.

"There are a couple of things that strike me as interesting." He was stringing it out, whether for drama or because there was nothing terribly incriminating, it was hard to tell.

"These are the pages you identified from her office review." He pushed two-thirds of the documents off to one side. "And these are the ones you identified as documents she requested from Arthur." He separated out several pages from the boat pile. "She could have asked for extra pages to make sure Arthur couldn't figure out what she was focusing on. Like budget projections."

"That's what I've thought, too. She was smart. But I think she may have overestimated Arthur's interest in the numbers."

Blake smirked, and I stepped on his foot under the table to keep him from commenting.

"When I compared the two sets of documents, it was clear she had areas of interest for follow-up. She didn't apparently ask for more information on things such as cash flow, debt, expenses, assets, payroll documentation, depreciation schedules, taxes."

"That seems like it covers almost everything," Blake observed.

"Not quite." John turned a few pages around to face us. "She asked to see the internal control structure. In addition, she wanted a second look at invoices and contracts with vendors, including how the bidding process was handled. She also asked for budget projections, but I think that may have been a distraction or a way to view potential fraud within the larger framework."

"Were a lot of the invoices related to BluSky?" I asked.

"A number of them were. But they also hired architects, interior decorators, and some marketing specialists. They even hired a lobbyist."

"I think the Board's oversight might have been lacking."

"That wouldn't surprise me."

"Help me understand where the potential for fraud comes in given these areas of interest for Sabrina." Blake was studying the red checkmarks and starred portions of the documents John had put in front of us.

"A construction company would be at the top of my list," John explained. "They can overcharge or even skimp on materials and skim off the top. It's been a problem that's occurred in a lot of places, although not so much in our state. Our construction community isn't as extensive as in larger cities."

"What about someone in the chain skimming off money from grants or donations?"

"It's possible. But there are safeguards in place."

"You told me that board members can be too trusting. That long-time employees in need of money are the most likely to commit fraud."

"That's harder to discern from an audit."

"I think it comes back to Butch," Blake said. "I don't trust the guy. If he wasn't directly responsible for her death, then he did or said something that resulted in it."

I found myself nodding in agreement.

"A day without sunshine is like, you know, night."

John and I both stared at Blake. "What does that mean?"

"It's something Steve Martin said. Sometimes the obvious answer is the answer."

Chapter 23

Showdown

To my surprise, John stayed for a glass of wine. Macavity came in to see what was happening, gave John the onceover, then disappeared back into the living room to spend the evening with his new friend, Cora.

"A handsome cat," John observed as Macavity departed.

I appreciated the comment, but I noted he had made no effort to engage with Macavity. Maybe after a second glass of wine—

The conversation between the three of us didn't exactly sparkle after we quit talking about the AHA audit and Sabrina. We didn't seem to have a lot in common, although from time to time someone would throw out a new topic as a trial balloon. It became clear that John wasn't a TV watcher or a comedy aficionado. Blake tried talking about team sports, with no takers. John mentioned a biography he was reading. That was received with a yawn by Blake and a blank stare from me. We all avoided politics and religion like we'd been taught to do when interacting with strangers. It wasn't until John asked if Blake was visiting his sister that we zeroed in on a topic. Blake confessed that his girlfriend had kicked him out, and John displayed sympathy and offered what seemed like sound advice in equal measures. Who would have thought he could play Dear Abby?

It was no surprise that John called it quits at two glasses of wine. And I admit to being relieved when he said he needed to leave. Junk food was calling out to me. I needed something salty or sweet, but I'd been hesitant to start chowing down in John's presence. Why I was concerned about his disapproval, I'm not sure. Ironically, Blake must have been feeling the same way. As soon as the door shut behind John, Blake got out the remaining chips and cookies. “Is that guy for real?” he asked.

“Hey, he was very nice to you. And it was good of him to review those documents for me.”

“He’s got a thing for you, that’s for sure.”

“I don’t think so. Not anymore. I’ve made it clear that we can only be friends.”

“You may *think* you’ve made it clear. But he may still be hoping for more.”

“Him and my mother.” I poured myself some more wine.

“It’s hard to give up hope.” Blake poured himself some wine. “I should know.” He raised his glass. “Sometimes, against all odds, we hope.”

“Are you quoting someone?”

“Probably—although it sounds more like a Hallmark card, doesn’t it?”

“Well, I’m impressed.” We clicked glasses.

Blake half drained his glass and asked, “What’s on for tomorrow?”

“Want another round with Butch?”

“No thanks. Unless *you* do.”

“I’m not sure I could count on kneeing him a second time.”

“Isn’t there someone else we could ask about BluSky?”

I gave that some thought. “Maybe I could ask Earl about them. He’s tracked all of their invoices. And I wanted to talk to him about if he knew why Arthur had switched audit firms.”

“You didn’t seem to think he was very forthcoming before.”

“He wasn’t. Yet, ‘Sometimes, against all odds, we hope.’”

Blake laughed. “Maybe you could nudge him with some of the facts you’ve uncovered. Some of the stuff John mentioned.”

“You’re right. He might open up a bit to avoid looking like he’s part of a cover-up.”

"Unless he *is* part of a cover-up."

"I suppose he could be the inside man, but it doesn't seem likely."

"Why not?"

"He doesn't strike me as someone willing to take that kind of a risk. But if BluSky has been skimming, it's not a very original scam. Earl could have noticed when doing routine checks."

"Okay, then we talk to Earl."

"We?"

"Well, you. Or maybe you and me. Whatever. Tomorrow."

"Tomorrow."

Talking to Earl was probably something I shouldn't be doing, but it beat sitting around doing nothing. Unless Ben called me with new information before then, Blake and I could continue nosing around a little. Hopefully avoiding any more physical confrontations.

Logan called around 9:00 p.m. to check in and make sure everything was okay. So did Sophie. Blake disappeared into the other room to watch TV. Macavity and Cora curled up together next to Blake on the coach. It was time for me to call it a night. I looked forward to finishing off my day with one of the books I'd brought with me. Unfortunately, I only got a few pages into it before falling asleep and crushing a couple of pages.

When Ben failed to check in the following morning, Blake and I headed downtown. We found a parking lot near AHA that charged way too much for a lot filled with cracked cement, faded demarcation lines and a fees collection box that looked like it had been vandalized. Even given its dilapidated appearance, there were only a few spaces left. We found one next to an old Ford Taurus with a dent in the driver's door. Blake was reluctant to leave his car there, but I convinced him we wouldn't be long.

When we arrived at the brick building where AHA was located, we stopped at the entrance and started arguing about whether it was better for me to go in alone or if Blake should come in with me. Several people stepped warily around us before we managed to make it into the lobby while continuing to disagree. It took a lot to convince him it would be best if I talked to Earl alone. Earl was a stickler for protocol, and although he had been instructed to share information with me, Blake didn't fall under the same umbrella. Reluctantly, Blake finally agreed to hang out in the tiny lobby.

"I'll act as greeter," he said. "Say 'hello' and direct people to the elevator."

"Good idea," I said, thinking to myself that I'd better get in and out before Blake got arrested for loitering.

A couple of people nodded at me as I made my way to Earl's office, but no one questioned why I was there. Nonprofits have a larger turnover than most corporations, and a lot of interns and volunteers coming and going, so they tend to be fairly relaxed about strangers in their midst.

Earl was in his office, wearing his uniform of gray and darker gray. I poked my head in and asked if he had a moment. He did his reflexive glance-at-his-watch routine, as if he were in high demand for all sorts of important meetings. My dislike of the man rose in my throat like acid reflux. Without waiting for an invitation, I stepped inside his office and closed the door.

Blake and I had decided what I needed to ask Earl about BluSky, but, seeing him sitting there looking like a Dickensian villain, I suddenly reconsidered my earlier defense of him as an unlikely candidate for fraud . . . and even murder. Call it a hunch, instinct, interpersonal acuity or just a foolish impulse. But the allegation that came out of my mouth surprised even me.

"I know you were embezzling money. I had someone analyze the financial records you showed me and compare them to those Arthur set aside for Sabrina." I paused to let what I'd said sink in. Earl waited for me to continue, his face expressionless. "What I don't know is whether BluSky was in on it or not. Were you partners in crime or were you playing it solo? Want to enlighten me?" If he was innocent, this was his chance to prove it.

"I have no idea what you are talking about." He sounded perfectly calm, as if I had said something about the weather rather than accusing him of a crime.

"I know Sabrina was investigating AHA's relationship with BluSky. You were either the instigator or the accomplice. You tell me which."

His pale brown eyes had turned mud colored. That was the only indication that what I'd said had gotten to him. He still seemed passionless, like someone extremely unlikely to make the top ten suspect list in any murder investigation. But then, I was assuming that the fraud and murder were linked. Maybe they weren't. It was possible Sabrina's murder had been a crime of passion unrelated to any fraud being committed by someone connected to AHA.

"I repeat, I have absolutely no idea what you are talking about. Now, if you don't mind, I have work to do." He looked down at the papers on his desk, dismissing me.

But I wasn't about to be dismissed without giving it one last try. "Someone told you about me retrieving the statue, didn't they?"

There was no visible change in his demeanor. He continued staring at the papers on his desk.

"The police will be able to figure out who you may have talked with about the statue. Or overheard talking about the statue. Once I tell them about your participation in the fraud, they will question everyone you've come in contact with during the last month. That's all it will take."

He continued to ignore me. I may have scored a mental punch, but there didn't appear to be any physical fight in him. Even if he had skimmed some money somewhere, I couldn't imagine him possessing either the energy or the will to kill Sabrina to keep her quiet.

I wondered how long I could carry on a one-sided conversation before I provoked him into saying something incriminating. If I *could* provoke this lifeless lump of a man into any kind of response. Silently conceding defeat, I gave up and headed for the stairs. End game. I'd given it my best shot. It was up to Ben to run with the meager facts I'd uncovered.

It was luck rather than skill or cunning that saved me. I had just started down the stairs when I noticed I had a shoelace that had come untied. If I hadn't bent over to re-tie it, I wouldn't have noticed that there was someone creeping down the steps right behind me. If I'd been standing, he could have shoved me down the long stretch of cement steps. Instead, I screamed when I felt his presence, leapt up and rammed my head into his midsection. That wasn't something I'd learned in a class; that was my survival instinct kicking in.

Within seconds there were several people crowded onto the tiny landing at the entrance to the stairs, wanting to know what had happened. Earl mumbled something about *me* attacking *him.* I countered that it was the other way around, but they all knew mild-mannered Earl, and none of them had a clue who I was.

"Someone call the police, please." My voice was shaking and was perhaps a shade louder than necessary for the confined space. The people on the landing peered down at us, then looked at each other, unsure what to do.

"There's no need for that," Earl said. "I don't intend to press charges."

"But why would she attack you?" someone asked.

"What's going on?" another voice chimed in. "What happened?"

"Who are you?" a woman asked me. "What are you doing here?"

While they tried to sort it out, I took out my cell and speed-dialed Ben. When Ben answered, I said, "You need to get over to AHA asap. I think I have your murderer."

There was a collective gasp as what I said drifted up to the group on the landing. Then everyone fell silent.

Next, I called Blake and told him where I was. I heard him say, "Coming."

No one seemed to want to look at Earl—all eyes were on me. But I was looking at Earl. He had gotten smaller, shrunk inside himself as if he had become an old man in an instant. An old man I had accused of murder in front of colleagues. I certainly hoped I was right.

All of a sudden, Earl pushed me aside and started down the stairs. Unfortunately for him, Blake picked that moment to come running up from below, flashing some credentials at the group peering down at us.

"My back-up will be here momentarily," he called up to them. "Stop where you are," he said to Earl.

Earl hesitated. Blake reached out and grabbed his shoulder, forcing him around. "Everyone," he yelled. "Let's go back inside." When no one moved, he yelled, "*Now*."

Maybe because I knew he wasn't official, I was amazed when everyone quietly obeyed. Even Earl let Blake escort him up the stairs and back into the main office area. Once inside, Blake kept a firm hold on Earl's arm while Earl's colleagues fanned out into a circle, waiting for the drama to unfold. There was mumbling back and forth, but no one was challenging Blake's authority. Maybe he looked like an undercover cop to them. To me he looked like, well, like Terry's younger brother.

I got Ben on the phone again and explained where we were. He assured me they were minutes away. "Please wait until the, ah, back-up arrives," I said to the group. Given that Blake and I had no authority, it seemed like the best way to ensure that Earl didn't try to escape again was to have everyone stay where they were.

Not that it looked as though anyone wanted to leave—one of their own had been accused of murder; they wanted to see how things played out. We all stood there, frozen in the moment, as if posing for a photographer. Although no one was smiling.

Literally no one moved and nothing happened until Ben and two officers arrived.

It took a while to sort things out. Blake handed Earl over to one of the officers who looked uncertain about what to do. "He's a flight risk," Blake said with the confident knowledge of someone who has seen or read enough police procedurals to mimic some of the language used.

Ben told everyone they could go back to their desks. They were reluctant to leave but were obviously still too stunned by the unfolding events to resist authority.

Then Ben took me aside and asked me to bring him up to speed. I explained that I had evidence to suggest that Sabrina had suspected Earl of fraud. That when I confronted him, he hadn't admitted it, but he had followed me into the stairway and tried to push me down the stairs.

Ben interrupted. "What were you thinking? Why didn't you let me handle this?"

"The evidence I have isn't exactly ironclad," I said. "I wanted to see if I could get a little more out of him before turning everything over to you."

"You think he killed Sabrina?"

"I didn't think so at first. But he was willing enough to get rid of *me*. Although I don't know what he would have done if the fall hadn't killed me. I mean, I didn't notice if he had a weapon—did he?"

"I didn't see one. But let's worry about that in a bit. Tell me why you think he killed Sabrina."

I quickly gave him a high-level overview of what I had learned by tracing Sabrina's investigation. It sounded more convincing than I'd realized when confronting Earl. The dots were all connecting in my mind. There's nothing like a life-threatening scare to focus one's thinking.

"It's possible he didn't intend to murder her," I said. "At least at first. I mean, he kept her alive for several days. Maybe she didn't know the identity of her kidnapper. Maye he'd hoped to cover his tracks and then release her . . . if . . . if I hadn't retrieved the statue."

"You can't blame yourself for her death. He may have been keeping her alive until he verified what she knew and who she had talked to. That is, *if* he is the murderer. There are still quite a few loose ends."

"But if I'm right about this, having the statue enabled him to frame Arthur."

"That's possible," Ben conceded. "We'll talk more about this later. Meanwhile, I need to know whether you intend to press assault charges."

"Should I?" I wasn't sure; it seemed an insignificant act given that he had most likely murdered Sabrina.

"It might help us hold him while we investigate. And I need those documents you referred to. Bring them with you to the station."

At this point, Ben was taking a lot on faith; I sincerely hoped I was right and that we would be able to prove my allegations.

On the way back to Terry's to pick up the documents, Blake's driving was a bit erratic. As he relived what he'd done, he kept getting excited. Each time he thought of some new detail he would press his foot down on the gas. I had to remind him that having escaped a plunge down a steep flight of cement stairs, I was not looking forward to ending up in a tangle of crushed cars.

Then, it suddenly occurred to him that I had saved myself *before* he arrived. "Were you walking downstairs *with* him? Or did he sneak up on you?" he asked.

"I thought I was alone and only saw him at the last minute," I admitted. "As he was about to shove me down the stairs. My body reacted even though my brain didn't."

"You were lucky."

"Don't I know it."

A young officer in a freshly pressed uniform took the files from me and disappeared down a hall lined with people standing or sitting on what looked like uncomfortable wood chairs. One woman was holding a crying baby, bouncing it up and down, trying to ignore the irritated looks from those around her.

A few minutes later, two more uniformed officers came to take our statements. I went with one, Blake with the other. In spite of the fact that I was both the potential victim and the one who had been investigating Sabrina's disappearance even *before* the murder took place, my interview finished before Blake's. I assumed he was giving the officer an earful, so I sat down at the end of the row of chairs to wait it out. I noted that the woman with the baby was gone and felt guilty for being thankful that I didn't have to listen to the baby's distressed plea to fix whatever was bothering him or her.

There seemed to be a lot of activity in the main room, but I couldn't make out what was happening. And Ben was nowhere in sight. It was very frustrating to sit there wondering what Earl was telling them. Would Ben get a confession out of him? Or would Earl maintain it was all a misunderstanding and then clam up until he talked with a lawyer? Even if he refused to confess, I felt certain truth would out. I remembered Aristotle's suggestion that truth sometimes needed a little help finding its way into the world. However, in this instance, I believed that once the police started looking more carefully into AHA's finances, logic rather than emotion or ethos would prevail.

It was amazing how quickly I had gone from thinking Earl was innocent to believing he was a murderer. Hopefully, this would get resolved soon and I would be able to move the *Aspara* back to my designated moorage spot and get on with my life. Assuming Butch would back off once he was off the hook for what had happened to Sabrina.

When Blake finally reappeared, he was pumped. "That was really interesting," he said. He filled me in on the details of his interview while we headed for his car. His enthusiasm made me smile. My guess was that they were probably so pleased to finally get him to stop talking that they were willing to overlook the fact that he had technically pretended to be an officer of the law.

Blake took me back to the marina to pick up my car, and I followed him to Terry's. I had decided to end my exile and return to the *Aspara*. It was a leap of faith in the criminal justice process, but I wanted it to be over so much that I was willing to take the risk.

When we arrived, we found Macavity in the living room, his head resting on Cora's soft stomach. He raised his head enough to let me know he had seen me, then went back to his doggie pillow. I paused long enough to snap a picture that I knew would make Logan smile. Maybe I would send it to Terry; it would please her to know that the two animals had become friends. I left Macavity with his playmate while I packed.

Blake had agreed to fill in as house and dog sitter, so I was free to leave. He seemed sad to see me go but perked up when I mentioned that he should drop by the *Aspara* some time. I even offered to take him out for a sail. After all, he had been a big help the last few days and having him show up when he did had prevented Earl from taking off before the police arrived.

As a farewell gift to myself, I grabbed a couple of brownies out of the freezer and tucked them in my pack. Then I put Macavity's carrier on the floor by him. He eyed me, checked out Cora, and obediently got up and went inside. He apparently didn't mind leaving his new friend if it meant going home. Cora pulled herself upright and whined a goodbye deep down in her throat. Not a parting destined for the big screen.

At the door, Blake hugged me and leaned down to say goodbye to Macavity. Macavity flicked his tail in farewell. Then together Macavity and I headed back to our marina home.

Chapter 24

Who, Me?

Macavity was so pleased to be home that he purred and rubbed my leg before taking off to make certain everything at the marina was as he had left it. I collapsed on the settee, finished off Terry's brownies, and leaned back against the pillows, totally relaxed for the first time in a while. It was good to be back, and very good to be alive.

The next night, Judd cooked us one of his special dinners, and the three of us polished off some very nice red while I relived—and embellished—all of the sordid details leading up to Earl's arrest.

Although the police were pursuing Earl as both a fraudster and a killer, there were a number of unanswered questions about what Earl had been up to and, even more puzzling, what his motivation had been. Had he been trying to get back at AHA for making his life dull and meaningless? Did he have a secret vice that he needed cash to support? Drugs? Gambling? A mistress he kept hidden? None of it seemed to fit with his mild-mannered, non-flashy persona. Then again, even knowing what I did, I still had a hard time envisioning him as a murderer.

Meanwhile, I was relieved to no longer have to look over my shoulder. Except for the occasional glance around to see if Butch was headed in my direction. I had called and left an apology on his phone, but I hadn't heard back. And I didn't want or expect to.

As soon as word got out, everyone I knew called to give me their two cents worth. Family member were predictable in their responses. My mother informed me that if I moved off my boat into a normal apartment or condo, I wouldn't get mixed up in any more sordid police incidents. My niece Catrin texted me to say that that next time I got involved in something as exciting as a murder that I should let her know before it was all over. My brother Dylan left a voice message saying that he and Angela were glad the murderer had been apprehended, and, furthermore, why on earth had I told Catrin it was a good idea to move into an apartment?

Friends had varying opinions. Sophie reminded me that I was her best friend, and she would continue to support me in any hair-brained schemes I pursued. Also, she was glad I had forgiven her for telling Dane about the statue. Terry called to thank me for helping her brother get through a tough time. And for house-sitting. And for the delightful picture of Macavity and Cora together. Hudson let me know how pleased he was to learn that Arthur wasn't a murderer. And it was time to come get my fish. When I did, Bubbles V was so excited to be back in my office that she almost swam through the hole in the fake lava rock, turning at the last instant to fall into line behind Friend.

John dropped by in response to a phone message I'd left him, thanking him for providing the key to solving the case. He brought me a coffee and let me know he would be happy to give me advice any time. We chatted for a few minutes. As he was leaving, he suggested we take in a movie some time. I didn't want to encourage him, but after all he had done, I could hardly say no. I didn't bother reminding him that he had shown little interest in movies the evening Blake, he and I had our little wine fest.

Several board members from AHA emailed a thank you. Jan even sent me a box of Fran's chocolates. None of them mentioned tightening up their fiduciary responsibilities.

The only one who didn't call or contact me was Arthur. He quietly returned to the *Knotty Lady* and avoided me until I forced an encounter by running after him one day as I saw him get off his boat. "It's okay, Arthur. Everything's back to normal," I called out.

He stopped and waited for me before saying, "No, it isn't. Sabrina's dead. And it's my fault. I should never have hired her."

"Being attracted to someone isn't a crime." Actually, I agreed with him, but he was a neighbor, a pathetic neighbor, but still a neighbor.

"I should have realized . . ."

"Maybe. But now you need to move on. Anyway, welcome back."

Two weeks later Ben showed up at my office unannounced. "Want a cup of coffee and some details?"

"You buying?"

"Absolutely." His mustache looked freshly trimmed, a thin, precise line above his upper lip. At least it wasn't a handlebar or a horseshoe. Those would definitely be disqualifiers.

We went to Beth's and I ordered a piece of apple pie along with a cup of coffee. I figured I could eat while he talked.

"You were right," he began. "BluSky was the catalyst for Sabrina's suspicions. Although it wasn't as straightforward as you might have thought. Everyone always wants crimes to have simple solutions. Some do, but a surprising number are messy mixes of motive and circumstance."

"Nice alliteration," I commented.

He smiled before continuing. "The way details are emerging, it looks like there were actually two separate frauds going on.

"First there was Earl's. It appears as though he has been skimming and cooking the books for some time. As a long-time trusted employee, no one was keeping an eye on him. They all thought he was the eye being kept on everyone else. The fact that he handled membership and donations with next to no oversight made it possible for him to thank donors while recording their gifts at a lower level. The biggest reason for his success was that he hadn't been greedy. He'd been in it for the long haul, taking a little here and a little there. If someone had discovered a shortfall, he could have claimed it was an honest mistake."

"Did he confess?"

"Only to the fraud. He knew we were going to figure it out. But we are also accumulating enough evidence to make the murder charge stick."

"But how . . .?"

"Then there was the second fraudulent enterprise. This is where things started falling apart. BluSky has been fudging on material costs for some time. That we can prove. What we can't prove but guess at is how this all became intertwined."

"Through Butch . . .?"

"Butch hasn't confessed to knowing about the inferior materials, but he undoubtedly did. Maybe he told Sabrina about it or maybe he said something that made her suspicious. We may never know. There was nothing on her computer, and we haven't found any other notes from her audit."

"That's suspicious in and of itself, isn't it?"

"It's possible she had made notes and that Earl destroyed them. That's another 'may never know for sure.' Unfortunately, real life is full of loose ends. You just have to try your best to establish as much certainty as possible."

"And rely on the 'trout in the milk' approach."

"You read Thoreau?" Ben looked surprised.

"Not for a long time. And I actually discovered that phrase in a list of quotations about circumstantial evidence. I liked it because he combined the natural with a commercial product to make a point."

Ben laughed. "Maybe they had skim milk then. Definitely enough water for a fish in that."

Ah, he'd just doubled his point score. First, he knew it was a Thoreau quotation. And he agreed that skim milk is watery.

"Anyway," Ben continued, "I think Sabrina mentioned the BluSky scam to Earl before she figured out Earl's con. He would have realized that if she kept digging, his fraud would most likely be discovered too."

I made a mental note to myself to make sure this information made it to Gerald and Harold. It was the right thing to do, and you never knew when you might need a source in the future. "What about framing Arthur?"

"That's where *you* come in." His mustache twitched mischievously.

"If I hadn't brought up the statue . . . Sabrina would still be alive." I'd been pushing the thought of that to the back of my mind, trying to avoid facing the fact that my impulsive act may have resulted in another person's death.

"No, that's not what I meant, Bryn. Absolutely not true. If he hadn't had access to the statue, he would have used a different weapon. Once Sabrina started tracking the fraud at AHA, her fate was sealed."

"But how did Earl find out about the statue?"

"One of the poker players is dating an AHA employee. Apparently, it was discussed at some length over coffee at AHA. No one remembers for certain whether Earl was present when they were talking about it, but they think it's a good possibility." One thing was clear—I would never be able to hold my head high at AHA.

"How do you explain Arthur's fingerprints on the statue?"

"Arthur was able to help us out there. Once he knew Earl was involved, he realized what had happened. Arthur is known to have a sweet tooth. But he also has a severe nut allergy. There were some cookies in the lunchroom, Arthur's favorite. Earl assured him they were nut free. Then, shortly after Arthur had eaten two or three cookies, Earl rushed in to tell him he'd been mistaken—the cookies had nuts in them. He offered Arthur an allergy pill. After taking it Arthur felt strange and went home early. He thought it was a reaction to the nuts. And the rest you know."

So, the night I'd been spooked by thinking there was someone prowling around the *Knotty Lady*, that had most likely been Earl, not Macavity. We'd almost caught him in the act of planting Arthur's fingerprints on the statue. Almost—

"One final question, why do you think he kept her alive for several days?"

"If I had to guess, I'd say he was a very careful murderer. He wanted to make absolutely certain she had told him everything about her investigation so he could cover his tracks. That's truly cold and calculating."

What I couldn't bear to think about was whether Sabrina realized her death was inevitable. She had been so full of life, and to have someone take it away in such a deliberate and passionless way seemed to me like the height of unfairness. Not that murder is ever "fair."

As we lingered over coffee, Ben said, "I know I mentioned this before, but Arthur was lucky to have you on his side."

"I wasn't exactly 'on his side.' I mean, until the end I still had him on my list of possible suspects."

Ben smiled. "Did you have all of their pictures taped to a whiteboard? With lines connecting them to key issues?"

"No, too high tech. I have a large, drop down peg board on the boat. I can pin up pictures, string yarn between events, timelines, and potential suspects. I even have different colored dots to prioritize people based on the probability that they committed the crime. When I'm not working on it, I hoist it back up on the ceiling."

Ben smiled. "I don't suppose anyone has ever called you out for having a smart mouth, have they?"

I gave him what I hoped was a sweet smile, "Who, me?"

Made in the USA
Las Vegas, NV
29 June 2021